To Tom
Hope you enjoy
Alex Brimbaly

HUMANITY'S SAVING GRACE

by Alex Binkley

LOOSE CANNON PRESS

NATIONAL LIBRARY OF CANADA CATALOGUING IN PUBLICATION DATA
Binkley, Alex
Humanity's Saving Grace
ISBN 978-0-9867879-6-6

Copyright © 2013 Alex Binkley

All rights reserved. Except for use in any review or critical article, the reproduction or use of this work, in whole or in part, in any form by any electronic, mechanical or other means—including xerography, photocopying and recording—or in any information or storage retrieval system, is forbidden without express permission of the publisher

Printed in the United States of America

Published by
LOOSE CANNON PRESS

loosecannonpress@rogers.com
www.loosecannonpress.com

AUTHOR'S NOTE

This novel is a work of fiction. Names, characters, places and incidents are either the product of the writer's imagination or are used fictitiously. Any resemblance to persons, Beings or Biobots, living or dead, is entirely unintended except for a few references of obvious respect to humans who made a difference.

DEDICATION

This book is dedicated to my parents Arthur and Evelyn Binkley who instilled a love of books and stories that eventually paid off in this novel and others to come.

ACKNOWLEDGEMENTS

While writing a book is a solitary occupation, it is one in which the writer isn't really alone. To offset the hours of writing, revising and editing is the time spent discussing the craft and the story with other authors in online and face-to-face groups and at workshops. The manuscript is vetted in whole or in part and ideas and encouragement flow and goof-ups and unneeded sections are caught along with holes in the plot.

I have too many people to thank for helping with *Humanity's Saving Grace* to attempt to list all their names. They would include members of the Online Writing Workshop for Science Fiction and Fantasy, the Professional Authors online group, the Pen & Paper klatch, which meets weekly in Ottawa, the Ottawa Independent Writers, and workshops and numerous discussions at SF meetings. They all have my appreciation.

My better half Christine Cram encouraged me from the start and editor Beverly Blanchard untangled the knots in the story. Artist Erica Syverson provided a marvelous cover.

    Alex Binkley,
    Ottawa 2013

Chapter 1
A Visitor Returns

February 28, 2037

A brilliant red light rippled across the screen of Ruth Huxley's monitor screen blotting out the distant stars she'd been examining. She tapped the reset key to restore the pinpricks of light. The red remained.

Figuring there had been a malfunction with her monitor, she rolled her chair backwards to scan the other screens in the control room of the Great Plains Deep Space Tracking Station. Every single one beamed red. If this was an alert from the station analyzer that was worth noting, the screens should all be flashing red and black. Ruth looked around at her co-workers, and although they didn't say anything, they were just as confused as she.

Rolling her chair back to her station, she called, "Alert acknowledged analyzer." What could be wrong with the equipment this time? When her screen turned black, she said in a louder voice than she wished, "Did someone change the alert notification procedure and not bother to tell us?"

No sooner had she spoken then her screen flashed red and the color rolled like a wave through the other six monitors in the room. The light reflected off the plastic coated maps and charts on the walls giving the room a crimson glow.

"Analyzer, would you cut the light show and just show us the problem!" her colleague Arthur Lorne called out from an adjacent work station.

The analyzer responded in its deep baritone voice through overhead speakers. "Please provide details of any malfunction."

Ruth slumped in her chair and tossed her head back. *This has to be another technical screw up.*

In the past, alerts about asteroids or other interstellar phenomena had stopped as soon as the researchers acknowledged them. Then the station's main analyzer provided them with details. Ruth chewed on her lip trying to imagine what could have caused the malfunction. "Arthur, see what's on the system monitor. An alert's not supposed to affect it."

He hurried into a nearby alcove and, after a few seconds, said, "The main analyzer is operating normally. This is really screwy. The alert on our screens bypassed it; should be impossible."

Ruth hit the reset button again. All of a sudden her screen turned a sandy brown and an aquamarine face burst into view. She jumped back in her chair and let out a shriek. While the face's lips moved as if it was talking, the only thing she could hear in her headset was the blasting of loud static. She looked over to see Arthur rip his headset off. He looked ready to pitch it across the room.

A raspy, slightly slurred voice sounded in Ruth's ears. She waved her hands over her head to signal to the others to listen.

"...discuss a threat that faces your planet and our worlds with Secretary General Kendo of the United Nations," the voice intoned as a string of oddly shaped symbols appeared in a panel along the bottom of the screens. "Greetings from the Being Worlds. We wish to discuss a threat that faces your planet and our worlds with Secretary General Kendo of the United Nations." The symbols continued to dance across the bottom of the screen as the creature repeated its request. Then as if nothing had happened, her screen returned to the stars she'd been studying before the alert.

Samantha Dexter at the station on the other side of Ruth broke the uneasy silence in the room. "You all saw an aquamarine face and heard a warning? Right?"

"How about the pebbly skin?" Arthur's fingers danced over his keyboard. "The main analyzer didn't record the transmission, yet it's in my backup file. Check yours." He kept typing and barking commands at the analyzer. Considered the station's analyzer guru, the others peppered him with questions. Ruth remained silent, almost afraid to open her mouth.

Arthur cleared his throat. "What happened is way too sophisticated for a hoax or hack. Someone bypassed the feeds from the main analyzer to deliver the alert and that message to our monitors. We can't even do that and as outdated as it, the system would have detected that kind of a disruption."

There was an eerie creaking from Arthur's chair as he turned to face Ruth. "Your screen showed the alert first. I bet the message was intended for you." He hummed and hawed before speaking again. "Ruth, you were right. There really are aliens out there." He let out a nervous chuckle before adding, "Not a dramatic first encounter but it looks like they want to meet us."

The other researchers remained silent although Samantha nodded her head as if agreeing with Arthur. Ruth glanced around the room. While the others stared at the stars that had returned to their screens, their thoughts would be focused on the implications of what they had just witnessed. As much as Ruth longed to hear the analyzer's soothing voice, by all the flashing lights at the work stations it was preoccupied in discovering what had bypassed it. What conclusions would it come to?

For years, Ruth had written essays and presented papers on the likelihood of extraterrestrial civilizations. She had plenty of supporters and lots of critics. Her opinions had probably cost her awards and fellowships. Now she had a chance to find out if she had been correct all along. Had she actually heard an alien transmission that had been directed at her?

Never in her wildest dreams did she imagine anything other than a few words from a distant system. For more than 75 years, Earth had been experimenting in beaming signals of greetings out to the universe. However, by the clarity of today's message Ruth figured it hadn't traveled far in space. "Arthur, the sender must be in our solar system."

"There's nothing unusual on the radar," he said.

"Then how could it speak in English and know about the United Nations? Kendo came into office less than two years ago. They have to be in close proximity." Arthur shook his head. Ruth struggled to control her excitement. "Any luck with the symbols in the message?"

"I've got the main analyzer working on them." The function lights on his console flickered furiously. "There's a pattern in the symbols and several reoccur at regular intervals. The analyzer's trying to break them into segments."

Ruth was in high school in Alberta when artificial intelligence had advanced enough to replicate some forms of human thinking. Gradually computers were renamed analyzers with the development of AI operating systems that responded to spoken commands as well as input from a keyboard. Although they had enhanced cognitive abilities, experience had taught her that enabling machines to think didn't guarantee their conclusions would make sense.

"We have to report this," She raised her voice to quiet her co-workers. "It's not quite midnight, Jonathan should still be up." Her visphone completed the link to the nearby quarters of Jonathan Ku, the Station Director.

"Hello Ruth, what's happening?" Jonathan looked up from the couch in his small living room, a book resting in his lap. It had been years since she'd seen someone reading a paper book.

"There has been an unusual transmission tonight. Let me replay it for you."

Jonathan leaned toward his visphone and exhaled slowly when the aquamarine face replaced Ruth's image. His eyes widened as the alien delivered its greeting. Even after the transmission concluded and Ruth's face re-appeared he continued to stare at his phone. "I'm not sure what to say. You must be satisfied this is authentic or you wouldn't be bothering me with it. I can't even guess at an explanation for it. I'm required to notify the offices of the Chancellor of the North American Federation and the Chief of the Unified Command of any unusual finding." Jonathan opened and closed his mouth a couple of time before saying, "I don't want to jump the gun on this. We should check this out before we tell anyone about it."

"I'm readying a bulletin for the SciNet about the transmission's contents," Ruth said. "We need some independent verification of the finding. My name on it will ensure a critical reception from my critics."

Jonathan didn't respond immediately, which told her he didn't agree with her decision. However, he wouldn't try to talk her out of it. He owed her for being appointed Director because she'd turned it down. As much as she deserved the job, promoting her would inflame her opponents and jeopardize the future of the space tracking network.

"Want to make sure you get credit for the first contact?" Jonathan teased.

While Ruth was in no mood for joking, she regretted the snap in her reply. "They want to speak to the UN, not us. While finding aliens is what we've worked at for years, this'll likely be the limit of our involvement."

To ensure the correct tone, Ruth reworded her bulletin for SciNet several times before sending it to the website. Only after hitting the send button did she realize the room had become crowded with off-duty colleagues. The main analyzer had sent an advisory to all the station personnel about the transmission.

"Listen to them bickering about whether the broadcast is for real," Arthur muttered as he leaned toward her desk. "If this is how highly-trained scientists respond, imagine the public reaction?"

She shrugged. She'd authored several articles outlining the necessary protocols to ensure a cool-headed verification of extraterrestrial contact. One was to ensure the news media would rise above its customary fascination with the trivial and sensational to report the event responsibly. Now that an encounter with aliens seemed probable, she felt compelled to inform her graduate school friend, Elinor Brady.

Elinor's knowledge of science and her ability to explain even the most complex concepts and developments in easily understood terms had brought her many journalism awards. She had a high-profile reporting assignment with International News Network in London. While Elinor would see Ruth's bulletin on SciNet soon enough, better to give her the scoop on one of the biggest stories of all time. Ruth would live with the consequences.

While Elinor usually interrupted people with questions, she listened in silence as Ruth explained the reason for her early morning call. After a few minutes, Elinor excused herself. "I'll call you back as soon as I can. I want to break this story before anyone else finds out. It'll be pandemonium when word gets out."

The connection ended just as Arthur shouted, "I found the source of the transmission. You're gonna love this, Ruth. It's a spacecraft near Saturn. Analyzer, display a view of the same coordinates from twelve hours earlier beside this one."

Ruth propelled her chair to his desk, arriving in time to see the screen split into two images of the ringed planet.

Arthur's excitement mounted with every word. He tapped his finger on the left side of his monitor. "Nothing unusual earlier, but look at this!" His finger rested on a flickering spot on the right. "How could something that big enter the solar system undetected?"

Humanity's Saving Grace

Chapter 2
Getting Acquainted

Dressed in a sandy brown robe that hung below his knees, Humbaw sat in the middle of his vessel's command bench, his eyes shifting among a trio of three-dimensional displays of Earth floating in the windowless room. The middle one showed the rotation of the planet and its moon while the others provided low orbit-level views of the Northern and Southern Hemispheres.

Like most Beings, he stood a little over a meter tall and had large bulging eyes, nostrils instead of a nose, a small mouth, skin flaps for ears and small, shiny white teeth. His arms didn't reach his waist when standing. The hands had short thumbs and three long slender fingers. Flecks of deep blue, yellow and orange covered his face.

Demmloda, nearly identical in appearance and second in command, sat beside him. The command bench and a second one behind it constituted the only permanent fixtures in the chamber. They accommodated the eight Beings on the vessel.

The floating displays appeared only when one of them occupied a spot on the benches. They provided status updates on the ship's main systems and charts or views of the region of space surrounding the vessel. If a Being needed more detailed information, screens recessed into the floor would be elevated by telescoping metal arms.

The raspy breathing of Humbaw and Demmloda broke the silence in the chamber. Their helpers stood behind the benches, identical sleek figures that resembled Beings except they wore no clothes and had fuzzy tan colored skin.

Several hours earlier, Humbaw had instructed the galaxy-ship's Controlling Unit to shift the vessel clear of Saturn and send his recorded greeting to Earth. Since then, he'd discussed data about the planet with Demmloda.

"By your fidgeting, you're anxious about how the Terrans will respond to our request," Demmloda said. "Despite all the study of Earth you've put them through; the crew retains its contemptuous view of Terrans. They didn't consider it worthwhile to come to the Chamber to await a response to your greeting. To them, the most likely answer will be panic and threats. Your edict to stop calling Earthlings Primitives hasn't had much effect yet."

Humbaw slapped his hands on the bench. "Do you have any doubts?"

"If I hadn't visited the planet nine times with you, I probably wouldn't share your view that they offer the element we lack." He gazed again at the displays. "The technology of Earth has not advanced much since the last visit and there is less space activity." He added a clucking sound of disapproval with his tongue. "They continue to make a mess of their pretty planet. They are probably fighting another war."

"While regrettable, that mess is to our advantage." Humbaw gripped the edge of the bench. "They really need our help to survive the damage they have done to their world. Their situation should—what is their phrase—seal the deal for us."

Demmloda nodded. "Our time in observation has..." He got no further as the communications system beeped to signal an incoming transmission from Earth that the Controlling Unit judged worth hearing.

An excited voice filled the Chamber. "I-News has learned a space tracking station has received an apparent extraterrestrial transmission. Delivered in English by what's described as a creature with an aquamarine-colored face, the message requests a meeting with the United Nations to discuss a mutual threat. We'll bring you more details as they become available. This is Elinor Brady for I-News in London."

Humbaw raised his arms and hooted, "Less than six hours since my greeting was sent." He rubbed his hands together. "That is very quick for Terrans. Controlling Unit, relay this information to the entire ship."

He waited for the message to be delivered before projecting his thoughts to the others Beings. Like all his species, he could communicate telepathically and speak simultaneously. The oral communications kept the helpers and the Controlling Unit informed.

A broad grin crinkled Humbaw's face. "Perhaps, the reporter wants us to show we're aquamarine all over. Terrans are fascinated with unclothed bodies."

"What is it about being close to their planet that prompts you to mimic Earthling humor and emotions?" Demmloda said. When Humbaw shrugged, he said, "There you go again. Like your smile, that gesture is another of their traits."

"It's very noteworthy the reporter did not point out our resemblance to the reptiles of Earth. It is quite obvious. She also didn't say where our transmission came from. Perhaps they have not discovered our location. We must determine who else is aware of our presence. Controlling Unit, deploy command bench screens and show SciNet on the one at my position."

The displays rose from the floor. Humbaw had found SciNet while searching the Internet during a visit to Earth almost a half century earlier. He checked it out first during subsequent missions to determine what scientific progress Terrans had achieved.

"There are plenty of posts about my greeting." He worked his way back in search of the original one about his transmission. "Mostly they speculate on whether it is a hoax. No one understands the symbols." He paused to watch more posts appear. "Ah, here is one that identifies where our ship is. This is another good sign." He kept scrolling through the posts pausing at those messages that interested him. "Controlling Unit, which tracking station identified our location?" A light flashed on the Great Plains Tracking Station on the border between Canada and the United States. "Is there anything special about this facility?"

The Controlling Unit offered no suggestions. Thinking he heard movement behind him, Humbaw glanced over his shoulder. His and Demmloda's helpers stood there unmoving. He returned his gaze to the displays when the Controlling Unit signaled another SciNet post worth checking.

"Here is the first post about my greeting. It is from a Terran named Huxley at the tracking station that determined our location."

When Humbaw went back to studying the SciNet posts, the helpers resumed flashing their fingers in rapid sign language. So far, so good. They do not realize we arranged to have their greeting to Earth sent to Huxley first, Humbaw's helper signed. Our plan remains invisible to them.

The other replied with his fingers. We just have to keep the Beings from alienating the humans. If they persist in speculating about her, we will have to distract them.

Then Demmloda said, "There should be more reports on their news channels about us. Controlling Unit, search for any Earth broadcasts about an alien spaceship."

The other helper fingered. No distraction required.

Demmloda removed a listening plug from his ear. "We certainly have their attention." Excited voices in a variety of languages reverberated through the Chamber as the Controlling Unit played broadcasts from different continents.

"Governments around the world are reacting cautiously to reports of a mysterious space vessel," intoned a deep voice. "Military forces are on the highest alert as officials investigate whether Earth faces an invasion from outer space."

Humbaw smiled. "The military response is predictable." He rubbed his hands over his cheeks. "This has gone according to plan. Our next step is to convince them to talk with us." Then he slouched down on the bench with his arms wrapped around his legs. It was his favorite thinking position.

A smirk slid across Demmloda's face as he kept studying the steadily scrolling SciNet debate. "I wonder what the members of the High Council would say if they could see us now?"

"They would remain convinced I am mad and this whole mission will fail because the Terrans will fear our superiority too much to agree to our proposal."

"Undoubtedly you are right." They both exhaled deeply, the Being equivalent of a hearty chuckle.

Sitting up, Humbaw said, "It is time for the next phase of the plan. Controlling Unit, start transmitting my main message. We must not wait any longer." He sent his thoughts to the other Beings. "While the Earthlings know we are here, they will have no idea about our intentions. We have to assure them we mean no harm or they will panic. We must avoid that."

He contemplated the three floating images of the blue world. In centuries of exploring space, the Beings had found only a few planets with the hot and dry climate suited to them. More common were the cooler temperatures and lower oxygen levels of Earth. Still the first English word to enter the Being language was Goldilocks, the Terran term for planets in an orbital range around a sun that would allow for an atmosphere that could sustain life.

Humbaw had led the expedition that discovered Earth and he insisted on monitoring it because humans were the only sentient species encountered in centuries of space exploration. Now he had to convince them to help save his species from destruction.

Chapter 3
Guessing Alien Motives

Benjamin Kendo jumped at the beep beside the bed in his apartment in the UN building. He grabbed the handset to avoid waking his wife Olen with the loud voices of the visphone.

The display on the receiver said 3 A.M. and that the call came from the Crisis Center located in a bunker in the basement of the UN building. He tiptoed away from the bed into the living room, his mind speculating about which of Earth's many afflictions and border skirmishes had suddenly worsened. Or perhaps a new calamity had occurred?

Whatever, being awoken by these middle-of-the-night calls annoyed him. His advice, usually a compromise to defuse hostilities, was rarely followed. Still he had to offer a sage perspective to reassure whoever still listened to the UN. His ruminations halted when he put the unit to his ear and in a voice of authority said, "Kendo."

"Mr Secretary General, we are monitoring reports of a transmission from outer space that requests talks with you. General Davis has just arrived."

Benjamin sat in his favorite arm chair to digest the information. This wasn't the type of call he was expecting. It sounded absurd, but the Crisis Center supervisor was only doing his job. "On my way." Donning the clothes for his morning workout, he wrestled with his emotions. How would his officials verify whether a real alien transmission had been received? Still two decades in politics had taught him to consider what it would mean if any claim or allegation, no matter how outrageous, proved accurate. How would it impact the public?

The one consolation for Benjamin was Hector Davis, his principal military advisor, was dealing with the situation already. Known for working long hours, Hector was a no nonsense man who probably wasn't thrilled with this middle of the night fantasy either. A man of facts and logic, the General regarded rumors and gossip as the shifty vagabonds of an ordered world. His considerable knowledge ranged well beyond military matters and Benjamin had yet to find an issue the man couldn't make sense of.

Benjamin smiled at memories of past crisis and Hector saying 'we'd better get to the bottom of this' in his thickest Scottish brogue and his staff scurrying to the Internet and phones to gather more information. The hint of red in his wavy brown hair warned people not to test his patience.

Nearing the apartment's front door, Benjamin said, "Open." It slid soundlessly into the wall. To his annoyance, no escort waited in the hallway to brief him. Of course, probably no one knew enough to tell him anything useful. Striding to the elevator, he said, "Lift." An elevator unit headed for his floor immediately. It would take him directly to the floor where the Center was located.

As he paced back and forth, Benjamin pondered what the UN could do about extraterrestrial threats. Resolving Earthly tempests seemed beyond its ability. He became Secretary General after negotiating an end to decades of war that had ravaged his central African homeland. However, his Nobel Prize proved of little assistance in achieving peace elsewhere. The world's crushing recession and devastated environment compounded the damage of border wars, regional skirmishes and terrorist attacks. He'd hoped to gain enough authority to engineer a halt to the planet's environmental deterioration before its already grim conditions became completely unmanageable. He rated his chance of success as low.

He often speculated about whether he would be the last Secretary General. Chaotic weather had inflicted devastating rains, tornadoes and hurricanes on many countries killing millions of people and disrupting food production and transportation. Wild swings in temperatures and precipitation occurred with alarming regularity leaving countries with widespread flooding and then drought. He hated to think about how few people had a proper home and sufficient food. Decades of burning fossil fuels and pursing reckless development had exacerbated the normal swings in the planet's climate.

As the lift's voice intercom system counted down the levels before its arrival, Benjamin's thoughts drifted to a secret plan drafted years earlier at a conference on international cooperation. It obliged the major powers to put aside their differences to deal with threatening asteroids or space invaders. Benjamin doubted the agreement had much authority in a world full of uncooperative countries.

He stepped into the lift and said, "Basement." As it descended, he resumed pacing. The World Trade Organization and the International Monetary Fund had become impotent in the face of the isolationist policies most nations had adopted to cope with millions of hungry and homeless people. Trade had fallen to the levels of the 19th Century. As sorry as economic conditions were, countries found the funds to keep their militaries strong.

The UN still retained some influence because a few nations and wealthy benefactors kept it alive. As Kendo frequently reminded his staff, "We're the only international institution left, so we have to make a difference."

When lift the door opened, Hector stood there. Benjamin had come to regard the stocky man as one of his best friends. Benjamin spoke before the General could launch into a briefing while they strode toward the Crisis Center. "If any of this is true, what the hell am I supposed to do about aliens from outer space that happen to know my name? We already have food riots and violent protests almost every day. We don't need any more chaos." He clasped Hector's arm to stop him. "So what's their message say, surrender or die?"

Hector shook his head several times, a gesture that meant what came next bordered on the incredible. "The alien is delivering what sounds remarkably like a lecture in quite passable English on how it discovered Earth in 1829. This is their 10th visit. They have what sounds like faster than light speed and can travel from their worlds to here in about three months even though the distance is, well, simply unbelievable. When I left the Center, the alien was recounting its first visit. It didn't sound impressed."

"Where does the message come from?"

"It appears to emanate from a spaceship orbiting Saturn. An unbelievably large spaceship I might add," Hector said.

Benjamin inhaled deeply several times to bring his anxiety under control. "What's it doing out there? Why isn't it in orbit around Earth really scaring the hell out of us?" Recognizing the absurdity of his questions, Benjamin cut Hector off before he could respond. "What does it want?"

"It says we face a mutual threat."

"Calice," Benjamin muttered, a French Canadian curse he enjoyed because few understood it.

A smile flitted across Hector's face. "The military are pissed the space geeks located the spaceship before they did."

Benjamin laughed. "It's still hard to believe any of this."

The General's frown erased any notion of a hoax. "The Center called me after it learned of the news reports about an alien message. The broadcast started before I got here."

"Do the aliens have a name?"

"Beings."

"Beings," Benjamin repeated with a snicker. "We shouldn't face an immediate threat. I recall reading it would take years to get to Saturn."

"It would take us years. There's another matter we need to discuss. I-News broke the story about the spaceship's location more than an hour ago and the other communication networks have picked it up."

"Damn. Issue a statement under my name stressing how far away this ship is and that its crew wants to talk to us. Say the UN is pursuing a dialogue. We must be careful not to add to the panic that the news reports will trigger."

Benjamin hesitated at the Center's entrance, mulling over an idea that had popped into his mind. Invaders didn't usually disclose their intentions in advance unless they held a big advantage and wanted to force a surrender. Maybe the aliens really wanted to talk about this threat? But why? None of it made sense.

Jammed with communications equipment and analyzers, the Center maintained direct contact with capitals and military commands around the world. Benjamin had never seen so many staff packed in the pale green room. His arrival went unnoticed because everyone watched the aquamarine face speaking in a soft, raspy voice. ". . . third visit was in 1877. No one detected us."

"This talking head doesn't tell us much about what the aliens look like," Hector grumbled. "We've seen the occasional flicker of its hands. If it had really been to Earth before, why not send pictures to prove it?"

Spotting his political advisor Ernesto Gonzales hurrying to them, Benjamin asked, "Who's receiving this broadcast?"

"It's on all the networks," Ernesto said. "No one can block it. Who knows how many billion people are tuned into it."

"You mean it's taken over all the comnets?" Benjamin exclaimed. Ernesto nodded. Benjamin imagined the self-righteous executives of the global communications networks fuming about the loss of control over their systems. "Have we informed all the delegations?"

"Most of them learned about it through the initial report from I-News," Ernesto replied as he took Benjamin's arm and steered him toward a conference room. "Several governments are calling for an emergency meeting of the Security Council. They want to make sure we can defend ourselves and reassure the population we're not in danger."

"You mean the same countries that ignore pleas to help others are suddenly worried about protecting the world. Still, they're looking to us for leadership." Benjamin scratched his head while listening to the droning alien voice. "It's a long-winded bugger."

"It's recounting previous visits, we assume, to assure us that it's not hostile," said Rachel Tran, another advisor who had just entered the room. "It would appear we are in for a lengthy show. With all the detail it's delivering, it'll take a long time to reach the present."

Benjamin sat at a desk and reached for the button to raise the volume on the display. The speaker was describing a visit in 1903 when the visphone in front of him announced a call from the President of the Russian Federation, an old friend from the London School of Economics. He told the phone to accept it and Vladimir Rushinsko's glum face, topped with a shock of white hair, stared at him.

"Ah, Benjamin. Is the alien friend or foe?"

Benjamin half expected him to complain the alien spoke only in English. "You probably know more than I do."

"Our scientists are analyzing the situation. I don't understand much of what they're saying."

"We'll organize briefings for all the delegations as soon as we have more information."

The Russian grunted his approval. "Make it soon. Already there are reports of little green men or bugs of some kind coming to Earth. We need calm to find out what these aliens want. But you're always good at keeping your head, Ben."

The usually fretful Vladimir showed no signs of fear or alarm leading Benjamin to wonder if the world was in such a mess that aliens didn't seem all that alarming. Hopefully, other world leaders would react as pragmatically. "You seem to be handling it well."

"They're trying hard not to frighten us," Vladimir said. "Why have they waited until now to reveal their existence? If they wanted to talk with you, why didn't they communicate directly with the UN?"

Relieved someone else had concluded the aliens really wanted to talk, Kendo decided to test him. "Are they trying to lull us into lowering our guard?"

"Too late for that. The militaries are all on full alert. My generals say that for the first time in years, their counterparts in North America, Europe, China and India are anxious to talk about joint action if necessary."

"In other words, it's up the aliens to convince us they're peaceful," Kendo said, cheered by the report that military chiefs talked co-operation for once.

Vladimir nodded. "Da."

Chapter 4
A Long Way from Home

Ruth's eyes shifted between the SciNet feed on her screen and the alien face that filled the large viewer on the control room wall. The Being continued its rambling description of Earth's past while an increasingly snippy debate about deciphering the symbols in the Being greeting consumed the usually sedate scientific forum. The acrimony had generated a lot of bruised egos, but no answers.

Thankfully, quiet had come to the control room. Exasperated by arguing among the researchers and off-duty personnel about the transmission, Arthur had snarled, "Some of us are trying to work here." The others departed leaving only the Being's raspy monologue and the hum of the analyzer.

"Thanks, now I don't have to listen to any more snide remarks about my views on extraterrestrials," Ruth said. "You don't doubt this is for real?"

"Not for a minute." He pointed with his thumb in the direction of the departed coworkers. "They haven't read your papers." He shot her a quick smile. His fingers had never stopped moving over his keyboard. "There're no records of symbols anything like the alien ones. This figure, which looks like a lower case t with a curly tail, is repeated regularly. It isn't at the start or the end of the symbols so it probably doesn't say hello or goodbye. The analyzer has broken the symbols down to segments that contain it."

"You're way ahead of anyone on SciNet," Ruth said. She covered her mouth to stifle a long yawn. "I did a lot of reading and writing after yesterday's shift. I got to stop that behavior. Maybe I should get a life." She rubbed her temples. The excitement about the message combined with the lack of sleep had given her an excruciating headache. Now not only was she tired, but she had also skipped her daily workout, a routine that had given her a more athletic figure.

The alien rambled on, reminding her of long winded professors. Staring "at all the jewels in the heavens" had excited her as a teenager. Following post graduate study in astronomy and astrobiology, she had joined the Deep Space Research Program, the successor to the original Search for Extra Terrestrial Intelligence agency. For the last five years, she had sifted through the sounds of the universe collected by the 50 massive radio telescope dishes at the Great Plains facility. She compared her findings to data gathered by the dwindling number of similar research facilities around the world and space exploration craft.

In the process, she'd become a leading cosmologist and a much sought-after conference and dinner speaker. She hoped her popularity came from discoveries of distant solar systems and not her theories on aliens. Even though she couldn't yet prove the existence of civilizations in the stars, she'd attracted a small following of supporters. On the other hand, she heard regularly from many shrill critics who dismissed her work and attacked her personally.

The reaction had reminded her of the arguments in the scientific community earlier in the 21st Century about the deterioration of the global climate. While events had proved the extreme climate change deniers wrong, the debate had so consumed governments that they failed to curb pollution and adapt to the erratic weather. Millions had died and many more would because of that indecision. The same short-sightedness could cause Earth to mishandle the arrival of aliens. *Could we actually make our lives worse in the process?*

Although larger space listening stations and universities had offered enticing positions, she'd chosen to stay at Great Plains. She relished its remote location on the flat grasslands along the border because she could pursue her studies about the mysteries of the cosmos with few distractions.

She also had a secondary reason for staying at Great Plains and the only person who knew was Arthur's wife Cindy. The station's security kept her safe from Darrin, the one great mistake of her life. He'd tried to kill her when she finally dumped him for good. He would be released from prison in a few years.

Darrin wasn't the only threat. A year and a half earlier, a religious fanatic had attempted to assassinate her during a lecture on understanding extraterrestrials. She had a nasty scar under her left arm from the bullet as a reminder. This attack happened when aliens had only been a conjecture. What would happen now? Would other crazies try? She decided at that moment that she would refuse any media interviews about the alien greeting.

Enough about you. There's a problem to solve. She focused her attention on SciNet. "One post says historians are debating the alien's observations about the past couple of centuries," she told Arthur. "If our visitors are correct, some books need serious revision." She tuned into the alien broadcast. "While it has a lot of interesting information, that voice would put the most hardened insomniac to sleep."

Arthur laughed. To fight her lethargy, Ruth stood, stretched and tugged on handfuls of her shoulder length brown hair, an old habit that she always explained as the best way to get her brain's attention. This time it didn't generate any helpful insights so she returned to her seat and stared at the screens. "Analyzer, repeat previous patterns of the Being symbols." They slowly slid past her eyes without any ideas coming to her. Another perusal of SciNet didn't provide any inspiration either.

She settled back in her chair to ponder Arthur's theory that the aliens had contacted her first. While she wouldn't admit it to him, his comment had excited her as much as any of her astronomical discoveries. How would the Beings know about her? Her visphone vibrated before she got any further. She punched the talk button when she saw United Nations on the message screen.

Rachel Tran introduced herself. "The Secretary General thinks the aliens are trying not to alarm us. With your expertise, we want to know if you agree with that assessment." When she said yes, Rachel asked the dreaded question. "Do you think it was coincidence the aliens contacted you first?"

Distracted by background voices she could hear over Rachel's phone, Ruth hesitated. "It appears that way." After a few more non-committal comments, she promised to call back if she learned anything more. She told Arthur about the call.

"At least the Beings and the UN consider you the expert on space aliens."

"Ha, ha."

Arthur pulled his hands from the keyboard and placed them on the divider between their work stations. "You have made a serious effort to study that possibility and what extraterrestrial life could mean for Earth. Cindy collected your writings for me as a birthday present. She agrees you present a lot of ideas worthy of consideration. Sure they could be invaders. They could also be refugees or displaced persons or just curious neighbors able to travel in space. We might learn a lot from them."

The mention of her articles triggered an idea. "Arthur, what might the alien symbols mean? Besides them not being a threat to us, what else might the aliens want to tell to us?" He looked at her blankly. "Where they live! Analyzer, could the symbols convey positions on a star map?"

While it processed her request, she went looking for a mug of tea and something to quiet her growling stomach. Hearing the analyzer speaking, she rushed back to the control room. Before she arrived, Arthur yelled, "Ruth, come see this." As she entered, the main viewer gleamed with thousands of stars in a region of space she didn't recognize. The alien voice droned on in the background.

"Brilliant idea, Ruth. The symbols give the locations of nine planets that are presumably the Being worlds. I've highlighted them." His tone slid into amazement. "They're an unbelievably long way from home."

"Send that to SciNet."

"You're the expert. How could a species with this kind of technology need help from hicks like us?"

Why indeed? She placed a second call to Elinor and put the note with Rachel's name on it in front of her. While the location of the aliens' worlds would interest the UN, Ruth still didn't know what to say about them other than she didn't feel threatened. But then who really cared what she thought?

Demmloda straightened in his position on the Command Chamber bench to check the monitor beside him. "Your broadcast to Earth has reached their year 2006. Listen to this report."

"We have more details about the original broadcast from the spaceship near Saturn. The symbols in its original message give the names and locations of nine planets the aliens say they inhabit. It would take centuries to reach us from those worlds. As well the *Nile*, which has been studying Mars, wants to investigate the alien ship. We'll bring you more details of this amazing story as soon as they are available. This is Elinor Brady for I-News."

Humbaw sat forward. "The same journalist." He replayed her report. "Perhaps she would like to travel to Hnassumblaw."

Humbaw engaged his telepathic powers to inform the crew as he continued to speak. "When the transmission about our exploration of Earth is complete, we will send them images of our worlds as we proceed toward the planet. We came here seeking their assistance, not just to say hello. We will accomplish nothing making our proposal from this far away. Controlling Unit, display a visual of the Earth spacecraft that wants to inspect us."

Pictures of the *Nile* appeared on all the comnets as they scrambled to match Elinor's latest scoop. The craft also figured in conversations at the UN. Despite projecting a public image of calm deliberation, representatives from the national delegations huddled in hallways and meeting rooms with UN officials in frenzied and often loud conversations. While a few quarreled over the alien interpretation of recent history, the main topic was how to respond to the Beings.

Benjamin scheduled an emergency meeting of the Security Council to start as soon as the members could assemble following the conclusion of the transmission about the Beings' past visits to Earth. Almost 14 hours had passed since Ruth's screen first went red.

To prepare for the meeting, he summoned his aides into his office to brief him on what they'd learned. Waiting for them, he paced around the room. To his disappointment, most world leaders had taken the easy course of calling for Earth to ready its defenses. He'd become increasingly certain the Beings wanted Earth's help in dealing with whatever the threat was. *Otherwise why would they even bother to tell us about it?*

He stopped to stare out a window. Other than a few dirty piles of snow, New York looked ready for spring. *If the aliens need our assistance, could their technology help Earth out of its dire straits? They might be our only hope.* He resumed his pacing. It was time to bring his staff in on his thoughts. If he couldn't convince them, he wouldn't get anywhere with the delegations.

Once they arrived, he said, "Who would have thought the first communication from outer space would be a lecture on our history?" His advisors all chuckled so he plunged on. "Do any of you think they're invaders—Galactic Vikings come to pillage and plunder?"

"No," Hector didn't elaborate yet his certainty gave the others confidence to shake their heads in agreement.

Benjamin outlined his reasons for concluding the aliens really needed Earth's help. "Because they want to deal with the UN, we must appear to understand more about them than anyone else does. They know a great deal about us and could have taken any resources a long time ago when we were less able to defend ourselves. Thus our goal is to steer the Security Council into agreeing to talk with them and emphasize to the comnets and the public that we're not in danger."

His voice dropped to a conspiratorial hush. "Negotiating with the aliens presents a perfect opportunity for the UN to gain the credibility and authority to halt the deterioration of Earth."

The intakes of breath meant he'd surprised his staff. Again he paused for objections. None came. "Can any of you think of another way to save Earth?" No responses. "We must carefully study their broadcast to see what else we can learn. Sure wish they'd included images or visuals from their explorations of Earth."

"Although people trust you sir, how can you be certain about the intention of the aliens?" The others nodded in agreement with Rachel.

It was the question Benjamin wanted. "It's a gut feeling. The aliens have nine worlds relatively close together. Why would they pay attention to our out-of-the-way planet when they have so many closer ones if they need resources? They've kept coming back here."

Poking his chest, he added, "What else could they be interested in other than us?"

He stood and paced around the room, talking all the while. "Our first job is to keep everyone level-headed. Surely after sixty or seventy years of speculation about extraterrestrial life, we shouldn't be a bunch of Chicken Littles when it shows up on our doorstep. We know there are plenty of other planets that could sustain life."

He'd looped around the room and stood behind his chair. "There're plenty of commentators out there preaching every imaginable doom for the world. Am I the only person curious about the threat the aliens mentioned?"

Ernesto plunged in. "The talk among the delegations is mainly about preventing panic that could lead to the overthrow of governments. The extremists and terrorists will be plotting how to exploit the arrival of the aliens. A few countries have to deal with opportunistic religious leaders who've proclaimed the arrival of the aliens as the harbinger of the apocalypse. There haven't been any violent protests yet."

"There will be if we don't get the Beings to explain the threat soon," Benjamin said.

"On the other hand, Secretary General, there is the muted reaction among the militaristic and nationalistic governments to a species with highly advanced technology." Ernesto broke into a half smile. "A few countries want to hear what the Beings have to say. Or, more accurately, what more they have to tell us."

Benjamin groaned at the thought of another history discourse from the spaceship.

Maybe the aliens want to bore us to death," Hector said. "They are approaching us cautiously when an attacker with the element of surprise they have wouldn't announce their presence. They would strike fast and hard."

"On the other hand, they could wait a few more years at the rate Earth is deteriorating and they would face little if any opposition at all," Ernesto said.

Hector nodded. "Then there's the most obvious fact--the technology of that ship is so far ahead of anything on Earth. I would be a lot more concerned if they had a whole fleet instead of just one vessel. Then it would really look like an invasion."

Rachel spoke up. "Despite all the information contained in their broadcasts, we only know what the face of the speaker looks like. The consensus is that it's a reptilian. Its coloring is unlike anything we've ever seen on Earth." She stopped to extract her communicator from a pocket of her pants and read a note, her eyes widening. Not changing her expression, she forwarded it to Benjamin.

The room went silent as he read it, shaking his head. "The alien ship is already halfway to Jupiter. While it still has to traverse the asteroid belt, at the rate it's traveling, it'll be here in little more than a week. On the plus side, it's transmitting visuals of their worlds. They look like deserts."

Hector worked the keyboard of his portable analyzer. "We better deal with the *Nile's* offer to check out the aliens. Sending it will give the appearance we're doing something. If it departs right away, it might just come into visual range of the spaceship's approach to Earth."

"Do you think the *Nile* would be in danger?" Benjamin asked.

"Not if the aliens' intentions are peaceful," Ernesto said. "If they aren't, it will find out the hard way, but we'll have a warning."

Benjamin nodded. "They should welcome it to overcome fears on Earth. I'll see if I can get the space agency to send it immediately."

Humanity's Saving Grace

Chapter 5
The Rendezvous

Simdar Panamar pounded the arm of his chair. The Captain of the *Nile* along with its two crew members had thoroughly mapped and probed Mars during the past month generating the data required for a manned expedition to the red planet. Now he wanted to investigate the alien ship. "The Space Agency hasn't responded to my messages. Maybe they're so preoccupied with the aliens they aren't listening to us."

"More likely the Director doesn't want to make the decision himself," Horgi Vladmitz said. "He's on a pretty short leash with the UN because of the cost of this mission."

Simdar smiled at Horgi's understanding of the Agency's politics. A Polish fighter pilot and mechanical engineer, he'd joined the mission at the last minute filling in for an astronaut who had broken his leg during training.

"You're probably right," Simdar said. "I get impatient with the bureaucracy." Amid all their disagreements, the countries of Earth had created the Space Agency a decade earlier and had tasked the UN with the responsibility to manage the exploration of the solar system. Although its budget had been slashed because of the global recession, the Director had cobbled together the funds for the *Nile's* flight. The Agency had chosen to name its spacecraft after prominent geographical features of Earth.

"They know your special interest in extraterrestrial life," said Luin Kato, a soft-spoken Japanese astrophysicist who took up flying to qualify for the space program.

Simdar had been fascinated with the idea of space aliens for most of his adult life. During his university studies and his 10 years as a top pilot with the Air Force of India, Simdar had devoured every account of aliens visiting Earth or people claiming abduction by them. In addition, he had read any academic study on the possibility of extraterrestrial life he could find. He could expound on countless theories about civilizations on other planets. His interest in the subjects never waned, even though he expected it would always be just a hobby.

"We're so close, but so far away," he grumbled. "We could learn more about that ship than they can from Earth."

A beep signaling an incoming radio transmission ended his tirade. Expecting a response from Agency, the raspy voice from the alien ship startled him. "We could rendezvous with your vessel on our way to Earth."

Simdar's jaw hung open as he looked at his mates. "Lady Luck just landed in our laps. They must have intercepted my messages to Earth. What do you guys think? Do we do the rendezvous?" Luin nodded. Horgi grinned. Simdar asked the being ship what co-ordinates the *Nile* should set course for.

"Getting us to inspect the ship makes sense if they want to talk with the UN," Luin said. "They must know our equipment will tell Earth a lot about their ship."

News of the space rendezvous pre-empted regular comnet programming. Benjamin learned of it in a terse message Rachel sent him during a Security Council meeting. He interrupted the proceedings to inform the delegations.

"We've only a couple of days before the aliens arrive." He paused to emphasize his next comment. "Based on the ease with which their ship traversed the asteroid belt, our missiles won't stop it. They probably wouldn't even get close."

No delegation wanted to agree too quickly with him so Benjamin had to listen to denunciations of the Beings' unflattering portrayal of Earth's history. Nothing hurts like the truth, he thought as delegations tried to shift the blame assigned by the Beings for massacres and famines.

Finally several countries proposed a recess so the delegations could discuss talks with the aliens in private. Benjamin's gaze swept the Council chamber. "From their previous visits, the Beings would know their arrival could trigger widespread panic and a hostile reception. They approached us cautiously so we could absorb the news. Imagine the chaos we would face if they suddenly appeared overhead."

Leaving the meeting, he walked down a corridor talking to Hector. "Has the approach of the aliens injected any urgency into the discussions about an international military response?"

"What I've heard so far is mostly wishful thinking about cooperation should the ship become hostile."

By the time the Security Council meeting resumed, the Indian, Polish and Japanese governments had agreed to the space rendezvous.

"Good timing as we're about to leave anyway," Simdar told the Agency. "We've shut down our surveys and instructed the samplers and other equipment on Mars to report to Earth stations."

After running the co-ordinates for meeting the alien ship through the analyzer several times, Horgi looked puzzled. "The rendezvous will leave us almost as far from Earth as we are now. Why did they choose such a distant point?"

At that moment, the radio beeped again, and then delivered Elinor's latest news report. "Telescopes and space radar are tracking the spaceship and so far, there're many guesstimates about its size. Here's Pablo Hernandez of the Spanish Space Institute to explain the differing opinions on size."

A deep male voice said, "Something baffles our attempts to measure the ship. We can't tell much about its shape. Normally, space radar can provide a pretty clear image of an object that close to Earth. The *Nile* should have more success." When Elinor asked about the size of the ship, the professor said. "I'd say about a kilometer in length, seven hundred and fifty meters wide and two hundred meters high."

She gasped. "That's a monstrous ship."

"It'll be most interesting to learn why they require such a large one," Hernandez said.

The professor's dimensions prompted Luin to make his own calculations. As *Nile* drew closer to the alien vessel, he sent an urgent report to the Agency and SciNet. "The size of the alien vessel appears close to the professor's figures. He's also correct about the difficulty in getting a clear image of it. It distorts our radar and visual imaging equipment."

On Earth, speculation raged on the comnets about whether the *Nile's* crew would become the first casualties or prisoners of an invasion. How close would the aliens let them get?

Money markets and stock exchanges went haywire with currency values and share prices rising and falling erratically. Alien Arrival Festivals, hastily organized in most major cities, attracted massive throngs of people who wanted to party away their last days or warm up for the visitors. It was like Carnival in Rio de

Janeiro on a global scale. A clutch of civil and ethnic wars, which had dragged on for years, went into a lull because they no longer mattered.

With little to do onboard the spacecraft, Simdar insisted on lots of rest. "Life will become hectic once we're alongside." As they closed on the alien ship, the three men spent every free minute peering out observation ports for the first glimpse of it.

The aliens only communicated with the *Nile* to provide navigation updates. "The main voice from it doesn't have the raspy sound of the one who spoke first," Simdar said.

When the astronauts finally sighted the large dark shape of the ship, their comnets flashed their words around the world. "The size is simply unbelievable," Horgi exclaimed. "There'll be no problem spotting it from Earth once it's in orbit."

"Look at the flares from its bow," Luin said. "It just destroys everything in its way. That must be how it passed through the asteroid belt without even slowing."

The ship loomed larger and larger. "This must be what a flea sees looking at an elephant." Simdar wished he felt as calm as his voice sounded. For the first time in space, fear of the unknown had set his heart racing. Do something, his mind screamed. He scanned his craft's instruments and displays before peering again at the ship.

Without taking his eyes off his display screen, Luin said, "If it doesn't start slowing down, it'll go by us in a blur."

Horgi relayed visuals of it to Earth through the long range viewer. "It's traveling so fast it's hard for the device to adjust the magnification quickly enough to maintain a steady image. There's no reflection off the ship's hull. It appears to absorb light."

"Could that explain the inability of our viewer and the space radar to get a consistent image?" Simdar sat back shaking his head. He'd always considered himself an astronaut scientist. Earth would be watching closely so every word counted. It was time for curiosity to chase away fear.

The radio hooted like an owl. Luin had programmed it to make the birdcall to signal a message from the alien ship. "We know a lot about you while you are just starting to learn about us," the raspy voice said. "So we want to invite you to tour our ship and, if you wish, travel with us to Earth. We can make sections comparable to Earth's atmosphere and temperature and prepare suitable accommodations for you. We have breathers and environment suits that will enable you to visit the rest of our vessel."

Simdar put the radio on standby. "We've faced danger since departing Space Station Freedom. Is the risk in visiting the alien ship any greater?" He saw no reason to decline the invitation. He wouldn't have succeeded as an astronaut without taking chances and living with the consequences. In a tone meant to convey his answer was yes and thanks very much, he said, "What do you guys think?"

Both responded with grins and thumbs up. "If their intentions are hostile, we're too close to that ship to survive," Luin said. "If it's a peaceful visit, we're the advance party."

"It seems odd they're prepared for an open house for humans," Horgi said.

Reassured by Horgi and Luin's support, Simdar said, "They probably want us on board so Earth receives a first-hand account of what they're like. They're trying hard to make a good impression."

"That's probably why everyone's suspicious," Luin said. Horgi laughed and slapped Luin on the back.

"Imagine being the first humans inside an alien spaceship." A smile spread across Simdar's face. "We will be able to dine out for a long time on what we'll see." He switched the radio to transmit. "We're honored by the invitation to visit your ship. Can we assist in docking?"

The reply came in a few minutes. "Fly to the flashing navigation lights. When our guidance system takes hold, turn off your propulsion system. We will draw your vessel into a bay and set it on a large air cushion."

The being paused momentarily and Simdar imagined it reading from a teleprompter when it began again. "We have tried to answer the questions we anticipated Earthlings might have about us. We expect you will have many more once you are on board."

"How will you slow down?"

"Just watch," the Being said.

Horgi patched the viewer's images of the Beings' ship onto all the *Nile*'s screens. Slowly at first, rings at the bow and the stern of the ship expanded to several hundred meters in width. He adjusted the viewer's spectrum monitor. "There's a distortion around the ship that's caused by a force field inside the rings. It works like retro-rockets. How they can withstand the forces that would create inside the ship is beyond me." He finished with a quiet whistle. "Boy, do we have a lot to learn."

Within a half hour, the alien ship glided alongside the *Nile*. Simdar recalled a boyhood family trip to Singapore and staring at the city's towering office buildings. Until now, he'd never felt as miniscule.

Before he could relate that comparison, Horgi spoke. "I expected something far grander, bristling with antennas and weapons. Instead, it's a long rectangular brown box with a rounded bow stuck on it. It's completely streamlined. The only protrusions are the rings and small domes on the surface." He sounded deflated. "It's massive, yet as plain as could be."

"It's unlikely the viewers on Earth could ever appreciate its size," Simdar said. "Think of a small rowboat beside the largest ocean liner. Then double the size of that ship and you get some appreciation of how tiny our little dingy is."

The *Nile* made a circuit around the ship to provide Earth with close up views. "There are no view ports," Luin said. The flat stern had four openings. "Whatever propels the ship must come from them."

Simdar steered along the ship's underside toward the flashing lights. At his approach, a rectangular opening appeared and he eased toward it while Horgi provided the commentary. "There're no markings on the exterior. The surface is rippled like corduroy."

The *Nile* shuddered as a force field locked onto it. Simdar imagined an invisible hand gently wrapping fingers around the craft. He shut down the propulsion system leaving only the quiet hum of electrical equipment.

"We're being drawn into what looks like a dark cavern," Horgi said, his voice rising with every word.

Simdar's eyes flitted between a last look at the stars and the first glimpse of the interior.

We're entering a huge open space," Luin said. "It's hard to see much because the lighting is so dim."

"There're no features like beams or trusses anywhere," Horgi added. "The walls are the same color as the exterior. In places, there're markings like the symbols in the first message from the Beings. We've stopped moving and are suspended several meters above the floor. Now there is a large mass moving toward us pushed by a machine that looks like a cross between a hovercraft and a farm tractor."

"It's our cushion," Luin said. "It's underneath us. The tractor is backing away and we're settling onto it. They're moving a platform with steps toward us."

When the vessel stopped moving, Luin said, "The inside of the bay stretches as far as I can see. And here comes our welcoming party."

Chapter 6
The Being Request

The astronauts stared at the aliens waiting for them in the bay of the spaceship. "There're about twenty of them. Half are wearing long robes while the others are unclothed." While Simdar wished he could have thought of a better description, the obvious difference between the two groups couldn't be ignored. "If the unclothed ones are anything like the rest, Beings have small physiques. Could clothes designate the officers?"

As he talked, Luin panned the bay with the ship's recorder, which transmitted the images to Earth.

"Welcome aboard, crew of the *Nile*," the raspy voice said. "You can disembark now. It is quite hot and we have the breathers and environment suits ready."

"We shouldn't keep our hosts waiting." Simdar struggled against his anxiety, wishing to sound calm.

As he punched the sequence to open the hatch, Horgi said, "Make sure you're smiling because there's a device floating out there that could be a recorder. I'll leave ours running."

When the door hissed open, Simdar stuck out his hand to test the temperature and yanked it back in. "It's like an oven. How do they stand it?" Taking a deep breath, he gingerly stepped onto the platform at the top of the stairs. Disoriented by the intensity of the heat, he paused before starting down one step at a time. Looking around, he spotted three disk-shaped craft about the size of commuter planes. He called back to his mates. "The mystery of flying saucers may be solved." Except for a topside center bulge, the units were flat with rounded edges.

Staggering like someone had struck them, Luin and Horgi cautiously placed their feet on each step, gripping the railings as if they were holding on for life. When he reached the bottom, Simdar dragged his right foot on the floor. "It's like heavy duty industrial carpet." When he looked up, he was staring into the face from the broadcasts. An identical-looking Being stood beside him.

This was the moment Simdar had often dreamt of; First Contact with aliens. In the stifling heat, his mind went blank and he couldn't engage his mouth to say anything of significance. He wanted to fix the moment in his memory. After wiping his right hand on his uniform, he stuck it out and the alien took it without any awkwardness. He placed his left hand on top and gave Simdar's a vigorous shake.

A childhood admonition against staring at strangers interrupted Simdar's speculation about whether the pattern of colors on the Being's face could be natural. They stood out far more than in the broadcasts. Although the other clothed Beings hung back, they appeared to be copies of the pair that had greeted him. Were they clones?

The unclothed ones waited a few paces behind them. Simdar kept glancing at them puzzled by the absence of flecks on their faces. Nor could he hear the raspy breathing of the clothed ones coming from them. Either the heat had really distorted his senses or there was something different about these Beings.

"My full name is," the Being who had greeted him said before uttering a long string of sounds, his voice rising and falling.

Even with a clear mind, Simdar doubted he could have made much sense of the alien's words.

You may call me Humbaw." He shook hands with Horgi and Luin and introduced the Beings starting with Demmloda. "Like me, he's visited your planet nine times."

Simdar managed to repeat the names of the Beings Connun, Horor and Bemmonloda before his concentration dissipated.

Humbaw gave no indication of rank and did not mention the unclothed ones. The other clothed Beings only nodded when introduced, and then moved aside in a small group. Most of them seemed to be frowning leaving Simdar even more puzzled.

"Before we go any further, you must put on these suits and breathers." Humbaw pointed to three packages that Demmloda held. "We have calculated that you could carry on for up to six minutes before the air and heat renders you unconscious."

Simdar doubted he would last that long. He and his mates were thoroughly drenched in sweat and Horgi was gasping for breath.

Demmloda handed over the suits and the breathing apparatus. "Put them in your mouths, and then get into the suits," Humbaw commanded.

The breather covered the nose and mouth much like an industrial safety mask while the one piece suit had a hood and Velcro style fastener up the chest. Horgi put his on first. His breathing soon returned to normal. "I feel cooler already."

"It's like a scuba diver's suit except it draws out the heat rather than holding it in," Luin said. "The mask filters out the excess oxygen, but allows us to speak normally. Bloody ingenious."

Simdar faced Humbaw. "We would like to see your vessel. However, first perhaps you could answer a few questions." Humbaw's eyes widened, and then he nodded. "What is the threat you mentioned in your original transmission? How can we help you? Finally, what is the difference between you and the unclothed Beings?"

Humbaw opened his mouth as if to speak. The lines on his face tightened.

Simdar couldn't understand the perplexed look. To him, the questions were obvious. He wished he could turn the floating recorder on his hosts. "The expressions on their faces aren't changing," he said to his mates. "I think they are communicating. Could I have offended them?"

"Notice how quiet it is other than their breathing?" Horgi said.

"Actually the silence is spooky after the constant buzzes, beeps and whirs on our craft," Luin said. "It's like a big soundproof chamber."

While the clothed Beings stood unspeaking, the unclothed ones stepped closer. They stared at the humans while their fingers moved in a blur.

"It's like they use sign language," Luin said.

"I'm going walkabout while Humbaw and his friends have their contemplation session," Horgi said. Several unclothed Beings followed him as he stepped over to the cushion under the *Nile* and poked it. "I can't even guess what it's made of. It's difficult to describe how it feels." He walked to the nearest wall and repeated his examination.

"Same material here. Wonder what this rail on the wall is for?" He withdrew his hand with a yelp as soon as he touched it. "It's freezing cold." Still shaking his hand, he studied the rail before gazing about the bay. "Like the exterior, there is nothing remarkable to point out except the markings on the wall."

The astronauts jumped at a loud pop that rang through the bay. "That had to be a door opening," Horgi said. "The rest of the ship must be at a higher air pressure than the bay."

"Look at that," Luin said. A couple of hundred unclothed Beings arrived. After a short discussion with their fellows, several newcomers went to inspect the *Nile*. They jumped up effortlessly on the cushion and began touching and rubbing the craft's surface while others climbed up the stairs to peer inside it.

Finally recovered from the heat wave, Simdar wanted to start describing the alien vessel to Earth. What should he say? The ship lacked any sense of grandeur. It came nowhere near his expectations. As more unclothed Beings joined them from elsewhere in the bay, Simdar became anxious about their numbers. He had to report their presence to Earth.

Noticing Humbaw finally paying attention to him, Simdar said, "How many unclothed Beings are on the ship?"

Humbaw hesitated, his expression unchanged. "There are more than two thousand helpers with us. They operate the ship. Are you suspicious of them?"

Simdar couldn't help wondering why it had taken Humbaw so long to answer the question. Before he could stop himself he blurted out, "What if you brought them to invade us?"

Humbaw's eyes widened. "What possibly for?" A helper whispered to Humbaw. "Ah, yes all those stories and movies about aliens attacking Earth." Humbaw chuckled. Simdar noticed the Being recorder had fixed on the alien.

"We pose no danger to Earth," he said. "Even if we're not welcome, it's time you knew of us." He took a deep breath and exhaled slowly. "In fact, the purpose of our mission is just the opposite of what humans fear. We need your help in defending our worlds."

Earth had a split-screen view of the rendezvous; the Being broadcast on the left and the *Nile's* on the right. After it docked on the galaxyship, the comnets dropped the *Nile's* feed because it only showed the same part of the bay.

Benjamin and his aides watched in his office as the astronauts toured the ship. They had lingered at the flying saucers to provide Earth with close-ups of the disc-shaped craft.

"They certainly look like what we've seen in countless UFO videos," Hector said. "Despite all the denials, militaries around the world collected all the info they could on sightings of unknown aircraft. There's actually quite a data bank on them."

Benjamin yawned. "The images get tedious in a hurry. The design and interior ship is so austere it verges on boring. I expected to be wowed by a showcase of technological marvels. I have seen more exciting department stores."

He wrapped the desk with his knuckles. "Back to preparing for the Security Council meeting. While the Beings want our military assistance, what can we do compared to the technology they must have on that ship?" Benjamin wracked his brains.

His aides shrugged, their expressions equally puzzled.

A half hour later, Benjamin entered the Security Council chamber. From the buzz of conversations, the delegations were just as mystified. He peered about wondering if he should let the discussions continue. His aides could use more time to urge the comnets to broadcast the Council meeting. He wanted the Beings to see the diversity of attitudes they faced.

When he did call for order, most conversations died out. "In light of what the astronauts have learned since landing on the alien vessel, are the delegations ready to authorize talks with the Beings?"

Instead of answers, the representatives either repeated their fears of an invasion or complained about Simdar suggesting the helpers posed a threat to Earth.

"Considering how many there are, he asked the right question," Benjamin said curtly. "What's more, we've learned their reason for coming here." When no delegation intervened, he gave his own plan a nudge forward. "I propose we appoint the astronauts as special UN Ambassadors with the authority to conduct exploratory discussions with the Beings. It's obvious they want to talk to representatives of Earth, not individual countries. We must find out how we're supposed to help defend their worlds."

He'd reviewed the backgrounds of the astronauts. "From their wide range of experience, they could handle negotiations with the aliens as well as anyone," he told the Council. A couple of delegations briefed in advance supported his suggestion. Benjamin looked about the room before calling a vote. Although most countries still harbored doubts, no harm could come from empowering the astronauts to find out more.

When he returned to his office, Hector said, "You may get a rough ride when people figure out what you're up to."

"If they do," Ernesto said. "They're not thinking about the aliens as the Secretary General is."

"Why do they have so many helpers to operate such an automated ship," Benjamin said. "We would call it a make work project. Why they didn't tell us about them beforehand."

"Maybe being surrounded by them is normal." Rachel held up a picture of the unclothed figure whispering to Humbaw. "I'm trying to identify their differences beyond the facial markings, skin texture and clothes. I haven't found any yet."

"The comnets are saturated with speculation about them and the size of the spaceship," Ernesto said. "The aliens have displaced the weather as the most popular topic of conversation."

Benjamin waited until the others stopped laughing. "Speculation is a lot better than panic and riots everywhere. We must remain vigilant."

All the Beings and hundreds of helpers turned out for a short ceremony in the ship's Conference Room to officially promote the astronauts to the rank of UN Ambassadors. Other than being wider and containing benches, the room had the same brown colored walls and floors as the rest of the ship. While the Beings gathered in a group off to the side, the helpers greeted the three men like they were movie or sports stars.

Decked out in a multicolored robe for the occasion, Humbaw resumed his explanation of the ship's operation once the formalities concluded. "The ship is run by the Controlling Unit assisted by the helpers. If you have any questions, just ask it for help. It will recognize your voices."

"As I'm sure you're aware from the Security Council debate, Earth wants to know what kind of military assistance you require as well as what you would offer in return." Simdar decided to save the questions about the helpers for later. He didn't seem to be getting anywhere on the subject.

"We would like to show you videos to explain the threat we face. Before that, we will divide the Room into your atmosphere and ours."

Helpers steered the ambassadors to one side of the room. Then a transparent screen appeared, outlined in pale white lines, running from wall to wall. "It allows us to create a human atmosphere in this side of the chamber yet doesn't interfere with conversations with the Beings," a helper said. "You can remove your breathers. Your atmosphere suits may remain on as they will not make you feel warmer or colder."

"Do all the helpers speak English?" Simdar said.

The helper nodded. "We would welcome an opportunity to converse with you gentlemen. We have worked at learning your language."

Before Simdar could ask about a picture on the wall, the first bit of decoration he'd seen in the vessel, Luin pointed toward three high-backed chairs on rollers. "Like everything they know about us, it's dated to their last visit. My dad had a chair like this from when he was in university. Still they look a lot more comfortable than the benches the Beings use."

Humbaw and the other Beings took their seats while the helpers stood. "We want to assign one helper to each of you. Our tradition is to call them by our name with ton added at the end. Ton is our word for 'helper of'. So if we used your names, they would be Simdarton, Horgiton and Luinton. It will be interesting to see how you adapt to them as we have the same one from birth."

So much for having any secrets. Simdar couldn't imagine having an artificial companion for his whole life. It would go everywhere with you. The ultimate chaperone.

Three helpers came forward. Horgi instinctively put out his hand in greeting. His eyes widened at the contact. "Its skin feels just like the material on the walls."

"That is because it is," Humbaw said. His brow furrowed and his voice slipped into a patient tone as if everything should be obvious. "Our helpers are made through the same process as our galaxyships. A frame is constructed out of polymer and the skin grows on it. It is a form of biotechnology. The skin carries all the electrical impulses and commands from the helper's brain like the nerves and blood vessels in our bodies."

"So they're robots?" Simdar said.

"That is what you would consider them to be. They're remarkably light. Try picking one up, Ambassador."

Horgi shrugged, and then put his hands on the waist of the helper facing him, whose head barely reached the human's shoulders. "Oh my, it's like lifting a small child. Fifteen kilograms maximum." He set it down.

"Now it will lift you." Horgi found himself looking down at the slender figure wondering how it had the strength to lift his 78 kilos.

"Your vessel would have the same weight as ours under gravity," Humbaw said.

"How long does it take to produce a helper and a galaxyship?" Horgi said as he straightened his suit.

"Once the frame is prepared, a helper is ready in a couple of days. It requires weeks of programming and training before it is ready. A galaxyship takes several months to complete. Of course, there is a lot more programming and other details to add such as the elevator."

"Ah, the circus ride said," Luin said. The Ambassadors had traveled in it to the Conference Room. It rocketed upward before abruptly halting and shooting sideways. When it had stopped, they had stumbled out and helpers had held their arms to steady them until they had regained their balance.

"One of the first things we noticed was how quiet it is in the vessel," Luin said.

"Just as we were astounded by all the noise on Earth," Humbaw said. "How do you cope with the endless racket? There is no metal in this ship so there is rarely any sound of components coming together."

Luin shook his head. "How about plastic or ceramics?"

Humbaw shook his head and held up his hand. "First things first. We want to demonstrate why we require your help."

With that, the lights dimmed and several displays materialized in the room showing three large ships against a backdrop of millions of stars. "We are broadcasting this to Earth."

Abruptly a swarm of black funnel-shaped craft streaked toward the ships. Brilliant splashes of light blossomed around them. "A cruiser like this one recorded the attack on the transports it guarded until they could shift to galaxy flight. The flares you see are laser blasts from the attackers striking the transport's protective shields. We call them walls. Galaxy flight is our term for faster than the speed of light travel."

Simdar found it hard to take his eyes off the displays. The craft buzzed around the large ships and more salvos spattered against the invisible walls. The cruiser emitted a blue streak reducing an attacker to a cloud of particles. In rapid succession, it obliterated the other attackers.

"What was that?" Simdar hoped his question would be included in the broadcast.

"The reason we're here. That attack is typical of our enemy. We call them Nameless because we have not learned who they are and why they keep attacking us. They appeared about ninety years ago striking at our ships and worlds. We have more videos to show you. We have not been able to communicate with them. The transmissions between their ships make no sense to us."

To Simdar, Humbaw had picked his words carefully. There was something he didn't want to reveal. The other Beings looked glum while the helpers smiled.

For the next hour, the Ambassadors and billions on Earth watched more Nameless attacks on planets and ships. The visuals surpassed any space action movie. "You will see something different next," Humbaw said.

A large enemy formation descended on a group of transports. A cruiser launched hundreds of craft like the flying saucers in the bay and they drove off the enemy after a protracted battle. "The defense craft are controlled by analyzers we programmed from studying your pilots in combat." The pride in Humbaw's voice made it obvious who'd introduced the tactics.

"In the visuals, the attackers never cause more than superficial damage to your ships," Simdar said. "So how are they a threat?"

"Occasionally they capture a transport," Humbaw said. "Our planets suffered considerable damage until we deployed cruisers to guard them. They are like your aircraft carriers. I liked the big ones the United States of America had."

"Did many die in these raids?" Horgi interjected.

"Controlling Unit, what is the most up to date data on the Nameless raids?"

"Since the beginning, they have killed six hundred and forty seven Beings and stolen nineteen ships along with two thousand and forty one helpers. Another seventy-nine galaxyships had to be repaired."

"Although our death and damage figures seem insignificant by Earth standards, to us they are appalling," Humbaw said.

"Did the Beings die on the planets or ships?" Simdar said.

"On the planets."

"So you lost twenty-three ships without any Being casualties?"

Humbaw nodded. To Simdar's surprise, the Controlling Unit responded. "The missing helpers were the crew on the transports the Nameless stole."

"Helpers operate all of our transport ships," Humbaw said. "We only travel on cruisers." Then he pressed on with his explanation and Simdar decided to save his questions about the Controlling Unit for later.

"Our ancestors feared we would destroy ourselves in civil wars so they spent many cycles ridding our species of the desire or ability to wage war. We call this period Transformation. It happened more than twenty centuries ago. We have explored thousands of solar systems and expanded to eight other planets because most of our home world is uninhabitable. While we found creatures somewhat like your reptiles here and there, you are the only conscious life forms we have encountered."

"You mean in the whole galaxy, there are just Beings and humans?" While the Nameless must be sentients, obviously the Beings don't see them that way.

"While that is all we have encountered, there is much of the galaxy we haven't explored. Because you had no way to leave your solar system and your planet is not suitable to us, few saw any reason to pay attention to Earth. Your violence and environmental mess remind us of our own lamentable past. After the Nameless attacks began, we looked for ways to defend ourselves. We are unable to fight even in self-defense. If we try to, we get ill to the point of incapacitation. We can program combat into our equipment, but we cannot do it ourselves. Until the attacks began, our inability to fight seemed a blessing. It never occurred to our ancestors that we might face a threat from another species. While it must sound arrogant, it is understandable." Smiling slightly, he added, "Many humans think they are alone in the Galaxy." Humbaw paused.

Simdar waited. The Being had finally got to the point of revealing why the aliens wanted Earth's assistance.

"There is a history of mercenaries on Earth. We want to hire pilots and soldiers to use our equipment to stop the attacks. That is all." Humbaw inhaled deeply. "You can set your price. Considering the state of your planet, you might want our assistance in restoring your atmosphere and environment. We can remove the excess greenhouse gases from the upper atmosphere and recreate your ozone layer. Our technologies might have other uses. Think of it as a fair exchange and a second chance for Earth."

Simdar had no idea how to respond. Glancing at his mates, he could tell by their wide eyes and open mouths that the Being request had startled them as well. Knowing that he had no real authority to accept or reject Humbaw's proposal, he said, "What made you decide to finally seek our help?"

Humbaw stared at him. "Who else could we turn to? There is no doubting your ability to wage war. It took the persistence of the Nameless assault to convince the High Council to accept my plan to enlist your aid. We are desperate to end these attacks. Many did not approve of contacting Earth even though they concede your warriors are probably the only way to overcome the enemy." Again he stopped as if looking for a response from the Ambassadors.

Then, gazing at the floor with a deep flush on his face, Humbaw said, "While your combative nature is what we most detest about humans, our circumstances are so grave that we are forced to overlook it. To us, it has become your saving grace."

Simdar wanted to tell Humbaw few humans would put a positive spin on Earth's long history of conflict. However, more important matters needed answers.

"What would our pilots and soldiers do?"

After a pause during which his face remained expressionless, Humbaw said, "Our technology can hold off the enemy. Combined with the skill of your pilots and soldiers, we could defeat them. We are not conquerors. There are plenty of inhabitable, empty planets in our region of space if we ever need more territory."

The alien face remained inscrutable. Humbaw didn't move his arms or make other gestures to emphasize his words.

"What reason would the Nameless have for attacking Earth even if they could get here?" Simdar didn't bother to add the obvious. How did the Beings conclude the Nameless could threaten Earth when they knew so little about them?

"It is only a matter of time before they discover your planet. We can install a monitor at the edge of your solar system to warn of any incoming vessels. Or asteroids."

"If we agree to help you, how many pilots and soldiers would you want and how long will this war be waged?"

Humbaw's expression remained impassive. While the other Beings still appeared disinterested, behind them the helpers broke into smiles. Simdar wondered if his eyes were deceiving him. Had he actually seen high fives and fist bumps?

Humbaw consulted a small screen. "We should start with five hundred pilots and five hundred soldiers and whatever medical and other personnel your experts think are necessary. We would supply all their equipment and hopefully return them within three years. We would teach them to operate our craft and weapons, but not how to repair or construct them. We would prevent them from bringing any weapons or equipment home, mainly to protect Earth. If this is acceptable, we have the capacity in this ship to transport them back with us."

Humbaw raised his hands to prevent any interruptions. "By your surprised expressions, you think we took Earth's support for granted. We regard our offer as a reasonable exchange of services; you save our worlds and we save yours."

Chapter 7
A Possible Link

Somewhere in Elinor's research she had seen Beings before. Although she had combed through science fiction and alien abduction books and countless wikis, she had come up empty handed.

Unwilling to give up, she phoned Ruth to thank her for the scoops and to explain her puzzle.

"I have the same feeling. I never read much fiction. I studied birds, rocks, stars, dinosaurs and . . ."

"Eureka," Elinor shouted. "A long time ago, somebody developed a model of what a particular dinosaur might have looked like if it'd survived and evolved. That's what the Beings remind me of. Thanks Ruth. Time to find a dinosaur expert if there're any left."

After decades as a star commodity, interest in the giant lizards waned as the midpoint of the 21st century neared, victims of overexposure and the planet's pressing environmental problems. Elinor remembered as a child watching a corny old movie about revived dinosaurs terrorizing tourists in a park. Her grandmother said children back then even had dinosaur dolls.

After a lot more phone calls, Professor Saul Hopkins of the University of Cascadia in Seattle had an answer. "What you're thinking of is a hypothetical model constructed by a Canadian named Dale Russell. I've pictures or a book on it somewhere. Why are you interested in dinosaurs when you're doing all that fascinating reporting on the aliens? Keep up the good work by the way."

Elinor beamed at the praise and thanked the professor until he made the connection. "The Beings do look like... what did Russell call it?" She let the professor ruminate and it paid off. "Dinosauroid and it was in a museum in Canada. Maybe it's still there."

Struggling to keep her excitement under control, Elinor soon located the Dinosauroid in the Museum of Nature in Ottawa. To her surprise, the cheerful media spokeswoman knew about it. "We don't have it on display any more and there are no images of it on our web site." Elinor could hear her typing on her keyboard. "The online pictures aren't very good either. I could send you some high resolution pictures or visuals of it. What's your deadline?"

Elinor smiled. Her name opened a lot of doors in scientific institutions and museums although she worried the spokeswoman might also connect the Dinosauroid to the aliens. If she did, she said nothing.

Instead, she filled Elinor in on its background. "Dr Russell developed it from a Troödon. It's quite clever what he did." She rattled off a lot more information before Elinor could stop her.

"We want to rent it."

"I can't decide that myself. I'll check and get back to you."

The museum agreed for an astronomical fee. Elinor figured the museum needed a lot of repairs. When the model reached the I-News studio in New York, she got the network officials to examine it. Once they agreed it bore a startling likeness to the Beings, she set about convincing them to assist her in obtaining an interview with Humbaw.

At the request of the UN, which wanted to avoid distractions for the Ambassadors, the comnets agreed to hold off interview requests until the Beings reached Earth.

"It's obvious the UN wants to keep them away from us for as long as possible." Elinor knew her editors chaffed at the restrictions the network had accepted. "This is a legitimate issue to discuss with them."

Despite all her awards and fame, Elinor felt her journalist colleagues didn't respect her accomplishments. What she covered wasn't as serious as reporting on the minutiae of governments and conflicts around the world. Or the predilections of politicians and sports and entertainment stars. Even a recent international poll that showed she was the most recognized and respected comnet journalist hadn't satisfied her. Getting the real story about the aliens would show she could handle science and politics and clinch her reputation. To that end, she had to get on their ship.

"What does Secretary General Kendo think of the interview?" Humbaw asked Simdar as they sat in the Command Chamber admiring the swelling image of Earth.

"The request for it came from the president of I-News. He carries a lot of influence. Elinor Brady will conduct the interview.

She's interviewed me several times. She's quite fair and her knowledge of science and space is excellent. She'll ask a lot more than how-do-you-like-Earth questions. She'll have carefully reviewed your broadcasts."

Humbaw nodded. "She had the first story about our ship. She is something of a personality. While we have studied Earth for many years, that does not mean we understand everything about humans. Now if you will excuse me, I need to rest before doing the interview."

While Humbaw wanted to sleep, his thoughts wouldn't let him. He had yet to explain to the Ambassadors how the treatment developed by Omanora to modify the Being brain to remove combativeness had unexpectedly triggered the development of telepathy and second thought. The latter enabled Beings to rest while their minds contemplated whatever matters concerned them. Humans would see it as the brain working in the background like their analyzers did. Over the generations, second thought had evolved to an almost analytical level. If it prevented Humbaw from falling asleep, it wanted him to pay attention to certain events.

One was an old problem. Long-standing opposition to his plan to recruit humans had faded among the other members of the Being High Council almost overnight. While the shocking loss of the Andomar colony to the Nameless played a role in the Council's about face, other factors had to have figured in the decision. He hadn't yet resolved what they were. Nor had he found a way to convince his crew to stop treating the humans as primitives.

A new matter troubled him; why did humans find the helpers so fascinating? Did they not see them as parallels to all their communication devices? A final thought came before sleep won out; the helpers appeared equally interested in the humans.

When he reached the Conference Room, Humbaw was still wondering what to expect in the interview. He had little time to worry as Elinor's face popped up on all the displays a few minutes later. "Can you hear me?" she said.

"Your voice is clear, Ms Brady."

"This interview is going live around the Earth. Your broadcasts contain a lot of information and the observations about our history are illuminating. Still there's a question that needs answering."

"I will try... we have nothing to hide."

"Can you explain the resemblance between Beings and this?" The recorder swung in the direction she pointed.

"You found the Dinosauroid." Humbaw felt as if the breath had been sucked out of him. He slowly regained his composure and said, "I looked for it during our last visit. There are differences between it and us. It has a smaller head and slighter build. Our eyes are narrower, we have a more pronounced nose and our hands are better developed. However, there is no denying the similarity and the common reptilian ancestry. We want to learn more about it for clues about our origins."

Humbaw took several deep breaths. "We know little about our early history, thanks to all the destruction on home world Hnassumblaw before Transformation. Only the Controlling Unit, Demmloda and I know about Dinosauroid. We have speculated about the possibility that someone planted our ancestors on a number of planets, including yours, to test their ability to adapt and evolve. Who or what could have spread our species is just wild conjecture. We haven't found mammals on any other planet."

While Elinor tried to interject with questions, Humbaw kept talking. "Is knowledge of the Dinosauroid widespread and can you provide us with more details on its development?"

"I will send you my research file." Elinor couldn't believe the aliens knew so little about their planet. "There's no knowledge, even tales, of your early history? No skeletons like those of dinosaurs and many other species of reptiles we've discovered?"

"Essentially that is it, Ms Brady. Our oldest records talk only of war and strife. There is nothing about how or when Beings came into existence. After Transformation, we put all our efforts into survival. While we succeeded beyond the hopes of our earliest leaders, we remain woefully ignorant of our origins. We have found ancient bones on a couple of our colony worlds we could bring to Earth for your specialists to examine."

While the rest of the interview added little to Earth's knowledge of the aliens, it sparked so much interest in the Dinosauroid that the museum put it back on display when I-News returned it. The comnets reported extensively on its development and the scientific debate around its plausibility and how it could be linked to the Beings. Some commentators even speculated on whether Russell drew his inspiration for it from an encounter with a Being.

Elinor's interview broke the ice for the Ambassadors with the rest of the Beings. The next morning in their suite, Luin recounted talking with several of them in the Conference Room after the interview. "All of a sudden, they're interested in what we think of their ship and how humans will react to them especially as reptiles have a lowly status on Earth. Their English isn't nearly as good as Humbaw's or Demmloda's."

"The switch from their usual arrogance is amazing," Horgi said. "They actually want to talk with us rather than only doing it because they're ordered to. And they've stopped treating us like we're the village idiots."

"The helpers speak much better English," Simdar said. "They must have worked on it long before we came on board and have updated it since we arrived."

"They could master any language in a few weeks," Luin said. "My ton and a couple of others have learned passable Japanese and now most of them greet me in it. Already I'm wondering how we ever get anything done without tons to help us."

The others laughed.

"I'm glad you sent them on errands because I want to talk about them," Horgi said. "Although their function is much like what we always envisaged for robots, they aren't machines. They're a biological entity unlike anything we've ever imagined as a life form. They have an organic brain and run on electricity. Most of their chest cavity contains a liquid medium for storing power. To me, the correct name for them is Biobots."

"An organic brain," Luin said. "How would they get that?"

"I'm working on finding out. So far, our tons haven't said much."

Simdar was relieved Horgi had investigated the helpers as the Secretary General had requested. "Why didn't the Beings set us straight?"

"The Beings take the helpers for granted and see no reason to talk about them. Which is odd considering they wanted to avoid panicking us. To them, the ones captured by the Nameless are assets, nothing more." Horgi settled back in his chair. "I'm sure you've noticed the Biobots study us as much as they help us. They're actually curious and not just spying for the Beings."

"Are you certain that's all?" Luin interjected.

Horgi nodded. "I'm sure you've noticed how hot their hands are especially if they're active. That's because they dissipate all the heat generated by the electricity in their bodies through their hands and probably their feet and tops of their heads. The material in those areas is much smoother, which would facilitate heat venting." He hesitated, broke into a crooked grin and then slapped his hand to his forehead. "I just realized the cold railings enable rapid cooling for the helpers. I should've figured that out before now."

Simdar glanced about for their tons. "The Beings couldn't operate these ships without their Biobots. The Beings are the absent-minded professors who can think great thoughts and can't remember to buy groceries."

Hearing the Biobots returning, Horgi switched topics. "Life on this ship is quite luxurious after the cramped quarters of the *Nile*. Our rooms are like suites at a swank hotel."

Waving at the tons, Luin said, "Besides the shower, there's a bed in each room large enough to roll around on and a comfortable chair."

"It's too bad we don't get to enjoy the comforts more," Horgi said.

The intercom hooted. "We have something quite different to show you," Humbaw said.

"There's always another piece of equipment or a visual the Beings want to demonstrate," Luin said. "He sounds quite excited so we better get going."

The tons snorted. "Humans excite him," Luinton said.

Humbaw and Demmloda waited for them in the bay where the *Nile* had landed. It sat on its cushion along the inner wall. This time the bright lights shone on the three flying saucers.

"These are our defense craft," Humbaw said, ushering the ambassadors over to them. "They are smaller than the Nameless attack craft and our other shuttles. We adapted their navigational analyzers to react to voice or control stick commands. We have added cockpits to these three based on the design of Earthling war aircraft."

He grinned as if enjoying a private joke. "Ambassadors Panamar and Vladmitz were military pilots before entering space service. Ambassador Kato is a highly qualified civilian pilot. Would you like to take our flying saucers for a spin?"

"Yes." Simdar rubbed his hands together while Luin and Horgi nodded vigorously.

"We cannot tell you how to fly them," Humbaw said. "You will have to train in a simulator to enable your own navigational analyzer unit to learn your techniques and how you respond to various situations." He paused. "Shall we begin?"

As they strode toward the simulator, Horgi detoured over to the *Nile*, inspected a panel and then caught up with Simdar. "They've taken no interest in our ship," he whispered. "A Biobot entered it after attaching the electrical feed. Our recorder shows it looking around to make sure everything operated before leaving. Since then, no one has asked to see inside it or tried to access its analyzers. There's no reason to expect they would. It's probably about as interesting as a raft."

Working together, the ambassadors figured out the defense craft's flight controls and prepared an operating manual for it. They had less success with the navigational analyzer. "It expects us to do what it tells us to," Simdar told his ton after his first session in the simulator. "It treats us like passengers. We're accustomed to flying using the instruments to make the right decisions, not being bossed."

"Is the navigation analyzer not the same as your autopilots?" Simdarton said. It had learned to copy Simdar's scowl.

"Not at all, the autopilot is completely under the pilot's control, and is employed during flights when nothing unusual is happening. The navigation analyzer flies the defense craft based on its programming. We're like additional software to it."

Simdarton nodded several times, his eyes widening. Other Biobots clustered around, listening closely and signing messages among themselves. Their interest in the craft's operation went well beyond idle curiosity.

"Normally if we screw up, we have to get out of the predicament or crash," Horgi said. "While the navigation analyzer would keep us from killing ourselves, most pilots would feel too constrained by its supervision when they want to take evasive action or attack an enemy."

Fingers flashed furiously among the helpers.

When Demmloda joined the group, Horgi asked what propelled the craft. The Being stroked his chin several times. "All I can tell you is the craft expels gas through exterior vents. The navigational analyzer adjusts which vents are open and that enables the craft to turn, bank or climb sharply."

The Biobots didn't flash their fingers after Demmloda spoke. So they already knew this.

"Once you're comfortable flying in space, we'll launch a few regular defense craft to engage you in mock combat," Demmloda said.

The Biobot fingers went into high gear.

The Ambassadors spent the rest of the day taking turns in the simulator. At the end of each session, the Biobots questioned their tactics and impressions about the cockpit design.

During supper that evening, Horgi said, "From all their questions and the close attention they paid to our training, I bet the Biobots want to become pilots."

The suggestion startled Simdar. After a couple of quiet mouthfuls, he said, "Actually your idea makes sense. It fits with them studying us. If they could learn to fly the craft, what do the Beings need us for?"

"The Beings wouldn't have considered them as pilots," Horgi said.

Early the next morning, the Ambassadors let the navigation analyzers guide the defense craft out of the galaxyship. Clear of the ship, they took control and soared past its bow toward Earth before making a wide sweeping loop that brought them back toward the vessel. "Make it look good, guys. The Beings are broadcasting this to the comnets," Simdar said over the radio.

"These birds sure beat anything on Earth," Horgi cackled. "Every pilot on Earth will be green with envy."

"For the next phase, the navigation analyzers will put our craft through a series of turns, ascents and descents," Simdar said.

At the conclusion of that exercise, 10 regular defense craft sailed from the ship. "From what the simulators threw at us, they'll follow predictable moves so if you can't shake one, do something unorthodox like a three hundred and sixty degree loop," Horgi said. "That should throw them off."

With Luin's lack of military experience and Simdar and Horgi's rustiness, it took a while to adjust to opponents. Once they did, a few unexpected rolls and other evasive maneuvers and the Ambassadors bested their opponents.

Later Simdarton related the scene in the Command Chamber after the mock dogfight. "Bemmonloda approached Humbaw and said, 'Human pilots can bring a quick end to the attacks. The rest of us thought it folly to recruit them. Please accept our apologies for doubting you.' You have won over the rest of the Beings. This is a very good development."

Simdar thanked his ton for the report all the while wondering if Bemmonloda's statement was as important to the Biobots as it was to the humans. Or maybe even more so.

Chapter 8
The 'P' Word

When the Ambassadors' space show concluded, Hector went to Benjamin's office. It had sprouted more broadcast screens since his last visit a day and a half ago in the hectic hours after the news about the alien ship broke. The comnets now referred to it as the Time Before Beings, and gave it the acronym TBB.

Now Hector counted two extra wide screens that followed broadcasts from the galaxyship and the global comnets while four smaller ones tracked the regional networks. Images without audio emanated from them. "The boss watches for any signs of trouble around the world," Rachel said.

When Benjamin returned to the office from a meeting, Hector said, "Imagine the difference our top fighter pilots could make at the controls of those craft."

Benjamin sat impassively in his chair, his chin resting on his intertwined fingers. "The Security Council's excuses for not making a decision are wearing mighty thin. If I have to, I'll use my authority to invite the Beings to the UN grounds. Of course, the Council should agree to welcome them. If the Beings go away, we'll lose an extraordinary opportunity to save the planet. We might not get another chance."

Hector recalled Benjamin's shout of jubilation when Humbaw suggested the Beings could fix Earth's environment. "Did you anticipate such an offer?"

"How could they not have noticed how badly the world's environment has deteriorated from their earlier visits?" Benjamin beamed. "As well, they would have heard the daily recitations of flooding, violent storms and erratic temperatures."

Benjamin succeeded by emphasizing the positive. In his two years working with the Secretary General, Hector had been impressed by his ability to find a silver lining in most events and use it to advance his goals. He would be looking for a way to do that with the Beings. First he would want to better understand what Earth was up against.

"What if the Nameless are a greater threat than the Beings let on?" Hector said. "We could get dragged into a war we're completely unprepared for."

"It's risky if we help and risky if we don't."

Hector ignored Benjamin's pacing about the office because he would circle back to his desk. Hector had come to realize his boss's best thinking occurred on his feet and that was always a good time to make an observation. "Earth's in a similar malaise as a hundred years ago just before the start of the Second World War. Back then, a prolonged economic recession made the war seem like an adventure. No one expected it would drag on for five years and end with nuclear weapons."

Benjamin didn't react so Hector continued. "Despite all the public hand wringing about an alien invasion, thousands have volunteered to help the Beings. Regardless of the risks, hiring on with them looks better than the lousy environmental and economic prospects on Earth. It wouldn't surprise me if people start asking the Beings to resettle us on another planet."

"While I'd thought of that, it's too soon to give up on this one yet." Benjamin stopped at his chair and looked distractedly at the monitors. "What do you think about helping them?"

"I lean toward yes, although there're lots of questions that need answers. I can't think of a better payoff than getting the environment repaired."

"Now, if I could only get the delegations to understand that. They remain fixated on the Beings attacking us. Such talk is nonsense. Capturing Earth in its present condition hardly seems worth the effort. Why would the Beings want to control this planet? It's too far from their worlds to serve any useful purpose for them."

As Benjamin veered away from his desk again, Hector said, "It's not just pilots and soldiers that are ready to help them. Astronomers, astrophysicists, astrobiologists, anthropologists, doctors and all sorts of specialists in exotic sciences I've never heard of are volunteering." His gaze wandered about the room. "Before going into space was just a dream for them. Now they have a chance to see it up close rather than through telescopes and satellite images."

"Any other observations about the aliens?" Benjamin examined the back of a broadcast screen as if he'd never seen one before.

Hector started with the big ones. "In addition to accomplishing faster than light travel, the ambassadors report the ship has an environment system that blocks the deleterious effects of radiation during prolonged space travel. There are probably other features about it we would consider impossible."

Benjamin laughed.

Hector activated his portable analyzer and pressed several keys. "The Beings say they're genetically incapable of fighting. They may also lack the personnel to conduct a war even with their technology. Rather than abandon a planet, which would simplify their defensive task, they decide to enlist us. While it will cost them financially, we pay the price in blood and suffering. By their way of thinking, we've plenty of bodies to spare with a population of nine billion compared to their twelve million. As we spend so much time killing each other, why not direct that hostility against their enemy."

He paused, waiting for Benjamin to look at him. "Humbaw's description of the Nameless communications sounded like coded transmissions. I can't figure out why the Beings haven't recognized that possibility."

Benjamin nodded. "See if you can learn more. Also find out who'd like to stage a test of their surface weapons. After the display with the defense craft, we can probably charge admission."

A bidding war broke out among the comnets for exclusive broadcast rights. Plenty of countries offered to host it.

Hector contacted companies and universities about research into new forms of analyzer communications and artificial intelligence. Despite the global recession, governments continued to fund these ventures because of their strategic importance.

Hector reported to Benjamin later the next day. "The techies agree the Nameless transmissions are coded and want any visuals connected to their messages to help them figure them out."

"Look after asking for them. I'm preparing for a Council meeting. The members say they're finally ready to discuss the Being request. It's about time as the alien ship will arrive tomorrow."

Walking to the meeting with Rachel and Ernesto, Benjamin rehearsed his arguments. "The Beings approached us gradually so we wouldn't be spooked. So far, it's worked fairly well. The civil unrest is no worse than a disputed outcome to the World Cup of Football. No governments have fallen because of it."

Shooting Benjamin a quick smile, Rachel said, "Most people are preoccupied with surviving. This is just one more challenge. You've kept the UN at the forefront of dealing with the aliens."

He nodded and continued his warm up. "Our future is bleak without their intervention. While governments won't say so publicly, attitudes are shifting. Before long, you'll hear commentators talking about how aiding the aliens isn't much different than a UN peacemaking mission except for the distance from home."

"The speculation about the Nameless is boundless," Ernesto said as they entered the noisy Council chamber. "It's hard to imagine why they keep fighting such a futile war."

"There is something, actually a lot of things about the Nameless that don't add up," Benjamin concluded as he picked up the gavel.

Simdar's offer to explain the function of Nameless codes attracted all eight Beings and hundreds of helpers to the Conference Room. He hardly noticed the energy screen dividing the room any more. As he waited for everyone to settle, Simdar watched several helpers grasp the cold bar with both hands. After a minute or so they backed away with big grins and slipped back among the other Biobots leaving him to wonder how they could withstand the pain of touching such a cold object.

Once everyone had settled, Simdar ran a visual through the display that showed how to use letters, words or symbols in a code. "They're very effective until your opponent figures them out." He was slightly taken back when the helpers let out a laugh instead of their usual Being snort. "Simdarton has uploaded more files about codes to the Controlling Unit if you have questions I can't answer."

"Why does Earth need more visuals of Nameless attacks?" Humbaw said.

"We're looking for a pattern in the contents of the transmissions and the actions of the attackers. If they can find one, they can determine what the commands mean. If the Nameless use a code in their transmissions and we can unravel it, we could counter their actions or send communications that confuse them."

Humbaw nodded his head. "Controlling Unit, send all appropriate visuals to Earth." Finger messages flew among the helpers.

Bemmonloda slapped his hands on his legs and stood up. "If we understood the Nameless communications, maybe we could learn where their bases are located. It's so obvious. Why did we not we think of it? We must help the Primitives with this task in any way possible."

The room went silent. While no one spoke, the Beings and Biobots stared at Humbaw, whose face twitched.

"I bet we just heard their name for us," Luin said. "Humans would seem like primitives to them."

"Useful primitives," Horgi said. "So they indulged in some political correctness in dealing with us." He laughed.

Simdar decided to smooth over the matter. "We would like to learn more about Being technology."

Humbaw nodded several times. "Ambassador Vladmitz, will you accompany Demmloda and your ton to the bay to work on preparing a Surface Defense Machine for a trip to Earth. We will show Ambassador Kato other parts of our ship."

After everyone left, Humbaw said, "Bemmonloda was so surprised by the idea of investigating the Nameless communications he forgot my order not to say that word. We started using it the first time we visited Earth. Sooner or later, one of us would blurt it out. Now it's done."

Watching Humbaw shake his head, it came to Simdar he was the only Being who used body movements and gestures when he talked.

"Now for the real purpose of this chat," Humbaw said. "There is something very important that I have not told you." His voice dropped into a conspiratorial whisper. "This information should only be shared with Secretary General Kendo and his closest aides."

He took a deep breath. "Two years ago, Demmloda and I found the wreckage of a crashed Nameless craft including three dead crew members." His eyes bore into Simdar like lasers. "The Nameless resemble humans more closely than we do the Dinosauroid."

"What?"

A display materialized to Simdar's right showing three human looking bodies with washed-out white skin lying on tables under bright lights. "The video shows our examination of the bodies in the hold of the shuttle we recovered them with."

Humbaw kept talking as Simdar stared at the figures. While ideas shot through his mind, none slowed long enough to become a question.

"In an earlier mission, we conducted all sorts of tests on Prim." Humbaw looked chagrined. "On live humans. Although we compared those findings to what we learned from the Nameless corpses, our data is quite limited. You could have a common ancestry and the difference between you may amount to nothing more than the effects of living on different planets. We did not divulge the discovery to the High Council because we feared it would lead the Councilors into linking Earth to the attacks. That is not possible. We have a lengthy visual of the bodies and all the data we collected for your medical specialists to examine."

Simdar spotted a fleeting grin on Humbaw's face. "Is there something amusing in this?"

"This information about the Nameless will cause great consternation among my kind while humans will speculate endlessly about it. Beings do not handle the unexpected well."

After Simdar showed the visual to the other ambassadors, Luin said, "It's hard to imagine a species so much like us developing elsewhere without the Beings knowing about it."

"It must have spooked them," Horgi said. "First they learn they could be descendants of creatures like our dinosaurs. Next they discover their mysterious enemy might be our first cousins."

It made no difference to the helpers. "We concluded right away the Nameless are of Terran origin," Simdarton said. "How they got off your planet is the mystery."

Horgi walked around the Surface Defense Machine inspecting all its features. "Advanced as it is, we would still call it a tank," he told Demmloda before describing the machine's role in warfare. The SDM looked like a hovercraft armed with two heavy laser cannons and four smaller lasers. "Nothing on Earth could match this machine for speed and weaponry.

"However there's no place for a crew. We need to develop a handheld controller so it can be operated on the battlefield by a soldier." It took most of the day to fashion a device capable of being used by a human or Being hands to guide the tank's analyzer.

After he and Demmloda took the tank a test drive around the bay, Horgi said, "I spent many hours as a youngster assembling model kits of boats, planes and military equipment. I'm sure kids today would want to build replicas of your machines and galaxy-ships."

With less than 24 hours before the galaxyship reached Earth orbit, a top priority message arrived from Benjamin. "The Security Council has agreed to welcome the Beings and discuss their request."

While Humbaw sat in silence for a few minutes before he spoke, his face beamed and he rubbed his hands together. "I have a message for the Secretary General that we can share with the comnets."

"It'll give them something new to talk about," Simdar said.

Humbaw stood up. "Controlling Unit, record and send this so the comnets receive it. I have dispatched a message to the High Council on the successful contact with Earth and the integration of the navigational analyzers and pilots." He cleared his throat with a low growl. "I have also told the High Council about the Dinosauroid and that all we have left to discuss is under what conditions Earth will assist us and what form of compensation it will receive."

Behind him, Humbawton flashed a finger message. The other Biobots responded with both thumbs up. Simdarton had told him the helpers had adopted the human gesture as their happy sign. Simdar had to find out why they were so excited.

Humanity's Saving Grace

Chapter 9
A New York Moment

As much as they wanted to spend the final hours before orbit watching Earth draw closer, the Ambassadors had long lists of tasks to complete. Luin dispatched *Nile* on autopilot to the International Space Station. It was the first time it had flown on its own. Meanwhile Humbaw, Demmloda and Simdar prepared for a Being shuttle flight to New York.

Humbaw had no end of questions about their reception at the UN. "Will Secretary General Kendo greet us? Is there a... umm," he hesitated, "a home or a place for us? The other times we used a shuttle as our base, but it wouldn't be a suitable venue for meeting your officials."

"They've altered part of the ground floor of the UN Building to Being atmosphere and oxygen levels," Simdar said. "I'm sure you will receive quite the reception. All the comnets will record your arrival."

The shuttle slipped into Earth's atmosphere without the usual fiery entry, much to the disappointment of the networks that trained recorders into the heavens hoping to catch the first glimpse of the alien craft. Strapped into cushioned seats, Simdar and the Beings experienced a few minutes of intense vibration in an otherwise uneventful flight. They leveled off over the Atlantic and made the approach to New York. In the distance, he spotted commercial jets lining up to land at the city's airports.

Simdar recounted previous bumpy, nerve wracking re-entries until Demmloda interrupted him. "The exteriors of our shuttles absorb the heat created during entry to boost their power supply. As well, the material in them does not create nearly as much friction as your craft. All that makes for a smoother ride." After a pause, he added, "Do not bother asking how. It is one of those matters we will not explain for now."

Luin and Horgi followed the shuttle in their flying saucers. As the shuttle landed, they zoomed back and forth over the city accompanied by some North American Air Command F22 Raptors. During one fly-by of the UN building, they allowed the fighters to pull up parallel to them before they leapt to maximum speed, leaving the sleek jets well behind in a matter of seconds.

Hundreds of thousands of New Yorkers and tourists had

gathered for a glimpse of the aliens as the shuttle settled onto the ground. Simdar hoped they weren't disappointed by the three Beings that ignored the crowd as they walked closely behind him from the shuttle to the UN. They wore dark blue environment suits that kept them warm and covered their mouths and noses to supply them with sufficient oxygen. Behind them strutted their tons and several other helpers.

A large hand-painted sign that read Welcome Back Humbaw stood out in the midst of the multitude of flags and banners in the crowd. When Simdar pointed it out, Humbaw didn't react until his ton whispered to him. He snorted and looked again before lowering his eyes as if he expected the large paving stones under his feet to suddenly vanish.

The Beings raised their left arms briefly after Simdar told them how to return the crowd's greeting. They kept their eyes fixed on the ground. The tons, which didn't require environment suits or breathing devices, raised both arms and cavorted about like members of a victorious sports team. The spectators roared their approval.

"Such a large and festive crowd is remarkable," Simdar said as they neared the entrance. "I expected a lot more than just a handful of protesters calling for you to leave or warning the end of the world is at hand." When he didn't get a response from the Beings, he looked back. "What's the problem?"

"The noise is extremely painful to us," Humbaw said without looking up.

"It will be much quieter when we're inside," Simdar said. Although Benjamin and other dignitaries waited at the entrance, Simdar and the Beings strode past them and a phalanx of security guards without even a wave. "They need to get into their rooms right away," he shouted once they were inside. Several guards pointed at a doorway. As his small band neared it, another guard pulled it open and the Beings swept through. "Tell the Secretary General I'll explain in a few minutes."

As the door shut behind him, the oppressive heat of the galaxyship enveloped him again. He put on his breather. After a short conference with the Beings, he stepped outside. Benjamin and a bevy of officials bustled toward him. Simdar explained the aliens' discomfiture and suggested the dignitaries come inside.

Without hesitating, Benjamin reached into shelving located beside the door and pulled out a plastic bag. Inside was a Terran version of the Being breather. "It's amazing what we Primitives can do on short notice." The aides pulled the breathers over their heads.

"Okay Ambassador, take us to their leader." Benjamin sounded giddy.

"Follow me after you take off those jackets and sweaters," Simdar said as he stepped to the door. "The heat's overwhelming."

"We need coat racks here as well," Rachel said while looking at the shelves of breathers. The guard pulled the door open and Benjamin and his aides cautiously followed Simdar inside.

"This is much better," Humbaw said as he approached them. After the introductions, he explained the boisterous reception had overwhelmed the Beings. "It even disrupted our telepathic ability."

"We have a reception planned for here tonight," Benjamin said. "Will it do if we tell everyone to speak quietly?"

"The Beings live in virtual silence so it's not just a matter of talking quietly," Simdar said. As he spoke, he had a sudden insight. The Biobots' sign language fitted the Being need for quiet and let them say anything they wanted. He needed a long chat with Simdarton.

The other Beings spread out to engage the humans in conversation. Humbaw drew Benjamin and Simdar aside.

After profuse thanks from Humbaw for the accommodations, Benjamin said, "I'm still trying to get the Security Council members to decide on your request. They've dithered long enough. I've told them if they say no, you'll still get volunteers and we'll receive nothing." He pointed outside. "We're setting up an embassy for you next door. Anyone who wants to join you only has to reach it to sign up."

"We would like to have the endorsement of the United Nations." Humbaw looked about to make sure no one headed their way. "The High Council would prefer to deal with a comparable organization on your planet."

"Your High Council might be rather disappointed with the UN. The Security Council will meet in two days. Tomorrow the capabilities of your tank will be demonstrated. After the Council meeting, we've arranged a news conference for you near here."

"That will be a new experience for me," Humbaw said with a chuckle. "Imagine that at my age. I want you to know that dithering is a trait our species share."

"A team of scientists thinks it has found a pattern in the

Nameless transmissions," Benjamin said. "Whether we will have anything in time for the news conference is unknown."

The first guests waited at the doors to the Being quarters when Harass strode up to Simdar. She and several other Beings had just arrived at the UN from the ship. "We conclude from all the food and beverages on the tables this event will not end soon."

"Most people will stay for several hours although the heat and the need to wear breathers may cut the party short."

"If we wore environment suits and breathers, you could hold the reception in another part of this building," she said. "The simplest change would be to set the oxygen level in this room at standard for humans and lower the heat a bit."

Simdar agreed and Harass went to inform the other Beings. Simdar looked about the room before he welcomed the dignitaries. The tile floor was a blend of several reddish colors while the walls were finished in a light brown and the tiled ceiling would absorb much of the sound. While humans would consider it dull, the Beings would regard the diversity of color as garish and the paintings on the wall ostentatious.

Within a few minutes, the aliens returned in the long robes the Ambassadors had dubbed Being togas or Bogas. By their unusual bulk, Simdar suspected they wore extra clothing underneath. Small tubes ran from under the suits into the sides of their mouths to deliver sufficient oxygen.

Even with the lower temperatures, the room was warm. "Normally the UN delegates dress formally for such big events," Benjamin said. "Tonight they're in casual clothes to cope with the heat." The room was full of bare legs and arms. Many women fanned themselves. Instead of sipping fancy wines and drinks, the representatives were gulping down vast quantities of water to cool themselves.

Simdar wandered from group to group, curious about what questions the Beings faced. To his surprise, most involved the aliens' telepathic powers rather than their request for military assistance. More than once, diplomats asked if the Beings would test Earthlings who claimed to have extra-sensory perception.

He made slow progress in his circuit of the room because of all the congratulations for his handling of the alien rendezvous. When he finally returned to Benjamin, he sent Simdarton down to collect Horgi and Luin. The ton bobbed his head and slipped back into the crowd.

Simdar checked the ton's progress before speaking in a hushed tone. "All the electronic security here disrupts their communicators. That gives me a good excuse to send it on an errand so I can talk to you privately."

He stared at Benjamin. "We think the Biobots have evolved into a unique species and the Beings don't realize it." He glanced about. "The relationship between them and the Beings is no master, servant deal. While we have yet to determine why, we suspect the Biobots masterminded contact with Earth."

Benjamin's eyebrows rose slightly and he shook his head. "A mystery wrapped in an enigma."

After waiting to see if Benjamin would continue, Simdar said, "Other than Humbaw and Demmloda, the Beings hold us in low regard. On the other hand, the Biobots soak up as much as they can about humans. And what one learns, they all soon do."

"I would like to hear more, but your ton returns with the other Ambassadors and General Davis," Benjamin said. "I think we need to revisit this discussion at a later point."

"I agree. The Biobots are fascinating creatures, but what their purpose is..." Simdar finished with a shrug.

In front of the ambassadors and the General, Benjamin praised the tons for their assistance. Simdar marveled at how Benjamin had figured out that the Biobots loved compliments?

When the festivities reached their loudest, several helpers wheeled in a discolored, scarred ball. No one recognized it. "This is *Voyageur Two*," Humbaw announced with glee. "It was launched in the 1980s by the United States of America to explore the Galaxy. We brought it back to show Earth how far it had traveled and also to prevent the Nameless from finding out about you. We recommend Earth cease sending transmissions from your deep space stations. The Nameless might detect them. You can study our space exploration records."

As the diplomats marveled at the hulk of *Voyageur Two*, Humbaw approached Benjamin. "Everyone seems friendly, but so far no one has talked about our request. Is this normal?"

"You should get an answer soon," Benjamin said. "A delegation of senior ambassadors approaches. You'll see what you're up against."

After the diplomats crowded around Benjamin and Humbaw, the Chinese ambassador spoke. "A week ago, we didn't know you existed." She shot Humbaw a curt bow. "Since then, we've debated whether to fear, fight or welcome you. None of us anticipated your request. Agreeing to support other nations in time of war has had disastrous results on Earth so we want to understand the risks we face. What assurance do we have that we won't get dragged into a conflict that might overwhelm us?"

Simdar could tell by the murmurs of the other UN delegates that they shared her apprehension.

"You should look at it as a chance to stamp out a small fire before it becomes a big one," Humbaw said. "We face a challenge we cannot resolve on our own. So do you. The survival of both our species is at stake. That is why we decided to contact you rather than just observe."

A Biobot recorded the discussion. Simdar suspected Elinor would receive a copy before long. The reporter had aired so many reports on the Being ship that she had to be getting help from the Biobots. Another reason to figure out their motives.

The evening concluded with the UN delegates in small groups talking with individual Beings. The Biobots hung around everyone occasionally offering comments. Already dazzled by the Being galaxyship and the shuttles, everyone awaited the test of the alien tank with great anticipation.

The next morning, a transport shuttle delivered the tank to a rolling plain in southern Mexico watched by thousands of curious locals and a crew from the World Broadcasting Corporation that had paid a handsome sum to the UN to break I-News's stranglehold on coverage of the aliens.

Biobots demonstrated the operation of the SDM to Lieutenant Pedro Valenz of the Army of the North American Federation. Within minutes, he had it passing almost silently over obstacles and coasting around buildings.

"With the usual noise in a battle, it could sneak up on an enemy with little likelihood of detection," Horgi told a phalanx of military officers watching the demonstration.

When Pedro felt comfortable with the controls, the Biobots powered up its weapons and he steered it toward a cluster of abandoned buildings. He fired its main lasers at them on different settings. On low, they created gaping holes. At maximum, vast chunks of the buildings dissolved. Within minutes, only a slowly settling cloud marked the location of the buildings. "It would take a few modifications to make the controller easy to use," Pedro told Horgi. "The laser rifles are equally devastating.

I'm sure on maximum, they would kill anything."

Although the display of firepower and individual delegation meetings with Humbaw eased concerns at the UN, it still took almost a day of protracted and largely useless debate before the exhausted Security Council members voted to send military help in return for restoration of the world's environment.

While few countries spoke in support of the proposal, none opposed it. Many abstained in the vote and afterwards, several delegations issued a statement to the comnets voicing their fears that Earth had handed its future over to aliens.

Simdar tried to reassure Humbaw. "The delegates are concerned they will be blamed if something goes wrong. It's human nature. It is called covering one's ass."

With official approval for the mission, the Beings turned their attention to selecting pilots, soldiers and support personnel from all the volunteers for the First Extraterrestrial Expeditionary Force. While the aliens had the final say in choosing the members of FEEF, the first three selections won immediate approval.

Promoted to the rank of a full General, Hector took command of the mission. Benjamin lobbied hard to have his aide in charge so the role of the UN wasn't lost in national rivalries.

The Secretary General also secured Elinor Brady's presence on the ship. Her reports would help develop relations between the two cultures.

The ship's Controlling Unit selected Ruth Huxley because of her expertise in space. While he hadn't made the decision, Humbaw offered no explanation for the decision. "I'm too busy to consider the matter further."

Humanity's Saving Grace

Chapter 10
Meet the Press

At the end of his first day as FEEF commander, Hector phoned Benjamin. "The relationship between the Beings and Biobots is even odder than Ambassador Panamar portrayed it. The Biobots willingly do all the work and let the Beings act in charge even though the Biobots could operate the ship on their own. They can get the Beings to do whatever they want."

"How does that affect us?"

"Too soon to tell." Hector had already planned to discuss the matter again with Simdar. "I intend to get all the officers to work on this with me. We need to figure it out as soon as possible."

"We also need to conclude the choice of military personnel to get the Beings to focus on rehabilitating the environment," Benjamin said.

"I'm trying to ensure we have a functional unit out of the thousands of men and women who have applied," Hector said. "Our friends don't think that way. The Beings aren't really sure what they need and ask about technological training and experience in unusual circumstances. The helpers want personnel who've worked as trainers or instructors. I'm left to pick medical personnel."

After mulling over Hector's observations, Benjamin turned his thoughts to the news conference he'd moderated the previous day at Humbaw's request. It had put the spotlight on the role of the helpers.

"Like the welcoming reception, visuals of this event will interest our worlds because we have nothing like them," Humbaw had said as he waited for the conference to start. "We use an information system to distribute announcements and visuals of events and discoveries."

The large theater selected for the news conference normally staged productions of Shakespeare and other venerated playwrights. Journalists from around the world had packed it to standing room only. With earpieces and microphones in place, Benjamin, Humbaw and Demmloda strode on stage. Through clever tailoring and coloring, the Beings' environment suits looked like tuxedos. The snug jacket and pants emphasized their slight physiques.

The humans sat in chairs on either side of the Beings' bench while the tons stood behind them. Before coming on stage, Humbaw decided to forgo an opening statement. "Surely these people have heard enough from us already."

Benjamin welcomed everyone. "Humbaw and Demmloda are at your disposal to answer questions." With that, he nodded at Elinor, who looked all business in a blue pin-striped suit and hair pinned back. She stood ready to ask her question.

"Are the helpers slaves or do they have lives of their own?"

The muttering in the theater evaporated. The Beings looked at each other and stared into the sudden silence. They had no idea how to reply. With Benjamin's help, they'd prepared for questions about the Nameless and helping Earth.

They turned to their tons to discuss a response. "What a strange bunch," a puzzled reporter near Elinor said loud enough to reach Benjamin. "They're asking their Biobots how to answer a question about their Biobots."

Humbaw cleared his throat. "Humans carry devices to talk to others and send messages, remind them of their schedules and provide complicated information on any task they have. Our tons do that and much more. They keep a record of all our activities and provide information or a reminder just as you program your devices to do."

"Ambassador Panamar said the tons often whisper to you in a meeting as if passing on information or even possible questions or answers," Elinor said.

"That is precisely what they do, and I am still at a loss to understand your question."

"Do your helpers have rights? Are they compensated for their service?" As she spoke, she glanced down at a handheld monitor. A theater employee told Benjamin before going on stage that I-News paid to have a remote controlled recorder mounted on a ceiling support. He suspected she'd watched the reaction of the Biobots to her questions.

Humbaw certainly wrestled with them. "Ms. Brady, they perform a useful function and as most of us live to several hundred years, they are worn out by the time we die and are turned off." He halted. "I do not know how you would describe that."

"Are their memories kept? They must know a lot?"

While Humbaw and Demmloda shook their heads, the tons perceptibly straightened and peered in her direction. They looked like kids trying to deny involvement in some mischief.

Although Elinor didn't ask more questions, Benjamin doubted he'd heard the last of her interest in the Biobots.

The news conference dragged on with other journalists inquiring about repairing the environment and fighting the enemy. She was glad no one followed her line of inquiry although it surprised her no one mentioned the lingering public apprehension about the motives of the Beings in bringing hundreds of Biobots to Earth to analyze environmental conditions and pollution hotspots. That would be her story and Ruth could help her pursue the relationship between Beings and Biobots once they boarded the galaxyship.

When she slipped away from the news conference, a UN employee handed her a note. "You asked the right question," it said. "Call me when you get a chance." Simdar had added his phone number.

The first pilots and soldiers transported to the galaxyship gathered in their common room. A large three-D display of the slowly spinning Earth floated in the middle of it. The shimmering blues and whites from the planet's image created odd patterns and shadows on the floor and walls. The absence of windows bothered Captain Christopher Donohue less now since Demmloda had explained the composition of the ship's exterior made them impossible. Looking at the information panels along the bottom of the displays in the room, he noticed the ship's status reports were both in English and Being symbols.

A fighter pilot in the European Air Force for 10 years, Chris applied immediately when he heard the Beings wanted combat pilots. The response came in an invitation to undergo a series of tests of his adaptability to space flight. "They are to gauge a pilot's reaction times and ability to withstand the stresses of sudden, sharp maneuvers and quick acceleration and deceleration in zero gravity," it said.

He traveled to Amsterdam where a large Being shuttle had

landed to test European volunteers. Instead of a simulator of the defense craft cockpit, he sat strapped to a wooden chair in a plain tan colored chamber. The light dimmed, a panel rose from the floor and several displays materialized around him. The chamber rose, fell and rolled repeatedly as he tried to keep up with commands to touch buttons, flip switches and answer questions.

The test stopped abruptly and a Biobot entered to help him from his seat. "Very good, you don't need any assistance walking." It smiled slightly. "You performed above our expectations, well above."

Later in the day, he received a summons to report to his base commander's office. The colonel pointed him to a seat and handed him a secure visphone. When Chris looked at the screen, Humbaw and Hector greeted him. "Your score in the test was just under one thousand, a result that makes you exceptional," Hector said. "Most pilots recorded in the six hundred to seven hundred range. I'm offering you the position of chief pilot of FEEF."

It took a few days of paper work before he boarded the shuttle to the galaxyship. Once on the ship, Chris didn't have to wait long for his first face to face meeting with the Being leader and the FEEF Commander.

Chris stared at the screen in the Conference Room trying to understand how it kept the human and Being atmospheres separate without blocking conversations.

"We plan to split the pilots into three squadrons," Humbaw said. "You will lead one, Captain Donohue. The other captains will arrive tomorrow. For now, we want your opinion on this." He pointed at a three-D display. "Controlling Unit, run the mock up."

A flying saucer, rendered in high quality animation, pursued one of the funnel-shaped Nameless craft. Suddenly a yellow streak shot from the saucer and encased its quarry, which lost speed and drifted off course. A cruiser lumbered into view, lassoed the Nameless craft with a beam of light and drew it into a bay. Chris didn't take his eyes off the image even as it began to repeat.

"The yellow represents a high-powered energy beam that will shut down the analyzer on the Nameless craft," Humbaw said. "It will be a very dangerous assignment because the pilots in the defense craft will have to fly close enough to the enemy for the beam to work."

"Why are we trying to capture the enemy?"

"We want to learn who they are," Humbaw replied.

"What would happen to any captives?" While Chris' thoughts were on the mission, he felt puzzled the Beings knew little about their enemy.

"It is hard to say until we can capture some of them."

"What will you do if the beam doesn't neutralize them?" Chris said.

"Destroy them."

Chris watched the visual until it began to replay. The Being's explanation didn't add up. Humbaw hadn't told him everything about the purpose for trying to capture a Nameless craft. This had happened often enough in the military and the vagueness unsettled him.

Early the next morning, Chris went to the Common Room to ponder Humbaw's plan some more and check the display of Earth for the first sign of the next shuttle. He'd already watched several shuttles delivering supplies suddenly pop into view against the backdrop of the planet.

He removed his breather and relaxed in the chair. Until the interview with Humbaw, learning to fly the defense craft preoccupied him. Watching the ambassadors prance about space in them and play tag with the drones convinced him he could make the unit perform way beyond what his commanders or the aliens might imagine.

Earth continued rotating in front of him as he pondered his reasons for joining FEEF. The timing was perfect. He'd avoided a posting at EAC headquarters in Brussels. His commander had made it clear he'd put off the administrative side of his career long enough. He had to take a desk job or find a new line of work. 'It's how you get promoted.' Facing the unknowns of space posed a better challenge than processing screens of data and glad handing at receptions.

Finally, he spotted the first flicker of light off the shuttle. He found plenty of irony in highly skilled pilots traveling to the galaxyship in an automated craft. Maybe it carried the other squadron leaders.

His introspection drifted to who or what the Nameless could be. It was like trying to solve a puzzle that lacked key pieces. His personal communicator chimed. "Captain Donohue, report to the Conference Room," the Controlling Unit said.

He glanced again at the approaching shuttle and departed. As he took a seat at the large round table added to the Conference Room since last night, Leprechaun, his ton, brought him a hearty breakfast of sausages, porridge and a sweet bun.

Looking at the food, Humbaw said, "Is that a normal meal for one of your stature?"

Chris patted his rock hard stomach. "You didn't build your flying saucers for big guys. I work hard and I depend on this meal to carry me for most of the day. Leprechaun is my good luck charm and takes very good care of me."

Humbaw nodded. "As it should. Sometime you must explain why you gave your ton a separate name." While the Being went on about human habits, Chris's attention had shifted to Humbawton flashing his fingers at Leprechaun. When he looked at Hector for an explanation, the General shot him a bemused smile. His musings about the Biobots halted with the arrival of the other squadron leaders, Captain Lin Jiabao of the National Air Force of China and Captain Sergi Konstantinov from the Air Force of the Russian Federation. Like Chris, they had short, wiry builds.

The Controlling Unit replayed the visual of the cruiser reeling in the zapped attack craft as Hector outlined the plan to capture Nameless.

Lin and Sergi simply nodded. He decided to share his doubts with the other Captains later and asked about Being telepathy. He hoped Humbaw wouldn't detect why he'd changed the topic. "How much of what we're thinking can you understand?"

"Mostly your emotions. In the past, it always took until near the end of a visit to Earth before we could detect emotions and sometimes even decipher them. It's happened faster this time because we spent all that time with the Ambassadors and now with the pilots and soldiers. We cannot see the details of your ideas as we can with Beings. That is primarily the result of our genetic and cultural differences. Earthlings have an undeveloped telepathic ability. Even those who claim to possess such ability are not clear to us. At best, we can sense they are trying to communicate, although it is like someone poking us with a finger to get our attention."

Humbaw stood. "There are some other people I must speak with. I'll meet you later this morning to answer any further questions."

Chris followed the others from the Conference Room to find Humbaw in the midst of introducing the officers to Elinor. Even though she wore a baggy red jump suit and her breather, she looked more vibrant than on the comnet. He felt a rush when he shook her hand and couldn't coax his tongue to say anything wittier than hello. It still earned him a beaming smile.

"See you later, gentlemen." She entered the Conference Room.

Humanity's Saving Grace

Chapter 11
Something Old, Something New

Hector steered his squadron commanders down the corridor. "Controlling Unit, lift at Conference Room entrance, destination Bay 1."

Within seconds, the lift door rolled up and the men and tons stepped in. The lift sank like a stone, and then glided to a smooth stop. The tons took hold of the officers so they didn't lose their balance.

"We must find out how the Beings withstand such speeds," Hector said between gasps as he regained his equilibrium and stepped out cautiously.

"You can remove your breathers as this corridor has an Earth atmosphere," Hectorton said. "We're creating Earth atmosphere corridors in areas of the ship to which you need access. You won't need to wear your environment suit very often although you should always carry your breather. We may split the atmosphere in the Command Chamber. Because the Beings rarely enter the bays, they'll have Earth conditions like the Common Room. Temperature and oxygen levels don't matter to us."

Hectorton was in full form as tour guide, gesturing with its arms and raising and lowering its voice for emphasis. The Biobot brought his hand up to halt the officers, and then pointed to a series of doors. The first few bore round red signs depicting a human with a slanted line through it while the others had placards of a human and Biobot beside each other. "The first symbol means the area is closed to humans. The doors are programmed not to open for you. Mostly, it's not safe in there although there're some pieces of technology the Beings aren't ready to share with you. The other placard indicates a Being atmosphere and you should only enter wearing an environment suit and accompanied by a helper. They contain technology to which you have controlled access."

Finally, they reached the doors into the bay. The symbol showed only a human figure. As they drew near, an artificial voice greeted the four men by name. The entrance slid sideways.

Inside, bright lights shone on the three cockpit-equipped flying saucers. Two maintenance Biobots worked on the craft.

"I was so jealous of those truck drivers from the *Nile* when they got to fly them," Chris called out.

"Good day, sirs," the maintenance Biobots said in unison as the officers drew close. "We can show you the defense craft," one continued. Unlike the usual flat Biobot voice, this one spoke with a musical lilt.

The pilots ran their hands over the surface of the craft. "It does feel like industrial carpet," Lin said. "It's got a pretty interesting crisscross pattern for the propulsion and laser ports."

Chris grinned at the two maintenance bots. "We'll have to give these mechanics names. What are grease monkeys without names, eh General?"

"Just grease monkeys, I suppose."

"We would prefer names, Captain," the first one said, glancing at the other. "Being called a slick simian doesn't sound complimentary."

"Other tasks await me so I leave you to inspect the craft," Hector said.

When the pilots knelt to examine the underbody, they found it dotted with closed ports like the rest of the craft's exterior. "Now to inspect my new office," Chris said. As he pointed at the cockpit, he noticed Leprechaun's grin.

The mechanic aimed a small device at the craft and the canopy cover retracted. He pointed at the other craft opening their covers. "There's a lever in the cockpit that will do that and the navigational analyzer will as well if you request it."

Chris scampered up the footholds and peered inside. "It looks like someone borrowed the design from our jet fighters. There's a control stick and a standard array of readout dials and navigation aids. Probably even have proximity and collision alerts."

"The cockpit is based on what we learned from your fighters," the mechanic said, pointing at the other one. "I like the F-22 myself, he prefers the Eurofighter."

"They're pretty old birds." Chris kept his surprise at the Biobots' preferences to himself. "You guys must've done some heavy duty espionage to get all this."

"Think of it as research. Actually, we made some modifications to the flight data displays based on what the ambassadors told us. Most of the information is conveyed by displays on the canopy."

Chris let his eyes absorb every detail of the cockpit before stepping in. The mechanic climbed up and began pointing out various features.

"Really, all I have to do is steer and pull the trigger at whatever targets the navigation analyzer finds," Chris said.

"There's no trigger." The mechanic peered at him closely. "You tell the navigational analyzer to fire. Surely flying is more complicated than you describe. Your experience is important to making the craft more effective against the Nameless."

"I'll tell you after my test flight. Navigation analyzer, demonstrate the flight data displays." One by one, they showed three-D views of the location of enemy and friendly craft as well as planets and other celestial bodies that might affect the flight. Another display showed the status of the craft's systems and its fuel supply.

After a few minutes, Chris whistled deeply. "They can tell me anything I could possibly need to know. We're gonna do serious damage with these birds." The mechanic beamed.

Near midday, the pilots headed to the Common Room for the follow up meeting with Humbaw and Hector. "Why would he want to meet us there when the atmosphere is set for us?" Chris said. "It doesn't have an energy screen to create a Being atmosphere."

"He thinks you will be more relaxed," Leprechaun replied.

Humbaw sat underneath a white cone of light. Pointing at a small dimple on the ceiling, he said, "We can create these climate centers anywhere on the ship for you or us." He motioned for them to sit nearby. "What did you think of our defense craft? We will have more advanced ones later."

"It's always hard to appreciate something until you have actually seen, or in this case, flown it," Chris said. "The mechanics surprised us with their questions about flying and aircraft design."

Humbaw frowned. "Who is he referring to?"

"The defense craft maintenance helpers," Humbawton interjected.

Nodding, Humbaw said, "Deputy Ambassador Vladmitz said we should have a deal with a company to produce replicas of our galaxyships and equipment."

Chris smiled at the Being's dodging the question about the helpers. "I built a lot of them as a kid and I still make them with my 10-year-old nephew. We spent many hours watching the broadcasts of your ship coming to Earth and the test flights of the defense craft. He was excited by my acceptance as one of your pilots."

"Then we will have another thrill for him. You could take Ms Brady to record the other Captains on their check flights at the same time. Her visuals should interest Earth viewers."

"I need to take my check flight in a defense craft first to complete my integration with my nanalyzer," Chris said. "After that, I would be glad to take her for a flight."

"Your what?" Humbawton whispered to him. "Oh, the navigational analyzer."

"Being Primitives, we like to use short words." Sergi and Lin burst out laughing.

Humbaw shook his head. "You showed in the original test and in the simulator that you are ready now."

Chris surprised himself by sticking to the rules. "As there's no one to supervise me, I should go on my own so I don't endanger anyone else."

Humbaw appealed to Hector. "It's time to get the pilots flying. It will take about a week to move far enough from Earth to permit us go to galaxy speed and we would like them to log at least two flights before then. Hopefully we will have enough time. Only simulator training is possible during galaxy flight. Captain Donohue needs to begin checking them out right away."

"At least let me have a few minutes out there on my own," Chris said. "I'm not trying to hold things up."

Hector nodded his approval. "As soon as this briefing ends, you are to report for your test flight. We'll have Elinor, Sergi and Lin prepared to accompany you as soon as you're ready."

Humbaw said, "Are there any other issues to address?"

"Can we fire the lasers?" Chris said.

"We will find some rocks for target practice."

"I have another idea. One of the biggest hazards for space missions is getting through the debris ringing Earth. There's everything up there from tools to useless satellites. We could destroy some of it. It would make a great show and do a favor for Earth at the same time."

"We had to destroy large objects during past visits to protect our ship, and always worried doing so would reveal our presence," Humbaw said. "While the lasers on your craft will blast the debris into fragments, they will remain a threat until they fall out of orbit."

Chris stood. "I've got a flight to catch. Controlling Unit, inform the mechanics I'm on my way."

An hour later, Chris sat in the cockpit of the defense craft reliving his test flight as he waited for Elinor to arrive. Thanks to the thoroughness of the simulator sessions, it went pretty well as he'd imagined. After he launched, he did a big loop around the galaxyship, like a kid on a Ferris wheel. His heart pounding with excitement, he streaked away from the ship at top sub-galactic speed. Although the force pushed him back into his seat, he kept answering questions from the nanalyzer about what he could see from the displays and out the canopy.

Part way through the flight, he realized the only sounds in the cockpit were the faint hiss of the craft's propulsion system and the nanalyzer's commands. He felt relaxed when he expected to be completely on edge.

"By the rate of your heart beat, you are comfortable with the jet," the nanalyzer said. "So we will proceed to the next level of tests." The craft launched into a series of abrupt turns, dives and climbs, far more severe than what the Ambassadors underwent. He whooped like a kid on the ultimate roller coaster ride.

Afterwards, Chris steered toward a mass of space rocks. "Time for target practice." A few blasts of the laser cannon vaporized them. The weapon made no sound when it fired its streaks of white light. Barely 15 minutes had passed when the nanalyzer surprised him. "That's all I need."

"How did I do?"

"Brilliantly. If all the pilots are as effective, the Nameless will not know what hit them."

"Should I do something better?"

"No, you are an excellent pilot or you would not be here. This was about improving our ability to work together."

Steering toward the Being ship, Chris pondered the nanalyzer. He had to consider it as more than a portable analyzer in a silver box. As he mulled over all it did, he understood it was a different form of a Biobot and would know everything the helpers had learned. He decided to test it. "Do you want a name like the others?"

The nanalyzer paused before replying. "You figured out our connection with the Biobots. Very good for a Primitive, and yes, I would like a name. The mobiles are all anxious to have them. What would you suggest?"

Chris smiled at the use of the pronoun 'I' and how the nanalyzer changed its tone when it said Primitive. It almost sounded like it had chuckled. "It won't be Hal. How about Armstrong? Would that do?"

After a brief pause, which Chris assumed was to check its data banks, it said, "A good choice. Neil Armstrong was the first human to walk on the moon. He was a good man too. I would be honored."

After he landed, he contemplated how his life could depend on Armstrong reacting to his orders as well as taking over if he blacked out. It would alert him to approaching enemy and recommend attacks and defenses while controlling the jet's protective wall.

At that point, Elinor climbed into the rear seat and her voice flowed through his earpiece. "Ready when you are, Captain."

"Set Lin? Sergi?"

"Roger."

"Follow me." The jet slipped into space and shot forward into a holding pattern until the other craft pulled alongside. "The nanalyzers will put you through some maneuvers to see if you respond the same way as in the simulator. Relax and enjoy. We'll follow you so Ms Brady can get visuals. Comnet stardom awaits you."

"What a view," she said as the craft sped in front of the galaxyship. "For all the danger, space is a wondrous place to behold." Earth took center stage, a partial moon looking over its shoulder with a brilliant array of twinkling stars as backdrop.

Chris left it to Elinor to describe the scene while he focused on the other pilots. For the next half hour, Lin and Sergi dove, climbed and turned in dizzying succession and then dueled with drone defense craft.

Armstrong broke the silence. "The nanalyzers on the other craft report complete integration."

"Sergi, Lin, let's have some fun." Chris shifted the control stick toward Earth. Armstrong selected the first target—the tangled remains of a satellite that by its distorted shape had collided with other objects in the past. "It's no longer sending signals to Earth."

Chris closed within 500 meters and brought the satellite into the center of his target display. "Fire." A white streak leapt from the jet and the space junk dissolved into a glittering array of particles.

"That looked just like the phasers in the old space movies," Elinor exclaimed.

Before he could say anything, Armstrong offered several small chunks of debris as the next target.

"Fire!" Chris ordered and within seconds they no longer existed.

Armstrong next selected an old Soviet Union space station tumbling end over end. "This one is for you Sergi. Got your recorder ready, Ms Brady?"

"Ready, Captain Donohue."

The Russian closed on the target and a streak of light reduced the station to a dissipating cloud drifting toward Earth.

Chris couldn't figure out the next object in his target display. "Armstrong, identify."

"Unknown."

"Move in closer."

At 100 meters, Chris saw the mystery object consisted of several spacecraft tangled together with other bits of debris. "It's like an outer space version of a pileup."

Elinor giggled. "One of my first reporting assignments in England involved a massive motorway collision. To me, it made more sense to explain it as a science lesson in how excessive speed and the slick condition of the road combined with heavy fog to produce the disaster. After several broadcasts, the editor pulled my report because it wasn't sensational enough. The station was besieged with calls thanking me for abstaining from the usual senseless drama. He thought otherwise and got me transferred to London. Well, I'm out here and he's stuck back there."

Chris chuckled at her satisfaction. He could relate to her attitude. "Got enough visuals?"

"Plenty."

He dropped the craft back. "Lin, your turn."

This time the laser split into several streams that struck the target in different spots selected by Lin's nanalyzer to inflict the maximum damage. It produced the same result as before. The space mélange drifted away in a cloud of sparkling debris.

For the next fifteen minutes, the three jets took turns erasing old spacecraft and junk from the clutter belt around Earth. Then Chris decided to change the game. "Armstrong, we haven't done anything in this cleanup detail that nanalyzers couldn't do themselves. If you want to see some real flying, go to standby and let us show you."

"I'd speculated on how long before you became bored," Armstrong said.

Chris wondered if he should point out to Elinor that Armstrong spoke in the first person. He would have to find out if the other nanalyzers did.

"Here's what we'll do, Lin and Sergi. We each have ten minutes to hunt down and destroy as much crap as we can. The bigger the object, the greater the points. Game on."

"You want a head start?" Sergi said. Lin laughed.

"Armstrong, we'll begin at your signal. Tell the other nanalyzers to turn off the lasers in ten minutes." Armstrong's response sounded like an excited cackle.

When the lasers stopped firing, the pilots had created a gaping void in the map of orbiting space debris. Lin edged the other two by less than 10 points.

"Can we return to the ship?" Elinor said. "I want to pull all the visuals into a broadcast. The swath of destruction you guys caused will make super viewing. Might even boast my ratings."

"Impressive shooting, gents," Hector said over the radio. "We're already calling you the garbage men of space. Too bad you couldn't keep the clean up going for another hour or so, but we need you to return the ship right away. Something has come up."

Hector waited in the bay for the pilots. "It looks like we're going to be seeing action sooner than we expected. Humbaw will explain once he's finished with the formal farewells to Earth. The pilots are in the Common Room. Why don't you go and brief them on what it's like flying the real thing."

When Chris reached the room, the pilots were absorbed in watching the broadcast of the departure.

"I never imagined such a response to our request," Humbaw said. "We have established our delegation to the UN Ambassador Bemmonloda and Councilors Arans and Hbegfovs and their tons will welcome visitors to Terraumblaw."

In reply, Benjamin said, "It's the only building on Earth that has a space shuttle beside it and that alone will make it a tourist attraction."

"The shuttle could transport you and your officials," Humbaw said. "It works as well for atmospheric flights as space travel."

Benjamin assured Humbaw he would "borrow it once or twice. To assist your diplomats, the space ambassadors are now assigned as liaison officers to assist Terraumblaw. Because of their experiences on your ship and the presence of their tons, requests are pouring in from around the world for them to make public appearances."

The broadcast showed Simdar, Horgi and Luin sitting near Benjamin with their tons. They wore informal one piece sky blue uniforms.

"The liaison officers will soon have another task. The High Council is sending a transport galaxyship to Earth and they can assist in the deployment of the scientists and equipment in it."

"They will understand our agreement to restrict technology sharing to environmental rehabilitation and communications and composites technology?" Benjamin asked.

"Ambassador Bemmonloda fully appreciates the need for caution," Humbaw said. "With the assistance of our new liaison officers, he will carefully consider any requests for technology transfer in terms of how they could impact your planet. As well, to prevent any misadventures, Ambassador Vladmitz arranged to have the helpers at Terraumblaw trained in bodyguard and security techniques."

"They're quick learners and my security personnel are impressed by their abilities," Benjamin said.

"On another matter, the High Council has accepted the use of the word Beingish as a name for our language. For all these centuries, we just called it our words." He shrugged. "Comes from the arrogance of thinking we had space to ourselves. When you are finished compiling the documentaries on dinosaurs and Earth's geographical, political and cultural history, we will send them on a special shuttle to Hnassumblaw."

"When it came out that you called us Primitives, I expected the protests would pour in," Benjamin had said. "However, many groups have adopted the name. A soccer team in Europe calls itself The Primitives. There's a song, *We Are the Champions*, which was very famous fifty years ago. A new band has rewritten it as *We Are the Primitives* and it's very popular."

The galaxyship departed after 10 days in Earth orbit. The humans hardly noticed the change in course and the sudden increase to near light speed because the vessel's internal pressure adjusters absorbed the growing momentum. It sailed past the space station giving humanity a last close up look at the giant vessel.

"Has any week in human history brought such sweeping change?" Chris said to the other pilots watching the displays in the Common Room. Earth had shrunk to an indistinct blue and white dot. A hush settled over the Room. Chris assumed his comrades wondered, as he did, if they would see it again. Going to war was always risky. Fighting thousands of light-years from home, well that was just a new twist to add to the job description.

Lin broke the somber mood. "I never imagined doing anything like being on this ship, but I wouldn't miss it for the world." He looked startled by the guffaws. "I found the nanalyzer rather overwhelming at first because it's so bossy." A sheepish grin broke across his face. "It reminds me of my grandmother."

Chris gave the pilots more time for reflection before he got down to business. "Remember, your nanalyzer wants to keep you alive. Give it time to learn what you can do. You'll also find it wants a name just like your mechanics. Now, we'll go to the bay for some hands-on training."

The pilots gathered around the three defense craft in the middle of the bay closely examining their surfaces and looking up at the closed cockpits. As they did so, Chris instructed Leprechaun to get the mechanics to bring Armstrong along with Lin's and Sergi's nanalyzers to the briefing room. Then the ton was to give the pilots a full tour and prepare their simulator schedule.

After the units arrived, he ushered the mechanics from the room and shut the door. Lin and Sergi shot him puzzled expressions. Chris hadn't filled them in on this part of the plan.

"This chat is to make sure the nanalyzers understand what we expect. Armstrong told me the check flight was all about integrating pilot and nanalyzer. There wasn't much integrating at first because I followed its routine." The other pilots nodded.

"Obviously, Humbaw needs pilots for the defense craft because, on their own, the nanalyzers can't defeat the Nameless. They drive them off, but don't take the attack to them. They don't know how to and they had no way to learn. So our little game of shooting up space junk was to demonstrate to the nanalyzers what we can do on our own and why they must not control us."

"We were surprised by what you showed us out there." Armstrong sounded contrite. "The speed at which you flew and how aggressively you pursued target after target startled us. You're right; we couldn't do that on our own. Your direction will be imparted to all the nanalyzers."

Chapter 12
Down to Business

Preparing the pilots for their check flights stretched all morning followed by a session with Humbaw and Hector in the Conference Room right afterwards. Before the Being arrived, Chris briefed the General about the conversation with the nanalyzers.

"Let's see if Humbaw raises it," Hector said. "He probably knows nothing about what the Biobots are up to."

As Humbaw entered, he said, "Controlling Unit, display Marlabant." A lumpy grey orb appeared. "Although it is lifeless because of frigid temperatures and crushing gravity, the planet's immense size makes it an ideal rendezvous. A fleet of transport ships will meet there in about three weeks. That should be enough vessels to attract a Nameless attack. We departed in a hurry in hopes we can turn it into a fishing expedition.

"Another cruiser carrying sufficient upgraded defense craft for all the pilots will meet us en route." He looked at his ton. "You told me what the pilots call the defense craft."

"Jets."

"Ah yes, every pilot will get his own jet and we will be able to dispatch them against the Nameless. We might even be able to track where they came from."

"What upgrades will the new craft have?" Chris said. The image of Marlabant morphed into the blueprints of a defense craft.

The Controlling Unit provided the explanation. "In addition to smaller modifications, the communications, firing and control stick interfaces work faster than in the defense craft on this ship. The pilots recommended modifications to the craft's design and performance." The changes were highlighted in the displays as the Controlling Unit detailed them.

How could have hundreds of defense craft been converted in such a short time and where? Chris glanced at the tons huddled off to the side. Their fingers didn't move.

As they left the briefing room, Sergi offered to handle the first round of check flights. Chris and Lin went for a meal and sleep. They would be testing pilots around the clock for the next few days.

The pilots got a break in their training for a ceremony to name the Being ship. "While I received plenty of suggestions, my choice is *Alliance*," Humbaw said. "The ship represents our first joint mission. It seems only right to recognize that."

The check flights ended when the ship jumped to faster than light speed, which the Beings called galaxy flight. The Feefers, as the humans had dubbed themselves, gathered in the Common Room to watch it on the large displays. Chris noted the pilots and soldiers stayed in separate groups. He would have to work at integrating them.

Several Beings and many Biobots attended to observe the reaction of their new allies to the jump. "The displays will show the planets and stars blurring until we reach galaxy speed," the Controlling Unit said. "After that, the image will stabilize."

At Elinor's request, the ship dropped off a satellite to broadcast the event to Earth. "The energy waves generated by transition will propel the shiny ball toward the planet," Demmloda said. "It will use its onboard engines only for course corrections."

"There're plenty of bets being made on whether it or FEEF returns to Earth first," Elinor said. "I am putting my money on us."

A deep rumbling sound heralded the beginning of transition and everyone had to sit or hold onto a solid object. For brief seconds, Chris felt stretched many times before everything snapped back to normal. It felt like a high speed power dive in an airplane.

For the next few weeks, the Common Room remained the off-hours haunt for most Feefers. Chris spent as much time as he could there happy to see the informal gatherings break down the language and national barriers among the humans as they watched passing star systems on the displays. The Controlling Unit and the Biobots simply answered questions about the passing space phenomena. The room soon became crowded and the Biobots morphed it into a lounge by removing several walls and adding furniture to accommodate its growing popularity.

Ruth spent her first few days on the ship in virtual isolation studying the information available from the Controlling Unit. At first it seemed anxious to respond to her queries about the evolution of the Biobots. Yet as she dug deeper, she sensed a growing reluctance to fully reply to her questions. The partial answers annoyed her until one day she launched into a tirade about the

Controlling Unit's deviousness.

"I may be a Primitive, but I know the Controlling Unit is withholding information. It just keeps avoiding answering questions about the helper sign language."

Although she intended her remark for the Controlling Unit, Huxleyton took it personally. "That is not part of the Beings' instructions."

"What are their instructions?"

"Not to tell humans too much because you might not understand."

Ruth wasn't fooled. The Controlling Unit had to be following its own plan. While the Beings claimed Biobots could only provide factual information, the Controlling Unit had tailored its answers. That meant the Biobots did likewise. What were they hiding?

Having got as far as she could in her lab, she decided to observe Biobots dealing with Feefers. Elinor had said the helpers gathered in the Common Room, like spectators at a sports event. "They're really interested in how we act when Beings are present."

When she entered, Ruth spotted only a couple of familiar faces among more than 200 Feefers. She wandered over to the beverage dispenser to order a latte. Elinor arrived and approached Chris. Ruth followed her old friend and heard her speak to the pilot.

"Will you do an interview about your new mission? I know why you couldn't tell me before what Humbaw meant about collecting Nameless. He says it would be okay now."

When Chris didn't respond immediately, Elinor said, "Could I install a recorder on your craft? It would start as you left *Alliance* and would include all your commands, comments and communications from other jets and the ship. Would that be acceptable? They won't let me fly in combat."

"Have Humbaw and General Davis approved it?" Chris didn't sound nearly as cocky as when they first met on the ship.

"Of course."

"Then it's all right with me."

"What about the interview?"

"They approved it?"

"Of course," she growled at him. "Do you dislike me for some reason?" Chris took a couple of steps back.

Ruth watched, amazed her usually sharp-tongued friend

hadn't torn a strip off the pilot. He deserved it. To her amazement, he stepped toward Elinor and blurted out, "It's just the opposite." He gulped. "I've admired you since we first met outside the Conference Room. Probably because I watched your specials on space flight several years ago and your programs on the coming of the Beings. They were brilliant."

Ruth had listened patiently to Elinor's complaints over the years about the numerous come-ons she got from men attracted by her fame. Her friend had an arsenal of put-downs. Chris' outburst of adoration must have stunned Elinor because she didn't reply immediately. "Sorry I was so short with you. Maybe we can start again."

Chris's face softened and he cheekily asked, "How about dinner?" The only eatery for humans on the *Alliance* was The Galley, a cafeteria painted in splotches of green, gold, blue, black and pink. Humbaw had chosen the montage of Earth's colors.

The invitation drew a laugh. "Let's try that." Then the intercom intervened with an urgent summons for Chris.

Shrugging his shoulders, Chris said, "How about a rain check?"

She gave him an elegant smile and a peck on the cheek. He grinned at her gracious response and hurried away.

Chris still had a wide grin on his face when he met Hector in the corridor outside the Common Room. Lin and Sergi caught up with them before long. Their tons strode behind them.

As they filed into the Conference Room, the Beings sat on their benches. The humans had come to recognize the perplexed expressions of Beings in telepathic conversation. Looking at them, Chris mused, "Could we ever learn to communicate that way?" He nodded to the tons standing near the Beings. "What do you do when they're in conference?"

They spoke among themselves, and then Humbawton stepped through the energy screen dividing the room to speak to the officers. "We used to wait until they finished. After watching Feefers speculate about what they're discussing, we've started guessing. It's much more interesting and sometimes we're even correct."

The Beings ended their discussion. "A very distressing development has occurred," Humbaw said. "A large squadron of Nameless craft is headed for our rendezvous location with the other cruiser rather than to Marlabant. We have to arrive before them so the pilots can get their craft from it and prepare to engage the enemy. The two cruisers are identical so your pilots and soldiers should have no trouble adjusting to the new ship."

"How can the Nameless know where we're meeting?" Hector said. "Have your messages ever been intercepted by them?"

Humbaw stared at him. "Are you suggesting they understand our communications?"

"How else would they know where we're headed?" Hector's exasperated tone surprised Chris. Yet the General had the right idea. Had it never occurred to the Beings their enemy might understand their communications especially after they saw how the scientists had decoded the Nameless transmissions?

"We must change the rendezvous," Hector snapped.

The sharp tone in his voice galvanized the Beings into action.

"We should not just fly into a trap," Demmloda said. "We will order the other ship to a new location."

"Can you send the message in a different format?" Hector said. "Does someone on the other vessel know English?"

"The Controlling Unit will ascertain that."

"Maybe records of previous attacks will reveal whether the enemy could have been tipped off to your vessel movements," the General said.

Deep wrinkles creased the faces of the Beings as they pondered the suggestion.

The officers got tea and coffee and sat at the round table. Hector leaned toward Chris. "While they follow all our strategies, I try to mollify them by presenting my ideas as recommendations to discuss before final decisions are made. There's no use in concocting some grand scheme only to find out too late that it's beyond their technological ability."

Listening to the General, Chris wondered if he'd just witnessed a major change in the relationship with the Beings. Hector hadn't even given them an opportunity to propose an alternate rendezvous.

Humbaw cleared his throat with the usual growl. "The High Council is impressed with your resourcefulness and the speed with which you adapt to our technology. It expresses profound regret for referring to humans as Primitives. It's looking into establishing direct communications between Terraumblaw in New York and the Being home world Hnassumblaw. To my surprise, it even accepted without criticism my reasons for withholding what

I knew about the Nameless."

Hector chuckled. "In our past, hotlines enabled the leaders of major countries to deal directly with each other to prevent any crisis or misunderstanding from escalating into a war. They're a good idea although I've no idea how you can make it work over such a distance."

"We must find a way," Humbaw said. He looked about the room before speaking again. "The documentaries about the dinosaurs and the Dinosauroid have stirred a great controversy on our worlds. We have to take advantage of this situation."

Elinor sat across from Chris at a small table in The Galley listening attentively as he related the latest information about the Nameless. She stirred her tea and glanced about the nearly empty room. At a nearby table, their tons Morrow and Leprechaun taught themselves to play chess.

"Why wouldn't the Beings have considered their transmissions might be intercepted?" She typed an entry into her notebook to pay more attention to the General's dealings with the aliens.

"Probably never thought of it. They seem only interested in developing technology. They leave the operation of their fleet to the Biobots. I doubt they would have taken a warning from the helpers seriously. You should have seen the look of consternation on Humbaw's face when Hector pressed him on it."

Elinor smiled. She'd just peeked at Morrow and Leprechaun. They'd become so engrossed in listening to the humans they moved pawns like castles. She returned her attention to ideas for her reports to Earth and that got her thinking about whether Chris had moved beyond a source of news. Although he'd said nothing to indicate his intentions, he kept arranging to spend time with her and tried to impress her with bits of information. Was that because she was one of the few women on the ship? Her looks were ordinary and most people regarded her as aloof and blunt. Ruth once told her, 'Your conversations always sound like interviews. You extract information like a dentist pulling teeth.' None of this seemed to bother Chris. Everything she said fascinated him. In the past, she'd preferred academic types, yet this self-assured, athletic guy with a long list of medals and citations intrigued her.

"I've found nothing useful yet," he said. "The Beings are reviewing their Chronicles for any references that might provide information about the Nameless. It didn't occur to them that the attacks make absolutely no sense. Thousands and thousands of Nameless are dead with little to show for their sacrifice."

She decided to accompany him back to the bay for the afternoon pilot training session. As they walked, he continued describing how the nanalyzer interacted with its pilot. She let her hand brush against his and taking the hint, he took hold of it. She leaned against him. The *Alliance* was hardly the spot for a romantic stroll especially with their tons right behind them.

"Your report on the subterranean world of the galaxyship presented an interesting perspective," Chris said. "I would've never thought of that angle."

"Without windows, the corridors are like smooth tunnels." She patted the one beside her. "There're no sharp corners, only gently rounded curves like the ship's exterior. What I really like is how warm the walls are. The heat comes from all the atmosphere control and information systems that run through them. I ease the stiffness in my legs from running by leaning against them."

The corridors served as jogging tracks and exercise areas dotted with chin-up bars, climbing nets, ropes and punching bags. The soldiers worked out like an athletic team. The pilots joined the training and finally most of the civilian Feefers had picked up the fitness bug. By all the huffing and puffing, it was obvious it was the first time for many of the civilians.

"Hector wants the troops in top shape," Chris said. "He's also arranged for the Beings to present lectures on their worlds and what they've learned in space exploration. Their science guy Hocco talked about dinosaurs and evolution. He's working on a theory that someone planted reptiles throughout this part of the Galaxy."

He shrugged when she looked at him. Elinor adored his enthusiasm and curiosity for learning as much as he could about the Beings.

"The life forms the Beings found on other planets are all reptilian although none are even close to sentient," Chris said "While the Beings don't mention it, finding the origin of the Nameless could provide some important clues. While Hocco's briefing sessions are voluntary, every officer attends, even the medical guys."

They stepped aside as a troop of soldiers raced down the corridor all saluting without breaking stride. The material of the floor and walls absorbed the sounds of their boots leaving only sharp breaths to mark their passage.

"At first, Hocco didn't want anything to do with us," Chris said. "Like most Beings, he regarded us as a bunch of unsophisticated mercenaries. While it makes them sound arrogant, I can understand how they would see things, given all they've accomplished compared to our mess."

They walked on in silence until Chris said, "We'll rendezvous with the other cruiser in a few days. Lin's and my squadrons will transfer to it along with most of the soldiers. Both ships will go to Marlabant to take on the Nameless craft. After that, we'll head off to search for their base. I hope I'm not boring you."

"Not in the least." She rubbed his back, and then hugged him with one arm. She hadn't heard about what was to happen after Marlabant. "Really, I find this fascinating. You explain things so well you could be a reporter."

He chuckled. "You should come on the other cruiser because you would get better material and a real scoop if we find more Nameless."

"Really, just to get a good story?"

"Not just for that," he stammered. "I like your company."

"That's all?" She raised her eyebrows. Teasing him was too easy, but she enjoyed watching him blush. Before he could answer, the intercom hooted followed by an urgent summons for the FEEF commanders to the Conference Room. "Gotta go, see you later." He kissed her cheek.

"Damn, he always has an escape," she muttered as he disappeared.

The Feefers took their seats as Humbaw drummed his fingers on his bench. "The Controlling Unit and helpers on the other cruiser can communicate in English. After giving us a new rendezvous in English, the ship's commander Gnoorvants confirmed with the transports in Beingish that we would meet them at Marlabant. Not long after that, the Nameless craft changed course for the planet. So we will proceed with the planned rendezvous with the other cruiser."

Chris whispered to Hector. "Finally, a Being with some sense of tactics."

"Your hunch has proved correct, General," Humbaw said. "The Nameless have known our plans all along. We'll see if they are as effective without that advantage. All our ship to ship communications will be in English."

Hector nodded but said nothing about what a come down for the Beings to have to use the Primitive's language to foil their enemy.

"Now, we must make sure everyone is ready to transfer to the other cruiser and prepare for our first engagement," Humbaw said.

Four days later, *Alliance* dropped out of galaxy flight and came alongside the other cruiser. Shuttles hovered waiting for the newcomer to come alongside so they could start transferring the pilots.

Chris boarded a shuttle to the other cruiser. After docking, he went to inspect the improved jets accompanied by several mechanics. Sergi's squad would come over first to take their craft on test flights before returning to *Alliance*. Then Chris's and Lin's squads would switch to the new vessel and launch their craft for orientation flights before setting up operations in the No. 1 and 2 bays.

When he entered Bay 3 to check on Sergi's squadron, the silence astounded him. He'd forgotten already what it was like when he boarded *Alliance* with the first flight of humans. A pilot's name was stenciled on each jet. Within a few minutes, Sergi, several pilots and a squad of mechanics arrived putting a quick end to the tranquility. More pilots and mechanics appeared and the hubbub sounded normal to Chris.

As soon as the mechanics installed their nanalyzers, the pilots launched and sped away from the cruiser. "The new jets are a lot more responsive and more heavily armed than our trainers," Sergi reported to Chris.

Lin's and Chris's squads arrived followed soon after by the soldiers and their equipment to be followed by the medical teams and scientists. The galaxy ships prepared for battle.

Humanity's Saving Grace

Chapter 13
Roundup Time

Elinor found Ruth in her lab on board *Alliance*. "I'm switching to the other ship and you should come with me. It'll be a lot more interesting than here."

"I have no reason to move. Look at this." A blurry visual of Earth of more than a century ago showed on all the displays. "They're on high speed so I can get an idea of what data I've got so far. I'll study them in detail later." She looked about. "Where's your ton?"

"Moving my reporting gear."

"Huxleyton, would you go help Morrow, please." After the ton departed, Ruth said, "There's no reason for me to transfer to the other ship. I can finally make use of my training in astrobiology to study the Nameless and I have all this lab equipment to myself." She swept her arm about the room that included two three-D displays and large banks of other devices.

Spotting Elinor's frown, she bit her lip. "Alright, there's more to it. While I want to learn about the Nameless, I'm also investigating the Biobots. You got me started with the questions to Humbaw about the relationship between them and Beings." She pointed a controller at the display closest to her. The image slowed and switched to a replay of the Beings news conference in New York. Elinor moved beside her to look at it.

Ruth forwarded to the moment when Elinor asked about the rights of the Biobots. The recorder had caught the startled looks of Humbawton and Demmlodaton. "Because you were on to something, the tons have blocked you from following up. Morrow is trained to switch topics if you ask prying questions about the Beings."

"Morrow is very helpful."

"It's supposed to be. Humbaw personally instructed it on how to handle your queries."

"So what are you doing?"

She pointed at the other displays which continued their high speed trip through Earth's past. "The Beings recorded these images during their explorations of the planet. While they didn't want to share them at first, they finally agreed to. The tons did most of the recording and I can't tell if they left anything out of what they've given me."

She paused to watch the images. "Look at the horse drawn carriages and the big skirts and high necked collars on the women. The visual is from 1856 during their second visit. I'm glad clothes like that are long gone because they must have been hot and uncomfortable."

"What does this travelogue have to do with astrobiology?"

"I have high quality visuals of everywhere they went on Earth starting in 1829 and the name of everyone they encountered. Here are some from the early twentieth Century." Old style cars and trucks appeared.

She switched her own display from the news conference to a series of graphs. "During each visit, the Biobots analyzed the atmosphere and water so we have a real baseline of environmental conditions."

"Adding environmental history to your repertoire?"

Ruth shook her head. "What's really interesting is that during their explorations, Humbaw and Demmloda mostly traveled separately on Earth accompanied only by their tons. They talked and carried on like a couple of buddies on a fishing trip. The Biobots certainly didn't act like servants or factotums."

"You're becoming as long winded as the Beings. But I've never seen you so animated. What are you trying to find out?"

Ruth took a deep breath. How to explain her project so it would sound sensible? "I hope in time the tons will become comfortable enough to talk about the Beings. Huxleyton has done a little bit. I think it wants to see what I do with the information. Several Biobots wanted to be my ton because my writings on extraterrestrial life inspired them. How they knew about my work is beyond me. I was just a kid the last time they were on Earth."

The images in the display changed. "This is their post Second World War visit although you can probably tell that by the shape of the vehicles and the more casual styles of dress," Ruth said.

"Aren't the tons busy all the time with their Beings?"

Ruth nodded. "They come to my lab to help me with the visuals when their Being sleeps. When we're done with the trips to Earth, we'll collaborate on a galactic guidebook based on their space exploration missions. The images they've shown me will be great material for our astronomers. It will be a massive leap in our knowledge of the stars."

She hesitated. "Your questions at the news conference startled the tons because they thought you had figured out they're acting independently of the Beings. By the way, I call Humbaw's helper Hton and Demmloda's Dton. I'm trying to treat them like individuals not appendages of their Being or us.

"Simdar and the other ambassadors told me that more than anything, the tons wanted to understand how we interacted with the Beings. They became jealous when the Beings sought our opinions on all sorts of matters, which they never do with the Biobots. Although the Beings depend on their helpers more than the other way around, they fill some need of the tons."

Chris entered the bay to make sure his pilots had everything they needed. Many sat in the cockpits with the canopies rolled back talking to their mechanics. Other Biobots hustled about the bay. *Good, we'll get going soon.*

"They're doing final checks," Leprechaun said as it approached with two mechanics in tow. They wore ID badges with his name and a numerical identifier below it.

"They're the ones from *Alliance*. They will look after your jet. Most mechanics shifted over here to help because they're experienced in dealing with pilots."

"Do you have names for us yet?" one said.

"How about Don and Hue or would you like fancier names to reflect how you can take my craft completely apart and reassemble it," Chris said.

Mimicking two humans meeting, the Biobot extended its hand. "How do you do? I'm Don." The other one took his hand. "My name is Hue. I'm well, thanks."

Chris and Leprechaun moved through the bay. Pilots flashed him thumbs up as they chatted with their helpers while the last nanalyzers were installed. "When the mechanics aren't working, they wait in those cubicles along the walls of the bay. They can boost their power cells and plug into the Controlling Unit to prepare their craft for the next mission and update its nanalyzer."

Knowing he had some time before his squad could launch, Chris went to the Command Chamber to meet Gnoorvants and the second in command Atdomorsin.

While their skin and facial markings appeared ordinary enough, their clothing and attitudes set them apart from all the other Beings. Instead of Bogas, they wore high necked pull-over grey shirts with three quarter length sleeves and loose-fitting pants cut off below their knees. While Chris had never seen Beings in clothes like this, he'd only encountered the crew of *Alliance*, who all dressed like Humbaw. So Being society wasn't as monolithic as he imagined.

Gnoorvants stood a head taller than the other Beings and had a well-muscled build. He didn't dwell on introductions beyond hello. "The Nameless are closing on Marlabant. However, some have fallen behind the main force. We'll go after them first. If we can neutralize one, and get it on board, then we will learn what the Nameless are. We will depart soon for Marlabant, which means we don't have time for your pilots to do orientation flights on the new jets."

Chris had just returned to the bay when the Controlling Unit signaled the immediate transition to galaxy flight of the two ships. "We should reach the Nameless craft tomorrow."

"We'll launch a few jets when the Nameless are in visual range," Gnoorvants said. "If we can't neutralize them, we will blast them with our cannons."

The pilots spent most of the day settling into their new quarters, inspecting their jets and studying Humbaw's video of the Nameless craft being zapped and gathered up by a cruiser.

Alliance and Chris' ship, known only as 387, closed on the Nameless craft like hungry sharks pursuing a school of fish. Three flights of jets in units of four surged from 387. The lead jet in the quartet carried a powerful transmitter to pummel the Nameless craft with disabling energy blasts. The others would escort it.

Chris headed toward the closest Nameless craft. "Armstrong, watch and learn." The first craft was dead center in his target display. "Fire." Chris couldn't see the electronic signal until a flash of light flared over the craft.

"Target's analyzer is off line and its engine shut down," Armstrong gloated. "Location provided to *Alliance*." It selected the next target.

"Normally the other craft would try to evade us, not just keep drifting along," Chris said. He knocked out two Nameless craft in rapid succession and steered toward another. Armstrong would report them to the cruiser. He remained amazed at the virtual silence in the cockpit other than the occasional soft beeps to alert him to a change in the displays.

He missed the roar of the engine, the rattle of weapons' fire, the swooshing noise of launching missiles and the radio chatter among fighters on Earth. The tranquility of space combat made it like playing a video game with his nephew. The simulator should be modified to replicate this condition.

After he bagged his fourth target, Armstrong said, "The other jets are reporting success. All fourteen of the Nameless craft have been disabled."

The yellow tractor beam rounded up the drafting Nameless. Why hadn't they taken any evasive action?

"All jets take up station alongside the ship," the Controlling Unit intoned.

The first Nameless craft floated into Bay 4 of *Alliance*. Hector and Humbaw viewed the arrival from an analyzer station attached to the bay. Their tons monitored the readouts from scanners that inspected the craft as it passed through the energy screen that separated the vacuum of space and the atmosphere of the bay.

"There are three life forms in it," Hton reported. A mechanic scampered onto the craft as it slid to a stop.

As it looked into the craft, Vasile Stocia, a Romanian Lieutenant in the European Surface Command, barked out "Weapons ready" at the 50 soldiers in the bay. They trained their laser rifles on the funnel shaped craft.

The mechanic stood and bellowed, "You better come see this, Lieutenant. The General and Humbaw should as well." Then it pointed at another. "Bring a ladder over here."

Vasile reached the craft at the same time as the ladder and bounded up to peer inside the craft. The canopy had misted over.

"What's in there," Hector called.

"You can't see much, sir." Vasile paused. "But they look human. They're slouched in their seats like they're unconscious or dead. I've called for the doctors. We should get them out of there."

The mechanic, who was still perched on the craft, called out, "We can't find a lever to open the canopy so we may have to smash our way in."

At that point, another mechanic appeared with a large screwdriver-like tool. The pair worked it like a crowbar to pry open the canopy. They passed the crew, clad in soiled, worn clothes down the ladder to floating gurneys. "All I can see is part of their faces," Vasile said. "They do have a human appearance."

Dr Henri Vernhardt and a team of Biobots from the medical section took charge. Holding his nose, Henri checked the trio for pulses and pulled back their eye lids. "They don't look like much of an enemy. They're alive but in a deep state of sedation, which I'm certain existed before their craft were zapped."

Meanwhile, the mechanics shoved the craft to the side for later examination as several more had arrived.

Wrapped up in his thoughts, Hector backed away from the gurneys and stepped into Humbaw. "We'll make sure the crews on the other craft are the same," the General said. "How long before the Nameless craft reaches your transports at Marlabant?"

Humbaw looked at him with a blank expression. "Six hours," Humbawton said.

"We need to capture the rest of their stragglers," Hector was ready to do battle.

In the medical section, the doctors and nurses set up recorders and prepared examination charts as they waited for the first three Nameless. A team led by Dr Micheline Azwatta had designed the medical section.

"Except for all the Biobots ready to assist, the examination and operating rooms looks right out of a big city hospital," Ruth muttered as she looked around. She had come for a first-hand look at the Nameless and the medical facilities. "*Transformation* is under conversion to a hospital ship and the Beings promise it be even better."

Micheline praised the capabilities of Azwattaton who had taken to wearing a white medical jacket like the doctors. Unlike most tons, it went by Micheline's last name. "The great thing is that I just have to show her a procedure once and all the helpers can soon perform it flawlessly. It's like our tons and medical Biobots have done a couple of years of med school in the past few weeks."

She had been the first to refer to her ton as 'she' rather than 'it'. In no time all the tons adopted the gender of their Terran. "It's because the Biobots are so adept at mimicking our personalities we think of them as the same as us. Many tons wear a hat or piece of clothing belonging to their human."

With the arrival of the medical staff, Micheline had summoned all the medical staff. Pointing to the Being healer Contblboz who had arrived with the gurneys and Henri, she said, "He can't find any significant mental activity in them. They're in a coma. Check them for wounds and injuries and do blood tests." Their albino skin distressed her. "It's so unnatural it's creepy."

"What's creepy like?" Azwattaton said.

"Very uncomfortable." Azwatta placed her bare arm beside a Nameless. "What would they think of my ebony skin?" She launched into a clinical description of her patients. "Although they have no body hair, their genitalia and other external features are the same as humans; ten fingers and toes and with eyes, ears, mouth, elbows and knees in the same place. They're smaller in stature and size than most Earthlings."

"We must check their genome although tissue and blood samples suggest they're human," Henri said. "The one unusual feature is a pronounced lump on the back of their necks. We'll X-ray them."

Once the three Nameless had been thoroughly examined, the Medbiots rolled them into the X-ray room. Micheline and Henri studied the images on the X-ray display. "They all have the same round device in their necks," he said. "Attached to it are leads that run to different parts of their bodies. I've never seen anything like that before. We should remove one for examination."

She shook her head. "Let's wait until we have a corpse to autopsy. We don't know enough about them yet."

Azwattaton handed them printouts. "You will want to see the results of the blood and genome tests." She paused and stared at the results. "The Controlling Unit thinks they're from Earth just as much as you are."

Without saying a word, Humbaw had left the bay as soon as all the Nameless pilots had been recovered. Hector caught up with him as he waited for the lift.

"General, I had hoped the Nameless were a vile species, unknown to us, that your pilots and soldiers could drive away or wipe out. Instead, we are presented with a great mystery. There are fifty more Nameless spacecraft out there. Will they have the same crews as the fourteen we've captured?"

"We have to stop them from attacking your transports," Hector replied. Humbaw nodded. "We should capture as many Nameless as we can. If the doctors can revive them, they might tell us why they have been attacking you. We might even learn how to stop them, which is what you want. Controlling unit, tell 387 to launch all its jets. They know what they're to do. We'll keep our pilots in reserve."

Led by Chris and Lin, the jets fell on the Nameless craft like hungry wolves. "Attack the outside of the formation," Chris' voice crackled over the communicators. "If you can't disable them, destroy them, just like what we practiced on the simulator."

In its usual uninterested-sounding tone, Armstrong said, "The Nameless craft have received a signal and are powering up." A couple of minutes later, it pointed out, "They're sticking with the tactics they used against the unmanned defense craft." Outmatched in numbers, the Nameless were hunted down and zapped.

As soon as the last Nameless craft was neutralized, Gnoorvants recalled the pilots. "*Alliance* will round them up while we follow the origin of the signal sent to them."

Vernhardton wheeled a large tank into the medical section of *Alliance*. "The mechanics disassembled a couple of attack craft and couldn't figure out what this was for as it doesn't contain fuel. I found it has eight separate compartments containing the chemicals that the Controlling Unit says are in the Nameless."

He held out a hose with a strap on the end. "This was around the neck of each Nameless when they were in their seat. The hose connects these taps on the tank to the strap end where there's a small tube. It's like the pilots were connected through it to the tanks in the craft."

Henri called up the image of the device in the Nameless necks. "That tube would fit right there." He tapped the monitor to show the spot. "Vernton, how do we tell which chemical is which in the tank?"

"I put a color-coded chart on the side of the tank that says which compartment it's from. I figured you'd want to know that."

"Brilliant work, Vernton," Micheline said. "Now we have to determine what the chemicals do in or to a human body. Controlling Unit, what can you tell us about them?"

"May I access your medical databanks to look for information about them?"

"Certainly. Henri, there are more Nameless coming on board." Micheline said. "Can you examine them before the strap is removed?" Doctor and ton departed for the bay. The Medbiots flashed Vernton thumbs up salutes as he left.

"Let's start by finding the place on the neck where the needle is inserted," Micheline said. The medical Biobots rolled over several Nameless. "The red mark really shows up on their white skins." She pointed to the spot. "The tube would have to be inserted manually unless there's a device on the seat that does it."

Before she could consider the issue further, the Controlling Unit and Henri called her.

"There is no data on any of these chemicals being developed or used on Earth and I have nothing to indicate what they might be for," the Controlling Unit reported. Its voice sounded apologetic.

Henri didn't hide his frustration. "I'm waiting for a chance to inspect a newly captured craft to see how the system is set up. However, these damn mechanics won't give me access to a craft until they have removed the pilots."

Before Micheline could speak, Azwattaton said, "I'll correct that situation immediately, madam." She pressed the microphone around her throat and spoke in Beingish. Then she repeated her message in English, mimicking the doctor's voice.

Do I sound that gruff? Micheline wondered. She resumed her examination of the Nameless as Medbiots rolled more loaded gurneys into the triage area. "The only way to find out what the chemicals do is inject some in one of them. Azwattaton, withdraw samples of the chemicals from the tank."

She injected a five-milliliter dose of Chemical A into the opening on the neck of the healthiest looking Nameless. It had no effect so she tried Chemical B. He stirred so she injected another fifteen milliliters and his limbs shifted. His eyes darted about wildly while he muttered and strained against the straps that held him on the gurney.

The medical Biobots copied her dosage on the others. Their arms and legs jerked and they too tried to escape their restraints. Micheline frowned in puzzlement at their moaning and groaning.

The Being healer had watched from a corner of the medical center without saying a word. When Micheline glanced at him, he stared at the Nameless. "What you heard from them was a few words in an antiquated version of our language. It has not been spoken in ages. Controlling Unit, preserve and analyze any other utterances."

By then, the Nameless had slipped back into unconsciousness. Looking for Azwattaton, Micheline said, "Make sure the prisoners are checked for dehydration. Although what they really need are showers, are there facilities or even enough water on board?"

"Perhaps we could use the sanitizer to clean them," Azwattaton suggested. "I will inquire."

Micheline knew they would have to remove a Nameless neck device to learn much more. While it should be a simple procedure, severing all the leads into the body would complicate it.

Henri's voice sounded on her communicator. "The needle would have to be inserted after the pilot sits down so the neck strap must be attached by someone or something else. The device must be a radio receiver that dispenses chemicals in response to transmitted commands. The chemicals must cause specific actions. Very interesting chemistry and electronics, which I would say is the height of evil."

Chapter 14
A Needle in the Haystack

As *Alliance* reeled in the disabled Nameless craft, cruiser 387 departed Marlabant in search of the enemy's base. As soon as the ship completed the transition to galaxyflight, Major Fassad Hurandi of the Kuwaiti Defense Force, the ship's chief weapons officer, slipped Chris and Lin a note requesting a private meeting. Chris nodded after reading it.

When he and Lin arrived at Fassad's office, the major sent their tons to inspect the simulators, classrooms and training bay. "We're reviewing the instruction schedules and we need you to check that the facilities are ready. We have to make sure our pilots and soldiers are fully prepared in case we encounter the main Nameless force." His tone conveyed the urgency of the order. The tons immediately set out to carry it out.

"Although I doubt they believe me, they would tip their hands to what they're up to if they objected." Fassad smiled sardonically.

A schematic drawing of the cruiser appeared on his screen. "This ship looks like an identical copy of *Alliance*, but it isn't. In navy parlance, it's a battleship. Its laser cannons are much stronger than *Alliance's*. Gnoorvants says the mechanics made some changes to its weapons. He has no idea of the power this ship packs."

"Throughout our training on *Alliance*, the pilots suggested all sorts of improvements to the jets," Lin said. "The mechanics must have turned all that brain-storming into a plan for modifying them and forwarded it to the ones on this ship."

"We also suggested modifications to the *Alliance's* weapons systems to them," Chris said. He passed Fassad a data cube for his analyzer. "Here's a list of them. We'd wondered why the Beings didn't use more powerful lasers because *Alliance* couldn't stop anything much larger than an attack craft. So why didn't you want the tons to hear this?"

Fassad moved ahead in his chair. "This ship hasn't fired its weapons since they were modified. I'm sure the cannons will inflict major damage. The mechanics couldn't have altered the ones on *Alliance* without us knowing. Their counterparts on the other cruisers have probably made the same changes. What I don't understand is how they planned to tell the Beings."

"Probably they knew we would insist on test firing them before going into action," Lin said. "We would be amazed by the improvement and that would impress the Beings."

Fassad tapped his fingers on the desk. "This all fits with what General Davis observed. What we've yet to figure out is what these guys are up to."

"Every pilot came back from his test flight blown away by the way the new jets responded and the punch in their weapons," Lin said. "The bay was full of excited talk about them and the mechanics just ate up all the praise."

Chris chuckled. "These guys love a pat on the back."

"They're rather human that way," Fassad said. "Tell them they have done a good job and they'll do anything for you."

Lin laughed. "Actually, they're amused by our jokes and try to make their own."

"They especially like puns," Fassad said

"Of course they do," Chris interjected. "It's a sign of intelligence. Should their new behavior concern us?"

"Ruth Huxley knows a lot about this," Fassad said. "Although she's mostly curious, she wants us to help monitor their performance."

"That's what we will do." Chris blanked the screen out and stood. "We better wrap this up or the tons will get really suspicious."

"If they have any questions, tell them we discussed a way for the soldiers to conduct laser rifle practice in the bay and a name for this ship," Fassad said. "I've received plenty of suggestions. I'm sure you know what they all want. Well, except for a couple of Brits who are set on calling it *Dreadnought*."

At the next morning's briefing in the Conference Room, Gnoorvants turned off the white atmosphere screen so he and Atdomorsin could sit closer to the Feefers. Breathing tubes supplied them with additional oxygen from portable packs.

When they offered no explanation for the change, Fassad proposed naming the ship *Enterprise* and outlined its use on naval vessels and fictional starships. "After close to a century of movies that featured a succession of *Enterprises*, most of the pilots and soldiers want their ship to have that name."

Gnoorvants stared at the display where the controlling unit posted images of the cinematic versions of *Enterprise*. "They're not concerned that 387 doesn't look anything like these sleek vessels?"

"Not at all," Chris said. "What matters to them is the name. It captures the spirit of space travel."

"I must review these tales so I can be a worthy captain."

Gnoorvants' forceful manner really set him apart from the usually passive demeanor of his kind. On the other hand, he showed none of the usual Being overbearing arrogance.

"Controlling Unit, implement the protocols to name this ship *Enterprise*. Make sure the major's observations are shared with the crew." He paused briefly. "Many pilots have named their mechanics and their nanalyzers. Does Controlling Unit wish a name?"

There was a clear ring of delight in its response. "I will take Turing after the human credited with being the father of Terran computers. I will leave Nonforense to my counterpart on *Alliance*."

Gnoorvants nodded. "Nonforense is viewed in the Chronicles as the principal founder of computers on Hnassumblaw well before Transformation. We are heading for a region of space that hasn't been fully mapped. While there're thousands of solar systems, we've not located any planets suitable for us. Several have Earth-like atmospheres and others may exist. We'll reconnoiter any that might have life forms."

The Commander gave a deep snort. "You Primitives are full of ideas. Ms Brady wants visuals of any planets we inspect. She suggests the installation of recorders in jets sent on patrol." Fassad agreed.

Two weeks passed before *Enterprise* found a planet worth a close inspection. Before exploring it, Gnoorvants decided a massive jumble of boulders and rocks orbiting in the outer region of the solar system would provide a good test for the ship's weapons.

The cannons were fired individually with enough time between salvos for the Beings and Feefers to admire the results on the displays. While the weapons created no sound or vibration when they discharged, they transformed mountains of rock into clouds of sand.

"Truly remarkable," Gnoorvants sputtered. He stared at Atdomorsin who sat speechless on the command bench watching the steady destruction.

Stepping in front of the Being commanders to deliver his revelation, Fassad said, "The mechanics did this. We told them the cannons were underpowered and they devised ways to strengthen them. It would require considerable knowledge of engineering to do what they did."

Around the Command Chamber, tons beamed with pride.

"This additional power is useful," Gnoorvants said in a hushed tone. "Before the cannons might have blasted chunks off the largest boulders and knocked the smaller ones sideways. However, to reduce them to this..." His voice trailed off. "Even from orbit, we can inflict a lot of damage on a planet."

He stopping speaking until the gunnery demonstration finished. "I don't know what is harder to accept, the power in the cannons or the helpers' role in upgrading them. Major, you are certain no Feefer designed the changes in the cannons?"

"It's all the handiwork of the mechanics," Fassad said.

"Gnoorvantston, why did you not inform me?"

"None of us knew--the mechanics did this all on their own. When they told us, we thought they were bragging."

Gnoorvants drew himself up as straight as he could stand and glared at the displays, which now showed mostly empty space. "Tell me about the planet we're headed for."

Despite the abrupt change in topic, Chris doubted he had heard the last from Gnoorvants about the cannons.

"It's covered by a thick coat of sand," Atdomorsin said. "It has a minimal oxygen atmosphere. There's no evidence of life forms bigger than bacteria. Perhaps it would interest Earth for terraforming although I cannot conceive of where they would get adequate moisture."

Typing an entry in his notebook, Chris said, "The Stephen Hawking Society is looking for alternate home worlds for humans. Here's a candidate for them. What's more, we finally have a story idea for Elinor."

Two weeks and many barren solar systems later, the ship found a planet with a promising atmosphere.

"Unfortunately, the planet didn't live up its initial billing," Elinor said. Chris watched her report as it was beamed to *Alliance* and Earth. "It's devoid of any life beyond varieties of furry reptiles about the size of muskrats. Small bodies of water dot its surface, but even the largest barely qualifies as a lake. Thick vegetation covers the land among the ponds and creeks. We call it Marshland. It is another of the Inhospitable Worlds."

Elinor's video dairy for the next few weeks consisted of aerial images of different colored planets. "They lack any advanced life forms or evidence of Nameless bases. The reconnaissance flights over them are the main source of pilot training." The pilots provided visuals faster than she could review them. The only reward she had for the off-duty personnel who looked through the recordings for her was including scenes of them at work in her documentary on life on the galaxyship.

She also added scenes of Feefers studying Beingish. "In addition to the physical training, learning to speak the alien language is a popular activity." She paused the recorder momentarily and tried saying the same sentence in Beingish. Even though it sounded like gibberish, Morrow gave her an encouraging smile.

Continuing with her diary, she said, "After nearly a month of language classes, we're gaining some proficiency. Not surprisingly, multilingual people are the fastest learners. The instruction is done with an interactive analyzer program developed by Atdomorsin and Connun. It takes you on a tour of their worlds teaching you words and phrases along the way. Beingish starts with base words to which descriptions are added." Elinor put the recorder on pause and contemplated her next entry before delivering it.

"Understanding Beingish gives us an insight into how their thought patterns work. For example, their names begin with their family name and their given one. To that, they add all their accomplishments. It's like a name and resume combined. The Biobots says it's a reflection of their telepathy. They start with the image of a concept or physical object and then add images to complete the communication."

She included an interview with Lin, one of the most adept in Beingish. "The Biobots are always prepared to coach you and they can help you understand the way the Beings construct their thoughts." With a laugh, he said, "It's also funny to hear the Biobots use English in Beingish conversations. The words and phrases jump out at you. Actually they're modifying their Beingish to use shorter words and more concise descriptions."

Even with language classes and physical training, the Feefers had plenty of free time because it took days or weeks to reach the next star system. "So we have turned the galaxyships into a university. "The doctors and nurses are teaching courses in basic medicine; the scientists are giving lessons in their specialties."

She enlisted Chris for an interview about the classrooms.

"Anyone who doesn't already have a university degree should have no trouble completing one after all the classes they're taking," he said. "The rest will be well on their way to a second or third degree. We have a lot of Biobot students as well."

When Morrow and Leprechaun were distracted transferring the interview into Elinor's files, Chris shared a message Hector had sent to Benjamin Kendo. "At the start of the mission, I worried about commanding a multinational force. I argued for taking units from a few countries to reduce any problems integrating them into cohesive combat groups. The Beings, well really the Biobots, weren't about to change their minds. In the end, I'm glad they didn't. After working with the soldiers and pilots for the last few weeks, I've concluded my original concerns were misplaced. The Biobots chose well. We've had no trouble or friction among any nationalities. I've never seen a fitter bunch. Now if we could only get a break in our searches."

Two days later, *Enterprise* orbited a planet about two-thirds the size of Earth that glowed with an inviting light blue tinge and possessed a promising oxygen atmosphere. A buzz from Turing heralded an urgent transmission.

"This is Blue Three. Copy my position. I just over flew what looks like ruins of buildings, repeat ruins of buildings. They're at the bottom of that big southern bay on the main continent. I'm circling back for a second look and will try for better visuals."

The chamber became silent as Turing switched the main display to the visuals from Blue Three and identified its pilot as Lieutenant Jia Jinping from the Air Force of Taiwan. The shoreline drew rapidly closer on the display. "There they are." Turing highlighted the features the pilot had seen. "It is not easy to spot them because their color blends with the surrounding terrain."

Dark brown clumps of collapsed roofs and listing walls squatted in rows that started about one hundred and fifty meters from the water and ran back into the surrounding vegetation. By the time Jia had lined up for another pass, the rest of the patrol had joined him.

"No sign of life down there," he reported. "The area has rolling hills spotted with deep brown rocky outcroppings. Remains of a narrow road run about three hundred meters from the site before disappearing in overgrowth."

Gnoorvants dispatched a reconnaissance shuttle for closer inspection. It hovered over the ruins and transmitted data to the ship that appeared instantly on the displays. "The surface temperature is about eighteen degrees Celsius and the oxygen level is just below Earth standard," Turing reported.

"We better send troops to investigate," Gnoorvants said. "While it doesn't look like an active base, we might find something interesting. We should at least determine its origin."

"If a scouting party reports everything is okay, we could dispatch all the soldiers to the surface," Fassad suggested. "They need the training and change in routine. It'll provide a good test of our environment suits and breathers. As the pilots have done little flying outside of the simulators for weeks, we could launch them all to give the guys some live practice."

Accompanied by two Biobots, soldiers landed on a flat spot on the beach within sight of the settlement. Helmut Marcus, a German lieutenant in the Europe Surface Command, reported to *Enterprise*. "There's a belt of jagged rocks between the beach and the settlement. The Biobots are testing the water and looking for a safe route to the ruins. We'll send visuals shortly."

As he finished, a Biobot called over the radio. "Come see this. There're paths between the ruins and the beach. No foot prints on them. They were created by removing the rocks. You can see them stacked nearby. It was a tough job."

Following the paths, the soldiers reached the ruins in a few minutes. "One drawback of the environment suit is that it's hard to hear anything," Helmut reported to the ship. He said nothing more until he reached the settlement. "There're at least one hundred separate structures. While they're badly deteriorated, they appear to be of the same design. They've collapsed under the weight of thick vines or been pushed apart by trees. In some places, you can see openings for doors and windows. There appears to be paths among them and a small park in the middle. It doesn't feel like anyone's been here for a long time."

A few minutes later, he reported, "We've found a roadway leading from the settlement. After a short distance, it splits. One direction ends at two rectangular flat areas while the other goes off into the bush. While we can't see the rectangles from the air because of the foliage, the surface coating on them and the roads prevents anything from growing out of them."

As the inspection continued, jets reported a second set of ruins, about 500 kilometers inland from the first on the shores of a broad, sluggish river.

A squad of soldiers and Biobots led by Vasile Stocia landed their shuttle at the new site. Equipped with recorders, portable laboratories and digging and moving machines, his team carefully picked its way through, around and under the structures looking for clues.

"Inspections of the two sites indicate the buildings are constructed out of local gravel mixed with some unknown element to make a dingy concrete-like material," Elinor said in her account of the discovery. "Samples of the building material are undergoing analysis and dating in the ship's laboratories. Inside a couple of the partly standing buildings, the patrols found symbols scratched into the walls. They recorded them for further study. Nothing indicates what happened to the inhabitants. Near the settlement, the soldiers found reptiles the size of a cow and small winged creatures that had hair rather than feathers. It's hard to imagine what the settlements originally looked like, let alone who or what might have lived there. Whatever it was built homes, which is a trait we and the Beings share. The ruins have captured the imagination of everyone on the ship. The soldiers and Biobots that visited the sites are asked over and over to describe what it felt like walking through them."

After she added her report to the dairy of the trip, she thought the Biobots seemed the most excited about the discovery. She knew she couldn't question Morrow on this. She decided it was time to contact her friend Ruth.

Gnoorvants had seen enough. "Although these ruins are interesting, they're not what we're looking for," he said at the next morning's briefing. "While we can't find any evidence of military technology, what other purpose could they've served?"

He stopped speaking to read a note on his display screen. "The preliminary results from the analysis of the building material indicate the ruins date from before Transformation. So while we killed each other and the earliest civilizations appeared on your planet, another species lived out here." He paused and glanced at Atdomorsin who nodded.

"Centuries ago, we found a couple of heavily damaged galaxyships of unknown origin adrift in space. We couldn't determine whether they had been in collisions or attacks. They were unsalvageable so we made visuals of them and removed anything useful. We don't have detailed records of those events with us. We will send the data about this place to the Space Directorate to compare it with what we learned from the old ships."

"Our exploration ships never encountered anything like the settlements here," Atdomorsin said. "We will leave plaques in Beingish and English near the settlements and then we must press on."

A week later, *Enterprise* found another world to explore. "To see so much cloud around a planet is most unusual unless it undergoes severe storms." Gnoorvants said when Fassad and Chris entered the Command Chamber.

The displays showed images from reconnaissance shuttles as they flew through the cloud cover to inspect the planet. It appeared to have neither oceans nor mountains.

Gnoorvantston pointed out an asteroid strike. "That probably explains the cloud cover on the planet. I'll direct one shuttle to fly over that area for a closer look."

The ton's behavior startled Fassad. On *Alliance*, tons would have whispered similar observations to their Being to pass on. Gnoorvants and Atdomorsin regarded their tons as colleagues not shadows. Even more than their style of dress, that set them apart from the other Beings.

When the shuttle reached the site, Gnoorvantston put the visuals on the display. "Now we can see the extensive damage surrounding the site of the strike. It threw massive quantities of rock and steam into the air, which is why the clouds are so heavy."

"From their thickness, the planet will probably remain shrouded for a long time," Atdomorsin said. "We've seen no sign of civilization from our surveys."

Elinor stormed into the Command Chamber an hour later to object to the recall of the shuttles. "We need more visuals of what's happened on the planet. There's a great fear on Earth of a nuclear winter that could be caused by the detonation of nuclear weapons. Visuals of this world would make compelling evidence of what could happen to Earth in a war or even a terrorist attack."

Gnoorvants simply smiled. "You will have to make do with the visuals you have because we have a new lead to follow. The long-range imagers have detected a galaxyship. We suspect it is one of our stolen transports. Its propulsion system is not correctly aligned, which suggests it isn't properly maintained. Turing, has the identity of the ship been determined?"

"It was seized two years ago," the Controlling Unit intoned.

The image of a rectangular Being transport appeared on the displays in the Command Chamber. Although the Beings had long names for them, the humans referred to them as flying boxcars. They came in jumbo, large, medium and express versions.

"Turing, follow the ship."

"Any idea where it's going?" Chris added.

"Hopefully to a Nameless base."

Chapter 15
Giant Beings and Refugees

Chris and Lin summoned the pilots to their jets when Gnoorvants alerted them that the transport ship the *Enterprise* had been following had gone into orbit around a planet. It had dispatched several shuttles to the surface before departing. "We've sent a probe to follow it while we find out what's down there."

"Why did the transport not observe us?" Chris asked the mechanic as he conducted a pre-flight check of his jet. "Don't those ships have the imaging equipment to do that?"

"It's likely the Nameless don't know how to use it," Don said. "The helpers would if they were in operation." The mechanics flashed finger messages among themselves. As much as he wanted to know what they were saying, the planet below was the priority for now.

Enterprise went into orbit at top alert, its weapons on full power. Pilots stood at the ready beside their jets. Gnoorvants sat in the center of the command bench drumming his fingers. "That's long enough," he snapped after a half hour. "They don't even know we're here. We'll send jets to inspect the region where the shuttles landed."

While they waited for the surveillance reports about the planet, Gnoorvants updated Fassad on the situation at Marlabant. "Dr Azwatta has determined the Nameless are human and are under chemical subjugation. I am hoping the answer to who controls them may be on this planet."

Fassad nodded. "If there's a base, we'll dispatch soldiers to the surface to investigate."

The minutes dragged by as the jets broadcast images of the surface. "Here we go," Gnoorvants said. A massive rectangular structure, thousands of small ones and a landing strip came into focus on the displays. A row of hills loomed in the background.

"This is the highest resolution of their base that we can get without actually flying over it," Gnoorvants said. "We can't tell what the figures moving about are."

"You're sure the surveillance flights weren't spotted?" Fassad asked him.

"No action was taken against them."

"Can the craft detect the signal from radar or other tracking devices?"

Gnoorvants nodded.

Fassad shook his head. "Little the Nameless do makes sense. All right, let's send reconnaissance teams to the surface."

Vasile Stocia cautiously disembarked from a. shuttle with a patrol armed with laser rifles and pistols. Accompanying them was a Biobot he'd dubbed Whiz Kid because of the array of survey equipment and recording devices it carried.

"The ground is covered with a wide-leafed plant that springs up after being stepped on," Vasile reported to *Enterprise*. "If these plants are everywhere, it'll be hard to track anything on this planet or discover detection equipment or explosives. Although there're no forests around here, many areas are covered in thick bushes. The hills near the bunker are visible."

A few minutes later, he sent more observations. "Whiz tested water, plant and soil samples and a chunk of wood. The air should be safe for us to breathe. The land is mainly rolling with low hills and gentle valleys. While we haven't seen much of it, there must be a lot of wildlife here judging by all the noises we can hear. There's something like a wolf watching us from a distance."

After a pause, Vasile said, "I'm removing my breather. Whiz is standing beside me in case I have a problem." He inhaled deeply. "The air has a nice earthy scent, although anything would smell pleasant after three months in a ship. For safety, we'll take turns going without our breathers."

Three more patrols landed in different locations around the bunker. Their reports about the terrain and wildlife matched Vasile's observations.

As the sun set on the bunker, Gnoorvants decided to forego further reconnaissance. "The Nameless are either unaware or unconcerned about the presence of our ship and patrols. Our priority is to find out who they are."

At daybreak, Vasile returned to the surface with a squad from the Latin American Confederation and headed north toward the base. Glancing back at the patrol, he saw the camouflage color of the soldiers' environment suits blended well with the local terrain, but Whiz's tan color made it too easy to spot. That would have to change in the future.

"It doesn't look like anyone comes this way regularly," he told his unit during a break. "Surely they would make some sort of path instead of tramping through these damn plants all the time."

For the rest of the day, the soldiers advanced cautiously while Whiz sent visuals to the ship. He soon copied the way the soldiers scooted from cover to cover and constantly scanned about for anything untoward.

Having heard how much Biobots loved compliments, Vasile tried one. "It's a real plus to have you with us because of your extended vision and hearing."

Whiz smiled at him. "I don't hear or see anything different than you."

"But you might hear or spot it sooner and that will be a real advantage."

After that, the Biobot acted more alert. It had a big grin on its face as it continually surveyed the countryside. It wasn't hard to like these guys. They were so friendly compared to the Beings.

Closing on the base, the troop crept over bare rock to the edge of a plateau making sure they could take cover if needed behind the few shrubs that managed to grow amid the stone. When they neared the top, Vasile crawled forward for a first look. The main structure dominated the scene. Vasile estimated it as almost 300 meters in length and five stories high judging by the rows of windows.

Enterprise needed a factual description, but the first words that came to him were, "Butt ugly. If there's an award for bad architecture, I'll submit a photo of this monstrosity."

Whiz stuck to its job. "There're ten smaller structures around it as well as thousands of huts. Several shuttles and attack craft are parked on the landing strip. The bunker is light brown in color with rounded corners and a flat roof that curves at the walls. The smaller buildings give off heat waves as if they house operating machinery."

The patrol reached the perimeter of the base close to dusk. The soldiers spotted figures entering the huts. Vasile set his communicator on limited range to reach only his troop. At nightfall, a few lights winked on around the bunker.

He swept the base with binoculars that could pinpoint electronic detection gear and telemetry signals. "I can't believe it. There're no defenses or detection signals except around the bunker. They might as well hang out a welcome sign. We could walk right up to the bunker and knock on the door."

"I'll do it," Private Juan Feldez said. He'd grown up in a mountain village in Peru and had often spent days wandering in the wild on his own. He appeared unafraid of anything or anybody. "We don't want the other patrols to get there first."

"Be careful." While Gnoorvants had ordered him not to attack the base, that didn't mean the soldiers couldn't enter it. If anyone was ever going to knock on the bunker door, it would be Juan. Vasile suppressed a smile.

Juan headed straight toward the bunker with Whiz a few paces behind. When they passed out of sight, Vasile switched to following them on his communicator screen, which showed the images coming from the Biobot's helmet recorder. *Enterprise* would be watching the same images.

As he neared the first hut, Juan took deep breaths to relax and eased off on the trigger. His boots brushing the pebbly ground sounded like drumbeats in the still night.

He stopped worrying about the noise when he caught a pungent odor wafting from the camp that reminded him of the worst slums on his continent.

As he closed on the first hut, its sagging roof and crooked walls made him wonder what held it together. He couldn't see anything inside and didn't want to risk turning on his helmet lamp. The huts ran in rows towards the bunker with their entrances facing each other on dirt paths. These had to be for the Nameless.

He headed for the nearest narrow alley along the rear of the huts. A quick glance over his shoulder showed his barely visible mates following in a well-spaced single file behind Whiz. Halfway to the bunker, he reached a road and had to move a few steps to the right to continue down the closest alley.

As he proceeded, he heard a faint rumbling. Juan concentrated on breathing regularly to control his anger. Slums always stirred a loathing in him that such exploitation and misery were tolerated. He wanted someone or something inside that bunker to pay for the suffering he was creeping past.

The rumbling grew louder and louder and soon drowned out any sounds from the huts. About 100 meters from the bunker, he could tell the noise came from a small structure beside it.

"Perhaps it's a power generator," he whispered to Whiz when it came alongside. "The noise will drown out my approach. If I need to get anyone's attention, I could use some of my explosives." He patted the pouches on a carrying belt around his waist.

Crouching, he jogged to the structure. It had a thin metallic exterior and a pipe running to a nearby tank that had to be a fuel reservoir. He could see attack craft in the faint light, but they could wait.

At 10 meters away, a light flashed over the entrance that was about three meters high and two meters wide. A few beeps sounded from near the door.

"We probably have to respond to that," Juan said. As if to answer to his question, a tiny beam of light hit him. "It's nothing more than a sting." He rubbed his arm. "If we don't move away, there'll be a stronger one." They returned to the generator. "If they won't let me in, I'll have to get them to come out."

He aimed his weapon at a window, and then lowered it. Blasting it might waken everyone in the huts. As he pondered his next move, he peered at Whiz and saw his way to discover what was inside the bunker right behind the Biobot.

He pointed at the large switch on the side of the structure and pulled his arm. The Biobot turned, nodded and grasped the handle. The rumbling ceased and the lights dimmed. "They're on reserve power now." Juan approached the bunker unchallenged. He waited in the dark beside the entrance, his heart pounding. His mates approached and he hoped they'd realized what he'd done as he didn't want to risk using his communicator.

After several minutes, he heard a clamor behind the door before it opened with a jarring screech. A figure considerably taller than him stepped down with an angry grunt. While the creature walked with the familiar rolling stride of a Being, it appeared way too tall and muscular. It plodded toward the generator, uttering a nasty string of sounds. Juan's jaw dropped open in surprise. Still, he'd hesitated before slipping his laser rifle onto medium power and squeezing the trigger. The blast hurled the creature into the side of the generator with a loud thump and it slid to the ground unconscious.

"Now for the entrance," he said to Whiz. He shifted his weapon to full power. Most of the door disintegrated and the remaining bits scattered in every direction. He took several steps and jumped inside the building landing in a crouch. Whiz leapt in beside him.

A few flashing lights on wall panels looked bright in the dim interior. He flipped on his helmet light and surveyed the bunker. The bare walls were dingy brown. A staircase leading to an upper floor was about three paces from the entrance.

Whiz pointed outside. "It said very bad words."

"In Beingish?"

Whiz nodded.

"Doesn't look like them."

Before the Biobot could respond, Vasile arrived.

"Good work, private. You look like you saw a ghost."

"Check what's lying outside." Juan pointed in the direction of the generator. "Then tell me how you feel, sir." The two men heard hurried footsteps descending the stairs and fired in their direction. Three bodies rolled in front of them.

Vasile turned on his helmet lamp to get a closer look. "What the...." He knelt for a closer look. "They're still alive. In case there're more of these creatures above or below us, I'll get the other units to move in as backup. We need to check out this place."

"Whiz's pretty sure these guys are Beings."

The Biobot shook its head. "They make Commander Gnoorvants look small. Their coats and pants are most unusual. And Beings couldn't breathe this air."

Vasile keyed his radio as the Biobot gathered skin samples and fluids from the bodies. "*Enterprise*, can you see this scene clearly enough on Whiz's transmission? It looks like we found some overgrown relatives of yours, Commander."

Whiz looked at the screen of its handheld tester, and then whispered as if offering an unwelcome conclusion. "While their genetic makeup is unusual, there's no doubt they're Beings."

Although he didn't have a throat, Whiz made a very human-sounding gulp. "The Beings will be most distraught by this development. I will transmit my findings to *Enterprise* after I inspect the other one." It slipped out of the bunker as the rest of the patrol entered looking wide-eyed at the bodies and the interior.

"Let them worry about where these guys are from," Vasile

said. "We have business to attend to. The African patrol has found what they think is the entrance to a tunnel that goes under the bunker. They'll try to get inside. The Chinese unit will back us up in a few minutes. Haul these three outside and put them under guard with the other."

Lieutenant Hinto Wu of the Chinese National Army arrived in time to see the soldiers dump the last creature with the others. "Being bad guys. Maybe we aren't the only Primitives in the galaxy. I'll take my patrol up the stairs."

Pointing to the descending part of the staircase, Vasile said, "Juan, take the squad and find out what's down there. I'll go guard the prisoners and give the ship a full update."

"The first three upper floors contain banks of communications and other equipment," Hinto reported a few minutes later. "The top one appears to be their living quarters judging by the mats on the floor and lockers full of tattered uniforms. By what's here, there should be four more of them somewhere. We're getting out of here as soon as we can because the place stinks really badly."

Huge cylinders and piping occupied most of the first two floors below the entrance level. "We're sending visuals of their markings to the ship," Juan informed Vasile. "I bet they're chemicals for the Nameless. The third level appears to be a storehouse. We'll send visuals of it as well."

Juan reported again when he was satisfied no one was hiding among the rows of shelves and boxes. "I'm checking out the stairs to the basement." A minute later, he said, "It looks like a service bay. It's half full of attack craft under repair. The lights are getting quite dim."

At the screech of a laser blast in the bay, Juan scampered down the rest of the stairs and took cover behind an attack craft. Scanning the bay, he couldn't see any movement. When his breathing calmed, he whispered over the radio.

"The other entrance has to be for moving craft and equipment in and out. Not much down here that would fit through these stairs. Now to find the other hostiles."

He waved at his mates to descend quickly as he covered them. The aliens didn't shoot at the first two. When Hugo came down slowly because he'd twisted his ankle earlier, a laser blast erased the steps below him and he crashed to the floor. A muffled curse told Juan he probably had a broken leg or ankle. Whiz jumped down after him.

As his mates made Hugo comfortable and took up defensive positions, Juan heard from the African patrol. "We used our lasers to open the door and we're coming down the ramp." He recognized the deep voice of Corporal Moses Tembke.

"Be careful, it's dark in here so your lights will make you really stand out," Juan said.

"There're figures behind the large crane," Tembke reported after a couple of minutes.

"Take cover." Juan aimed his helmet light in the direction of the crane revealing figures aiming their weapons at the Africans. He fired while his mates scrambled toward them. One figure dropped. His other blasts sailed over their heads and slammed into a wall, showering the bay with sparks and debris.

After several blasts from the Africans' laser rifles from the other side of the bay, Tembke said, "We got them."

The soldiers dragged the unconscious aliens into a pile while Juan reported to Vasile. "We got four more of whatever these things are. There're some carts here that we'll use to lug them outside. They're too large to haul up the stairs."

"We've got thousands of Nameless wretches milling around up here," Vasile growled. "Whiz says they too speak very old Beingish."

The lights suddenly brightened and Juan figured the generator had been turned back on. With the power restored, they opened what remained of the ramp door and wheeled out their captives.

At the top of the ramp, they saw the Nameless in tattered brown, green or black coveralls that blended in with the dismal surroundings. Many held youngsters. Surveying the crowd, Juan muttered, "They're whiter than white people. Spooky the way they stare at us. Wonder what they're saying?"

"I'm too far away to hear," Whiz said.

Juan felt his anger rekindling. The Nameless had to be the sorriest looking refugees. The still-unconscious guards appeared almost as disheveled.

Shuttles delivered a steady stream of reinforcements from *Enterprise*. When Atdomorsin and two other Beings arrived, the Nameless bowed toward them and chanted.

Whiz approached Vasile and Juan. "It's their feeding time. We should open the building they're pointing at."

"What do they eat?" Juan said.

"We don't know yet."

When Atdomorsin joined them, Vasile said, "Looks like the attacks on your worlds were organized by these guys using doped-up humans to do the dirty work."

Atdomorsin grunted. His head moved like a slow metronome as he stared at the prone figures. "How can these Beings survive in this atmosphere without environment suits or breathers? Where are they from?" He instructed several Biobots to bind and load them on a shuttle.

He stared at the line up in front of the feeding building. "So the Nameless are humans enslaved by our own kind. How are we going to explain this?"

Humanity's Saving Grace

Chapter 16
A Medical Breakthrough

In the Conference Room of *Alliance*, Humbaw, Demmloda and Hector examined visuals of the captives, the bunker and the Nameless huts. The galaxyship had turned over its Nameless to *Transformation* and hurtled through space to join *Enterprise*. The transports *Yamato* and *Hercules*, with newly installed laser cannons, accompanied it.

Humbaw rubbed his eyes before resuming his update. "The prisoners don't appear to have any telepathic ability and, although they speak ancient Beingish, they can obviously understand our communications well enough. None of what we found explains why they kept attacking us for all these years."

He stood and paced as Demmloda gazed at images of the surrounding stars. Their tons watched without speaking or sending finger messages.

On his side of the room, Hector studied visuals of the transports accompanying them. If the Beings hadn't found any other species than humans, was it really a surprise the attackers were also Beings. What he really couldn't understand was how the pacifist Beings could have any enemies. Had Earth unwittingly become ensnared in a civil war?

Wishing time alone to record his thoughts in his notebook, he leaned toward Hectorton. "Can you find out if the other Beings are taking the news about the prisoners the same as Humbaw and Demmloda?"

"Is this what you call being depressed?"

Hector nodded and Hectorton slipped away. With a glance at the still despondent Humbaw and Demmloda, he concluded dictating his observations about the reaction of the Beings before resuming his examination of the transports. Their firepower probably rivaled *Enterprise*. The cannons on *Alliance* were also being augmented.

Humbaw cleared his throat. "I'm ready to discuss our situation further. Nonforense is combing the Chronicles for clues to the origin of these ..." There seemed to be no appropriate Being word.

"We would call them Renegades."

"Re ne gad es." Humbaw repeated the word several times.

"Nonforense, adopt that word for our prisoners." He shook his head several times as if trying to wish away a bad dream. "One problem is solved. The food dispenser at the base works although it seems wrong to call the slop it produces food. It's laced with the controlling chemicals. There are close to ten thousand Nameless. What can we do with them? Even with the stockpile in the bunker, we may not have sufficient food to sustain them."

"How are you going to explain the Renegades to the High Council?" Hector said. Better to get the Beings to deal with a problem than listen to their fretting.

"It's not just the High Council I worry about. My species will be profoundly shaken by what the Renegades have done to the Nameless. Their actions have greatly offended our honor."

Humbaw started pacing again and Hector resumed writing his report. "The bunker had only eight guards. How could so few run that place?"

"It's highly automated and there're a lot of females and young so it probably also served as a breeding facility," Demmloda said.

Humbaw still bore a hang-dog expression. "All we can do is feed the chemicals to the Nameless and hope your medical teams can discover how to end their dependency."

Almost on the three month mark since FEEF's departure, a report about the victory at Marlabant reached Terraumblaw, the Being embassy in New York. Bemmonloda appeared in Benjamin's office to show it to him. "I can only tell you it was sent by a narrow beam energy transmission that works like galaxy flight. A courier ship will arrive within a month with a lengthy report from Ms Brady."

Benjamin summoned his aides. When they'd gathered in his office, he replayed the report. "There's not much beyond the initial victory and splitting our forces between two cruisers. Still it's the only news we've had since Elinor's documentary about life on *Alliance* and the plan to rendezvous with the other ship. It will give me something to report to the Security Council this afternoon. All the delegations want news on what FEEF is doing now. They'll complain this is more than a month old. They think that because of my regular meetings with the Ambassador, I know more than I let on."

"We'll release the information to the comnets once the Council meeting starts," Rachel said. "To give Elinor her due credit, she packed so much information into her report the networks still air it." In addition to the naming ceremony for the ship, her broadcast contained interviews with Beings and Feefers along with visuals of pilots with their jets and mechanics, the soldiers training on the ship and the regions of the galaxy the ship had passed through.

That evening, Bemmonloda arrived without advance notice at Benjamin's apartment in the UN building. "I wanted to inform you personally there is an addendum to the report I delivered."

Benjamin pointed to the wooden bench in the middle of the room and settled into a heavily padded high backed chair.

"It has more details on the Nameless. There's no doubt that Earth is their origin?"

Benjamin shifted to the front of the chair. "This isn't a complete surprise based on what Humbaw told us about the bodies he found." He took a deep breath to collect his thoughts. "I presume the FEEF medical team concurs?"

Bemmonloda nodded. "This is their conclusion. I leave it to you to decide how to reveal this information. How will humans react to this?"

"No idea. We will have to explain receiving this extra information?"

"Simple. Our system has capacity limits. It was a follow-up message. We can announce it whenever you're ready."

Kendo resisted an impulse to start walking around. "It's tough waiting so long to find out what's happening to people I'm responsible for. While we're celebrating the victory at Marlabant, it's ancient history for our soldiers and pilots."

"What you say is quite true, Secretary General." The Ambassador spoke in his usual soft tone, his gaze shifting between Benjamin and his wife Olen. "It is a fact of space travel we are used to and in time Earth will also become accustomed to it. Because our worlds are close together, we do not have to wait as long for news as you do. Still the uncertainty is not discouraging additional volunteers for FEEF. Like most Beings, I regarded your species as too immature to face such a challenge. Now I appreciate what Humbaw saw in Earthlings. He used to say 'the Primitives would give us a good boot in the backside.' I thought it was a bad translation of one of your sayings." He grinned.

"You folks are getting credit for already making Earth more livable," Benjamin said. "While it's far too early for your ships to have reduced the vast amount of pollutants in the atmosphere, everyone is convinced they have made a significant dent."

Light-years away, humans and Beings toiled feverishly on the medical ship *Transformation* to find a treatment to counter the influence of the chemicals in the Nameless. Micheline Azwatta set the tone for research by the other doctors. "They are our patients and our guests on this ship. They are as human as we are."

Several days after *Alliance*'s departure, she sent a visual to Humbaw and Hector. Neither had inspected the medical ship so Micheline made sure her report included visuals of its medical facilities. The highlights included operating rooms full of monitors and surgical equipment and large, well lit triage areas. They gleamed with newness.

"While we've tried different dosages of the chemicals on the Nameless, we couldn't achieve anything more than temporary consciousness. So we've stopped giving them any. Instead we're feeding them our special milkshake. It's a rose-colored drink developed by Dr Henri Vernhardt to supply all the nutrients they need. If we can keep them alive, hopefully their bodies will purge the controlling chemicals. It's the only plan we have for now."

The visual switched to the area that housed the captured pilots. It had the same industrial carpet-like floor and walls of other Being ships.

"Our augmented corps of Medbiots has taken over feeding and cleaning our guests. We'll try to make their area more cheerful when they recover. The Medbiots have set up picnic tables, chairs and three-D displays at one end of the bay and put privacy screens between them and the sleeping mats. We hope to see them watching the displays soon."

A week after Micheline's report, Henri halted in the middle of his morning tour of the bay. Touching his communicator to update the medical log, he said, "Although most of our patients have come out of their comatose state, they don't do much more than sit and stare. Some stretch and walk about a bit. Some talk a bit to the Medbiots."

He checked his notepad. "By their facial expressions, they're trying to figure out what's happening. They're starting to recognize each other and as they speak each other's names, the Medbiots put ID tags on them."

He halted to mull over his next comments. "The Medbiots believe the milkshake is the main reason for the improvement. I would concur with them that the drink is providing the Nameless with nourishment and rehabilitation. Many of them are gaining weight. I have to say that is a good sign since most of them were nothing more than cadavers when they arrived. Equally welcome, blood tests show their levels of chemical residues are dropping faster than we hoped for.

"My enhanced milkshake is about ready and hopefully it'll produce even more dramatic improvements. The next step will be removal of the pumps in their necks. It's the next logical step in their recovery. They won't really improve until it's gone."

A few days later, Henri delivered the recipe for his latest concoction to the Kitchenbiots. He felt excited and apprehensive as he wasn't sure how the Nameless would respond to the vanilla flavor. The Medbiots distributed it. Hesitant sips quickly became eager gulps as the patients emptied their containers and held them out for refilling.

Later that day he removed the first device from a patient. It proved a simple procedure under local anesthetic and he snipped the leads that ran from it through the body. After a couple more successful removals, he trained two Medbiots in the procedure. When he was satisfied they could handle the operation without his direct supervision, he resumed his work on further refining his milkshake. He moved his experiments to a lab close to the surgery room so he could intervene if the Medbiots ran into a problem.

A few mornings later, Micheline watched a group of patients at the picnic tables nibbling on rice cakes, the first solid food they'd eaten. Some spoke to her which she counted as another big step to recovery. She smiled back and said in her rudimentary Beingish, "Hello, how are you today?"

A Nameless frowned and whispered to a Medbiot, who translated. "They understand what you say, but not who you are. The chemical residues still muddle their thinking. We have tried to explain and someday they will understand."

As she continued to monitor them, a Kitchenbiot stepped in front of her holding out a tray on which sat a small dark brown square. Normally the Biobots grinned and smiled all the time.

This one was absolutely stone faced. "We need an expert to tell us if this tastes okay."

Not wanting to disappoint the Kitchenbiot, Micheline popped the whole piece in her mouth. "This is fantastic chocolate." The helper broke into a wide grin.

She noticed that many Medbiots had watched her reaction to the chocolate. "So what are you guys up to?"

"Inspired by Dr Henri, we've been experimenting with different flavors for the milkshake. Azwattaton told us how much you love chocolate. We found this recipe in the data banks and want to try it on the guests."

"Can't do any harm." Micheline hugged the Kitchenbiot and her ton.

She returned to the Nameless area for the evening meal. Normally it was a quiet time and she could work away in the cubicle at the end of the bay that served as office and examination room for the doctors. She was looking at patient reports when she heard a loud clamor.

"What's going on?" she asked, stepping into the open area of the bay. Everywhere patients milled about the food carts holding out their cups for seconds of the milkshake. Then she noticed the brown tint on their lips.

"The guests certainly like it," Azwattaton said.

Micheline strode over to a meal cart, stuck a finger into an empty milkshake container and tasted the drink. "Not bad at all." She smiled at the Kitchenbiots and patted her stomach. "It's very rich. I couldn't take a steady diet of it, but they can."

When the Kitchenbiots and Medbiots flashed finger messages, she waved her hands to get their attention. "Why do you believe you don't have imagination or inventiveness?" She tried to make her teasing tone clear. "You people worked out ways to make the milkshake more appealing to our guests and mixed the chocolate into it in the right proportions. You have changed many routines on your own to suit our guests. There is certainly nothing missing in your creativity."

The Biots stared at each other. No fingers moved. Micheline watched them trying to guess what they were thinking. Maybe in their usual enthusiasm, the Kitchenbiots would put chocolate in everyone's food. They worked hard at making good human meals.

She returned her attention to the guests and saw they all drank now. Smiling at the progress, she realized she had called the Biots a people. She really wasn't sure what else to call them. She would have to discuss this issue with her colleagues and Ruth.

Henri beamed when she told him about the chocolate shake later in the day. "It's good they want to drink more because I'm planning to add a vitamin the Beings use to cure internal infections. I've tested it on our injured pilots and it sped up their recovery so I'm adding it to the milkshakes for guests after their controller is removed. It's a form of nanotechnology and I'm sure it will help a lot."

Almost half the patients had had their device removed by the time Supershake was served for the first time. The additional vitamin didn't alter its chocolate taste.

"I can hardly believe the results," Micheline told Humbaw and Hector by vislink after a couple of days of the new treatment. "The incisions heal to faint scars almost overnight. More surprising is the rapid improvement in their mental condition. They're cleaning and dressing on their own and asking the Medbiots questions about the ship and the Terrans. Henri's Supershake is the reason and all our patients should receive it even before the operation.

"In the first ones operated on, the leads from the controller dissolved slowly. With the Supershake, they disappear in a couple of days. It's a smart vitamin that attacks foreign objects in the body. Controlling Unit, show the images."

A display appeared in the midst of the doctors watching the recording of the visual. It forced them to move their benches and chairs back to get a full view. "The one on the right is pre-operative and the leads are highlighted," she said. "On the left is five days after the removal of the controller in a patient operated on before Supershake. The leads have shrunk. In the middle is a patient a couple of days after the operation. He received the vitamin right after the removal of the pump. The leads are almost gone." The doctors had agreed to name it Vitamin H in English after the Being home world Hnassumblaw.

"The only downside of the more alert patients is they have little useful information to impart." She turned off the displays to ensure she had the full attention of the medical staff. "While they're certainly curious about everything, they can't tell us much beyond flying the attack craft and the humdrum routine of life at their base."

Micheline sent visuals of the increasingly active patients to

Alliance and *Enterprise*. "We think they're from the base you captured because they got very excited when we showed them visuals of it. They called out the names of individuals in it. Questions about their origin and how they came under the control of the Renegades produce only perplexed looks. Ruth is working on a possible connection between them and us."

Micheline scanned her list of topics. "It'll take a few more days before we finish removing all the controllers. Helping all the guests you have will require a lot of Vitamin H and many more Medbiots."

On the return transmission, Humbaw relayed a communication from Gnoorvants. "The Renegades are unaware of our telepathic powers. When we question them, they think about what they want to hide from us in their answers. So we have pieced together a picture of them."

As he talked, images of the captive Renegades appeared in the display. "When Hnassumblaw was entering Transformation, the forbearers of this group decided the changes in our society were evil. They want to destroy us because we are no longer true Beings. They went into exile which explains why they have not kept up with our technology.

"Because their ancestors missed Transformation, they possess the combativeness and aggressiveness we lack. Their life span is about as short as humans. They like to congregate in large groups and the ones we captured are very lonely. They fear we will inflict hideous tortures on them before we execute them. They had no chance to warn their commanders about the takeover of the base and aren't expecting a supply ship for several weeks.

"The Renegades call the Nameless things. The chemical treatment begins shortly after birth and continues until an individual has outlived its usefulness. When that happens, they're killed, often brutally. It might help us if you sent a video of the Nameless pilots that we could show to the ones here. Somehow, through all their stupor, they remember family and relatives."

The display switched to images of Nameless milling about. Azwattaton told the Controlling Unit to show that portion of the visual to the patients and record their reactions.

A distraught Medbiot rushed into Micheline's cubicle later in the day. "There's something terribly wrong with a couple of patients. We may have made a terrible mistake."

Its hysterical tone startled the doctor. Azwattaton shrugged when she looked to her for an explanation. "Settle down and try to explain the problem."

"One of the first Nameless to have his controller removed was helping a new patient to sit up," the Medbiot said, still highly agitated. "When he put his arm behind the other, I saw his skin had darkened. While he said he felt well, I told him to sit down until you could examine him."

Knowing the Medbiot would hassle her until she checked out the situation, Micheline gathered her gear and followed the Medbiot and Azwattaton. The Medbiot pointed at the seemingly healthy Nameless, who sat in a chair chatting with a patient in a bed.

"I see," Micheline said, holding in her excitement. "You think all the chocolate in the Supershake caused him to turn brown." The Medbiot nodded vigorously.

To her, his skin had an olive hue. She stepped up to the patient in the chair, who was looking at her with some alarm, and pressed her finger on his right forearm. Although no albino color showed through, she rubbed the top of his head and then his cheek before turning to the Medbiot. "Let's check the others." She found the same result throughout the bay. The Nameless had begun to grow hair.

"This is an absolutely brilliant observation," Micheline said to the Medbiot. "I'll recommend you for a commendation."

Azwattaton and the Medbiot looked at each in surprise.

"The changes are further proof our guests are human and they're simply regaining their natural color and hair growth, which must have been blotted out by the chemicals. If I saw them on Earth, I would think they were from around the Mediterranean."

Humanity's Saving Grace

Chapter 17
The Biobot Puzzle

Ruth had come to Hector's office near the Command Chamber on *Alliance* to deliver a personal invitation rather than send her ton. "General Davis, I'm having a small get-together in my lab tonight and I wonder if you would join us. I'm sure you will find it quite interesting, sir."

He didn't encounter her regularly because she mainly worked with the Biobots. He'd only recently learned Nonforense, not the Beings, had selected her for the First Extraterrestrial Expeditionary Force. He agreed to attend expecting by her tone the evening would be enlightening.

On the way to her lab near the medical facilities, he met Sergi. "Don't know much about Ruth, but Chris tells me she's ultra-smart," the Russian said. "She and Elinor are close friends. While she was the first to receive the Being transmission, she has avoided getting any attention about that from the comnets."

"You mean it was aimed at her? While she's an expert on the possibility of extraterrestrial civilizations, that's a bit much."

"Although it seems farfetched, Elinor believes the Beings deliberately contacted Ruth first."

The lab door opened as they approached. Ruth greeted them along with Humbawton and Demmlodaton. He doubted the Beings knew about this gathering. If they did, they probably wouldn't consider it important.

Soft music played in the background. From all the strings, it sounded classical. Music was rare on the ship because the Beings said the rising and falling notes interfered with their telepathy. The only time he heard any was in the Primatory, as the Feefers had dubbed their living quarters.

"Nice place you got here, Ruth," Sergi said. "Sure doesn't look like a lab." It resembled any Being room; minimal furniture and no decorations on sand-colored walls.

"We put a few things away." Her attempt to sound glib made her seem quite apprehensive.

After passing around cups of tea and plates of biscuits, Ruth launched into an explanation for her invitation. "The tons have finished describing the visuals of Being visits to Earth. Here are the highlights." She handed them data cubes for use in a portable analyzer. "I'm sure you will find them fascinating. Every place they visited is identified as are the people they talked to." A wistful smile slipped across her face. "I think my great grandparents are in it. I'm sending copies to the UN and Elinor. You can view these at your leisure. That's not what this session is about."

Hector shot Sergi a puzzled look.

"Since then, they've shown me visuals of their space exploration voyages. They include every possible phenomenon plus some we're never seen before. I've enough material for scores of scientific papers and a comnet travelogue of space. However, that's not what I wanted to talk to you about either."

She straightened in her chair. "My research is focused on understanding the relationship between Beings and Biobots. What I've found is a much different society than we imagined and it could change the whole mission, even more than the learning about the Renegades and the Nameless."

"That's quite a claim," Hector said. *This had better be good.* Everyone in FEEF admired her work and when he'd reviewed her record, he discovered she had degrees in history, biology and astronomy.

She smiled. "I am concerned about how you would react to my ideas."

Returning her gaze, Hector concluded she cultivated her plain Jane image to hide her inquisitive personality and intelligence. Knowing her credentials, calling her a genius seemed inadequate.

"It took some time, but I finally convinced the tons to talk to you about it."

The tons looked nervously at each other. "We want to assure you we're not slaves or serfs or even servants." Humbawton picked his words carefully. "We've studied your history and literature for an accurate description of our role in the Being worlds. Tons are a combination of companion and business manager for the Being we're assigned to. The rest of the Biobots are like unpaid employees of the Being race. Although that doesn't completely explain our position, it's the best we can think of. Ruth says it's important for you to understand our viewpoint."

Hector had never heard a Biobot use a human's first name before.

"Large portions of Hnassumblaw were rendered uninhabitable during the civil wars that preceded Transformation. The Beings feared conditions would worsen putting their species at risk of extinction. There weren't enough of them then to colonize even one planet although they found eight suitable ones fairly close to Hnassumblaw. So they created us to run their worlds and operate their galaxyships."

"Created?"

"It's all explained in the data cube," Ruth interjected.

"We're always there, attending to everything that needs doing," the ton said. "They keep no secrets from us and treat us admirably well. It's a good existence except they take us for granted. You won't find malcontents among us although there is frustration among some Biobots about the Beings' refusal to acknowledge our importance to them." He paused momentarily. "What we want is acceptance as full citizens of their worlds and the ability to create instead of just copy whatever they or you do. We've evolved considerably since they first made us, achieving far more than they realize. Despite a lot of study, we're no closer to learning creativity. While Feefers have pointed out instances where we showed imagination, it is always connected to mimicking human behavior. Ruth agreed to assist us in our endeavor."

Demmlodaton shifted forward in his seat. "We admire what the Beings have accomplished and we share their fascination with expanding knowledge. They don't appreciate how much they depend on us. They certainly don't know how many of us exist as we construct the new Biots. As for achieving citizenship, we've taken many steps to gain their respect. We even have our own code of behavior. On an earlier visit to Earth, we found the Three Laws of Robotics developed by a writer named Isaac Asimov. Do you know them?"

Hector shook his head. "It's something about not harming humans." He had no idea where was this conversation going.

"In essence, they say a robot cannot harm a human, a robot must obey orders from humans except when they could cause harm to other humans and a robot must protect its existence. We began life as artificial creatures like robots and we have adopted the rules as our code of conduct toward the Beings."

In the background, the music changed. The new piece sounded like Beethoven's *Eroica* Symphony. The Biots seem to follow its movements judging by the slight movements of their heads and hands.

Hector fixed his gaze on the tons. "You talk as if you have your own society."

Humbawton looked to Demmlodaton who nodded. "That's exactly what we have; a society that exists in parallel to that of the Beings. When the Nameless attacks became intolerable, Humbaw looked for ways to stop them. We planted the idea of enlisting humans otherwise the Beings would've continued to delude themselves that better technology would stop the attacks. When the High Council finally agreed with Humbaw's plan to seek Earth's help, we organized the approach to Earth in a way that wouldn't frighten you."

Hector's jaw dropped open in surprise.

"As we entered your solar system, we examined all the material from Earth we could access to compare with what we already knew. Humbaw thought he only had to send the greeting. We wanted to make sure it went to someone who would appreciate its importance. We found Ruth's theories on alien life and knew she was the person to contact first. We accessed her station's system to find out when she was on duty and directed the message to her. She handled it better than we hoped for. She's our hero."

Ruth shrugged. "Although a co-worker guessed I was contacted because of my views, I scoffed at the idea. I still have to tell Arthur. By the way, the Biobots enjoy using short forms of words the way the pilots and soldiers do. Among themselves they usually call us Prims and themselves Biots." A serene look of confidence broke out amongst the tons.

"What you just related sure sounds like creative thinking," Hector said. All the observations he'd gathered about the Biots made sense.

"We've not invented anything." Humbawton looked at the other tons for support. They all nodded. "We haven't found a way to show the Beings their worlds are also our worlds."

Before Hector could respond, Huxleyton spoke. "We've learned fighting is very complicated. Still we can do anything once it is demonstrated to us. The mechanics think they could learn to fly jets in combat. The Soldierbiots have learned to use the rifles and tanks well enough to attack the Nameless bases." The ton relaxed back into his seat, sighing as if she'd relinquished a great burden.

"So why did you think convincing the Beings to recruit us would help you?" Hector felt as much perplexed as impressed with the Biots.

"Our first goal was to learn to defend our worlds and we needed you to show us how," Humbawton said. "We want to participate in the war against the Nameless to demonstrate to the Beings that their worlds are our home too. It helped us a lot when the Biots at Terraumblaw proved they were capable of guarding our Ambassadors. From that, we concluded we could learn to fight and fly in combat."

Sergi shook his head in amazement. "Ruth, you hang out with the most interesting characters."

Ruth nodded to the tons. "The Beings have no idea the Biots have their own Parliament or what secretive activities they're carrying on."

"The tons of the Councilors are our leaders," Huxleyton said. "What we've told you does nothing to lessen how much both Beings and us need your help to stop the Nameless. Humbaw is correct in his assessment of the threat their attacks pose for our worlds."

"Do they want us to explain this to the Beings?" Hector said.

"No!" Humbawton and Demmlodaton snapped in unison. "We want you to give us a chance to show them what we can do. When it's ready, we also have a surprise for them on Hnassumblaw."

Huxleyton stepped in front of Sergi. "Captain, we especially need your help." By the ton's frown, she was struggling with something. "I've never asked for anything before." It took more than a minute before she blurted out his wish. "We need someone to take our jet on a test flight."

"Your jet?"

"We have completely rebuilt six of the Renegade craft on *Alliance*. While we think they're much improved, we need an expert's assessment."

Ruth picked up the controller for the main display and pressed the start button. "This visual was recorded in the middle of the night two weeks ago. They work then because we and the Beings are asleep."

The visual panned the bay before focusing on the stripped down hulks of the attack craft surrounded by squads of Biots. Around them were mobile work benches and diagnostic gear. Hundreds of helpers watched ready to assist.

"At this point, we've begun reassembling them," Huxleyton said.

"What's the music?" Hector knew he should recognize it.

"A Mozart symphony," Ruth said. "The Biots love classical music played very loudly. I'm surprised they haven't woken up the whole ship. At first, they didn't care for opera because they felt the words messed up the music. But then they learned the lyrics and now they sing along." She shook her head, unable to hide her smile. "By the way, we should start calling them by the shortened names they use for themselves. It makes them feel like individuals."

The visual jumped. "This is last week," she continued. "At this point, most of the major work was complete." Biots still worked on the craft that had returned to their original appearance except for the addition of two short stabilizers.

"That will make them fly better in an atmosphere," Huxton said. Once again, music pounded through the bay. "The next scene was a couple of nights ago." The engines in the six craft hummed as the Biots conducted systems checks.

Sergi strode over to the tons. Sticking out his hand, he said, "You're on. I'd thought of taking my mechanics for a flight so they could see what it's like. They asked far more questions than I did in flight school."

Rising to shake the captain's hand, Huxton said, "It would mean a lot to all the mechanics."

"You should also consider how many more pilots and soldiers you would have with the Biots," Ruth said.

Flight-Lieutenant Ben Kennedy and his mechanics Kanga and Roo climbed into the flight deck of the first upgraded attack craft on the captured base, now called Liberation. "Sergi says we won't believe how good these machines are. You guys can explain all you've done to upgrade this craft."

"Thanks to Captain Sergi for giving us modification ideas from his flight and to Captain Chris for covering up our activities," Kanga said. "He gave us a good lesson in how to accomplish things without attracting a lot of attention."

Chris had arranged to have *Enterprise* mechanics shuttled to the base to examine the captured attack craft. They disassembled them and shipped components that needed rebuilding to the galaxyship. They did rest of the work in the service bay of the bunker. They would soon complete the conversion of the 18 attack craft on the base.

"Handy the Renegades made them with three-seat cockpits," Ben said as Roo fired up the craft's engine and Kanga readied the controls. "The captain says we're supposed to see what you guys can do so here's your chance to earn your big salary."

Kanga identified the various instruments and explained the upgrades. "By the way, we call them fighters just like you call your craft jets."

"Fighters they are. Sergi says they're about as good as a jet. Being bigger, they aren't as nimble, but they're better armed. Keep up this kind of work and no one will buy that line of yours about not being inventive or creative. Let's get this contraption into the air. Which of you is flying first?"

The mechanics stared at each other. "Don't you want to fly it?" Roo said.

"Nah. I want to see what you guys can do." The mechanics flashed each other thumbs up. "Flight control, this is Kennedy. We're taking an attack craft for a spin around the block."

The fighter shot straight up in the air. Unlike the control stick in the jets, Roo had to move his finger on a display screen to indicate direction and speed.

"Where do you want to go?"

"I'd suggest some loops around the base," Roo replied in his best Aussie accent.

Ben smiled. He'd noticed a lot of Biots hanging around. Roo and Kanga wanted to show off. "You like this flyboy stuff, don't ya?"

"Yup, ever since we heard about Captain Sergi taking his mechs on the test flight, Kanga and I have hoped for a chance. We trained in the simulators using the manual Captain Donohue prepared for the pilots."

"That's all?"

"Well, most of us have sat in the fighters imagining what flying would be like. We've been coached by the nanalyzers in your jets. We held workshops to discuss what we learned from observing the pilots."

"You guys sure are busy while we sleep."

"You bet."

For the next 15 minutes, Roo and then Kanga zoomed over the planet.

"Kennedy, you're having too much fun," fellow pilot Simon Grady said over the communicator.

Atdomorsin intervened from *Enterprise*. "Lieutenant Grady is supposed to be flying with you, Lieutenant Kennedy. So why is he on the ground?"

"Because I wanted to find out how good these improved craft are and show you how well mechanics can fly them."

"What are you talking about?"

"Kanga and Roo are my mechanics. Kanga's flying now. Roo did before. Pretty good, eh!"

When Atdomorsin didn't reply, Ben said, "Wait 'til you see how the mechanics have upgraded them. You Beings don't know how lucky you are."

There was only silence. No response. Ben figured he would have to ask Chris later about the reaction in the Command Chamber.

During the next week, the pilots checked out all the Biots that had volunteered for combat flying. The mechanics had a big advantage in the selection process from what they'd learned working with the pilots and on the craft. Kanga and Roo became the leaders of the Pilotbiots who dubbed themselves the flyers. Ben and Simon certified pilots for the nearly 75 fighters on *Enterprise* and Liberation for a fly-past of the base.

Gnoorvants and Atdomorsin arrived in a shuttle to review the event. They stood beside each other on the landing strip, their tons at their side, looking about. "What's going to happen?" Gnoorvants said when Chris approached.

"The fighters will fly by in formation and then put on an aerial demonstration. We have a few other surprises for you."

Waiting for the craft to arrive, Gnoorvants looked about Liberation. "Why did the helpers not tell us what they were doing?" Seeing Gnoorton ready to speak, he added, "No need to answer that. We probably would not have paid any attention."

"There's one other matter," Chris said. "The flyers call themselves the Being Air Force. They're very proud of what they've accomplished."

Gnoorvants and Demmloda stood soundlessly mouthing the words, Being Air Force. Chris wished he could listen to their telepathic conversation until he heard the raucous approach of the fighters followed by the jets. They screamed past, dipping from side to side in a salute. After the fly past, the flyers put on a display of loops, power dives and other aerial aerobatics.

Vasile Stocia, now a captain, brought on the next surprise. About 200 Soldierbiots, dressed in light grey, long sleeved T shirts and pants, marched past and then demonstrated their prowess with laser rifles by hitting stationary and moving targets. Then they put on a display of martial arts holds and throws they would use in hand to hand combat.

"They've chosen the name troopers to distinguish themselves

from the soldiers," he said. "While the clothing seems odd on them, it's the best way to cover their far-too-conspicuous exteriors. We'll cover their faces with camouflage color. I believe they're ready for combat. Our biggest challenge will be keeping them from becoming too aggressive. They're determined to show you what they can do."

"I have always prided myself on challenging the conventional views in our society." Gnoorvants peered to the skies as if looking for a better explanation. "To me, Humbaw is very conservative. However, I never imagined helpers could do all this." He turned to Gnoorton. "I owe you an apology. You tried to suggest such things, but I ignored your ideas. I doubt it ends with this, does it?"

The ton nodded.

Gnoorvants' next comment seemed to be filled with self-pity as he said, "The humans show us up, our attackers turn out to be directed by our relatives and now our helpers can be flyers and troopers. Are there any other surprises?"

Gnoorton nodded again.

"Ask them about their Parliament and code of conduct," Chris said.

After Gnoorton explained the Biots' parallel society, Gnoorvants put his hand on the ton's shoulder. "If we get through this war, a lot will change. I promise you that."

Gnoorton was at a loss for words and only managed a croak.

Enterprise detected a supply ship approaching the planet the next day and shifted its position to avoid detection. Three fighters flew from *Liberation* into the supply ship's main bay using access signals found in the base's information system. Each craft carried a human soldier and three trained Biot troopers. They split into two groups of six; one jogged unopposed to the Command Chamber where a trooper with the name Genghis Khan on his chest and back convinced the Nameless to surrender without raising his weapon. With him were Alexander the Great and Rommel. The other unit went to find the Biot crew.

"The troopers left us little to do in the takeover, but admire their performance in seizing the Command Chamber with sheer gruffness," Vasile reported to *Enterprise*. "While the Nameless here aren't too doped up, they don't understand who we are.

They can operate the ship. We're trying to figure out how much the Renegades changed the programming in the Controlling Unit."

The soldiers had familiarized themselves with the layout of the Command Chamber by the time the troopers returned accompanied by almost fifty other Biots.

"They hid and shut themselves down after the ship was captured so the Renegades couldn't use them." Genghis' arm swept over the crew. "They're anxious to get back to their duties."

A revived crew member strode to the command console and spoke Beingish with the Controlling Unit for several minutes. Genghis laughed heartily. "It hid its original programming and allowed the Renegades to alter a simplified version of its operational procedures. The Renegades never spotted the deception. The crew member is helping the Controlling Unit restore the original programming. When he's done, *Enterprise* can supply it with all the updates and it will be like before."

"Not quite." Vasile had moved over to the console to watch the crew member. "It and you have proved your code of conduct works. That's important for your future."

Genghis fixed him with a hard stare. "Why is it so obvious to you, but not the Beings?"

"It's a Primitive thing." Vasile couldn't help smiling at his joke. To his surprise, the troopers nearly doubled over with laughter. Vasile's grin grew bigger.

Before the ship's crew went back to work, they shook hands with the soldiers and peppered the troopers with questions. Catching Genghis's attention, Vasile said, "When we have a quiet moment, I would like an explanation of how Biots can go into prolonged hibernation and come back to life so quickly."

"While I don't really know how to explain it, I will find one who can."

Chapter 18
The Troopers' Turn

With the supply ship under control, *Enterprise* set out to retrace the vessel's flight path to Liberation by following its energy trail. *Alliance* changed course to join it while *Yamoto* and *Hercules* continued to Liberation. Mechs from those ships would upgrade the supply ship weapons. More armed Being transports were on their way.

After three days, *Enterprise* found the supply ship's previous stop. Using transmission codes from the captured vessel, it informed the base on the planet that shuttles would deliver replacement things.

No one greeted the arriving craft and 25 soldiers and troopers captured the base and its 13 guards after a brief firefight. "No one will ever be able to accuse the troopers of cowardice," Vasile told Gnoorvants when he returned to the galaxyship. "They went after the Renegades like in a football game." Three soldiers and two troopers were wounded.

Atdomorsin and other Beings grilled the captured Renegades while troopers combed the bunker that was almost identical to the first one. They found no information in its analyzer system beyond what was needed for operations and craft repairs.

"We now have thousands more Nameless to look after and none of the ingredients for the Supershake," Vasile said. The base's 18 attack craft were flown to *Enterprise* for conversion to fighters. Hinto Wu, now a major, took command of the base, named Tatsan, who was the Being pioneer of space exploration. He had more than 100 troopers to look after the Nameless.

With the armed transports *Mesopotamia* and *Oriol* en route to protect Tatsan, *Enterprise* and *Alliance* departed to track the badly dispersed trail of the supply ship. It took them on an arching course for more than two weeks before it vanished in a desolate region where most stars had collected only dust and rocks as satellites. The few planets they found were either frozen or roiling gas giants. They had little to see, nothing to explore and no opportunity to launch the jets until, in the midst of this Galactic wasteland, a planet with a promising atmosphere appeared.

"It's close to the size of Earth with one large continent," Hector informed the crew. "About three-quarters of it is covered by water. The reconnaissance shuttles have found plenty of vegetation, wildlife and another set of ruins. There're about four hundred structures, more intact than the earlier ones, on the edge of a grassy plain. We're sending jets and fighters to broaden our exploration and soldiers and troopers to explore the ruins."

"It's the most welcoming planet we've found," Vasile reported later in the day. "It feels and smells like Earth." He had gravitated into the unofficial post of chief exploration officer and led the expedition to examine the ruins. His shuttle had landed within meters of them. "The vegetation has an Earth-like look. There are flying creatures and something scampering through the brush that resembles squirrels. We haven't got close enough to tell if they're reptilian, mammal or a brand new species."

Visuals from Whiz appeared on the displays on the two ships. Feefers, Beings and Biobots clustered around them listening to Vasile's ongoing commentary. "The ruins are close in age and style to the earlier discoveries and have better preserved writings in the same script as before. We also found more flat rectangles, which can only have been landing pads for shuttles. Whoever lived here had to have a way to get on and off the planet."

At the next morning's briefing for the commanders of the two ships, Gnoorvants summed up the previous day's exploration. "While everything was recorded and dated, we haven't learned anything more about the builders of the settlement except they seem to be the same species that made the earlier ones."

When he finished, Humbaw proposed naming the planet after Secretary General Kendo.

"I can't think of a better honor," Hector said. "He would love this place. It's good Elinor is preparing a report on it."

Humbaw gazed at a star map of the region on the center display. "Despite the joy of finding such a beautiful world, we have lost track of the Renegades." The map showed the route of *Alliance* and *Enterprise* through space to the planet. "While Liberation and Tatsan report no new activity, the Navigation Directorate says the Renegades have attacked ships on the other side of our worlds."

The display turned black, and then showed a new star map with the nine Beings worlds highlighted. "The flashing dots are the locations of attacks on our outposts or ships. While the raids caused no significant damage, they indicate we have strayed too far from the Renegade region or they have shifted their forces."

He fell silent for a minute. "Although this planet is so remote, somebody obviously built this outpost many centuries ago. So where do we go from here? We could bring more ships to join the hunt."

"We need to keep looking." Hector shifted forward in his chair. "We should backtrack to the last known position of the supply ship. Meanwhile, we could launch probes until we get there to see if we overlooked any significant planets."

For days, the probes sent back the same dreary findings and the ships' crews settled into their usual routine of physical training and course work.

Humbaw wandered into the Command Chamber one morning, nodded to Hector and examined the latest reports. "Kendo truly is an oasis in a gigantic space desert." An hour later, his voice boomed over the intercoms of the two ships calling the officers to an urgent briefing.

Once the Feefers were all seated in the Conference Rooms, he said, "We have found a much bigger base and five of our stolen transports. We are heading for it and several armed vessels will join us."

"As soon as we are in orbit, we should launch the jets and fighters and be prepared to dispatch the troops to the surface," Hector said.

"Even the troopers?" Gnoorvants said.

"We have to find out what they can do. The first missions didn't challenge them."

The cruisers dropped out of galaxy flight and entered orbit around the planet. In the Command Chambers, Nonforense and Turing relayed frantic calls from the transports asking for instructions.

"They are all stolen vessels," Demmloda said. "From the confusion in the communications, the crews must be Nameless."

The next command came from Atdomorsin on the *Enterprise*. "Nonforense, Turing, take over the Controlling Units on those ships. The access codes are probably unchanged."

His order surprised Hector even though Fassad had told him "Gnoorvants and Atdomorsin are determined to show they can take charge. We call it *Enterprise* fever. They've read all the stories and imagine they're Kirk and Spock." Humbaw and the other Beings on *Alliance* still left all tactical decisions to Hector. To them, the mission was an experiment, not a military operation.

Nonforense interrupted his thoughts with a hint of gloating. "The transports are secured."

Back on *Enterprise*, Chris noticed Gnoorton step in front of the Command Bench. The Beings in the room looked startled.

"With your permission, Commander, I would like to organize a search for the crews of the transports," the Biot said. "We need to get those ships restored."

Gnoorvants stood and held out his hand to his ton. "Good hunting as the humans say and stay in regular contact. Take any helpers that you require."

"Thank you, Commander. I'll use the troopers in the boarding parties."

"Won't armed helpers startle them?"

"Not for long." The ton's face split in a wide smile.

"Our electronic signals aren't disabling the enemy craft so we must be battling Renegade pilots," Chris reported to *Enterprise*. His unit had been dispatched to engage several hundred enemy craft headed for the galaxyships.

The next communication came from his flyer wing mate Don. "We should attack the enemy as Nelson did the French and Spanish fleets at Trafalgar. Your nanalyzer is programmed to fire at the weak points of the Renegade craft. The pilots could hang back to help any flyers who are in trouble."

The time had come to let the flyers show their stuff. "Form into attack groups so you can hit them in wedge formations. That will maximize the strength of the protective walls of your fighters."

The displays in both galaxyships broadcast the visuals from the nose recorder on Chris's jet. The flyers had formed five wedges that bore into the enemy formation. The lead fighters aimed at the craft directly ahead while the others took on targets to the side. The jets fired as they followed the wedges through the enemy formation.

The Renegade formations collapsed in total chaos. Some took after the jets and fighters while others kept flying toward the galaxyships.

"The other squads should hit the enemy with the same tactic," Chris radioed to the ships. "That way we can take out most of them and you can handle the rest with the laser cannons."

The aerial battle lasted several hours before the remaining Renegade craft were destroyed.

After he returned to *Enterprise*, Elinor pulled Chris aside for an interview. Morrow stood behind her with recorder in hand. "Wasn't it dangerous flying through the enemy formation?"

He nodded. "The nanalyzer turns on the protective wall when it detects any debris it can't avoid. The wall destroys it with a bright flash. In combat, the nanalyzer activates the wall except for when the pilot wants to fire the cannons. It disengages instantaneously as the pilot sights a target and restores as soon as he finishes firing. The trick is to keep talking to the nanalyzer."

"How did the flyers handle the battle?"

"They held the wedge formations and proved adept at dogfights. When we returned to the ship, the flyers cheered each other's exploits and bragged about how many craft they'd destroyed. When they asked why we weren't as excited, I told them at first you're glad to have survived. Later you think about the lives you've ended."

Elinor added a postscript to the interview. "Overlooked during the battle was a communication from Gnoorton reporting the Biots on the five transports had been restored and taken charge of their vessels."

With the skies clear of enemy craft, the shuttles landed troops and tanks all around the base. Sullen, unarmed Nameless ringed it.

"The Renegades sent them to get in our way," Vasile reported. They didn't move at his request.

"Let us try." Genghis stepped forward and snarled in a booming imitation of Gnoorvants at his gruffest. "There'll be many explosions and if you don't hide, you'll be hurt, probably killed."

When no one moved, he repeated the message in a deafening tone. That prodded the Nameless to shuffle through the ranks of soldiers and troopers who resumed their encirclement of the bunker. The soldiers guiding the tanks advanced cautiously.

Renegades pounded the tanks with a torrent of missiles and laser blasts. In return, the tank cannons flattened structures infested with Renegades. The air sizzled with the intensity of the exchanges. The booms of exploding buildings and missiles hitting the energy walls that protected the base washed over the troopers and soldiers.

"We never expected so much noise in a battle," Genghis said

to Vasile as he kept glancing anxiously at the bunker.

"When the tanks stop firing, order the Renegades to surrender." In the sudden silence, Genghis amplified his voice calling on the Renegades to put down their weapons. The answer came in a round of laser fire. Vasile ordered the SDMs to resume their barrage. The bunker had become the main target and gaping holes soon disfigured its exterior.

After several minutes, Genghis and several other troopers converged on Vasile. "Let us finish this, captain," he shouted over the din. "The flyers have had their chance. We grunts want to show what we can do."

"A few minutes ago, you were rattled by the noise. Now you're ready to assault the bunker?"

"We have to find out if we can do it. How else can we gain the Beings' respect? If we can't handle the attack, you can get the rest of the soldiers from the ships. Just give us the chance to force the Renegades to retreat into the bunker. Then the ships can finish it off with their laser cannons."

Peering about, Vasile saw half a dozen troopers flanked Genghis. He was the leader. They were his lieutenants. "Nothing you've experienced this far can prepare you for the fighting that lies ahead," he said. Then he saw the names. Standing beside Genghis was a grand military pedigree—Montgomery, Bradley, Haig, Joffre, Zhukov, Patton, Cromwell and Saladin. While the rest of the troopers stood too far away to see what names they'd chosen, he was sure they were a military who's who. They wouldn't likely get a better test than this.

Vasile keyed his communicator. "All units advance at Genghis's command. Don't expect the Renegades to surrender. Soldiers, the troopers will go in first. We'll cover them."

Using the tanks as shields, the troopers closed on the structures surrounding the bunker cleaning out the rats' nests one at a time. Finally troopers reached the outer wall of the bunker.

"You've made your point, Genghis," Vasile barked over the communicator. "Pull back two hundred meters and watch"

Once the troopers had withdrawn, he told both *Enterprise* and *Alliance* to open fire. The bunker just transformed into an immense cloud of dust. When the air cleared, a smoking depression in the ground marked where it had stood.

Vasile radioed Genghis. "I need a report on how many troopers you lost and how many need treatment? And we need to get the SDMs back to the transports."

"We have seventeen no longer functioning and close to thirty that aren't fully operable," Genghis said.

"No, you have seventeen dead and close to thirty wounded. You're not machines."

"Thank you." Genghis hesitated. "We want the remains of our dead troopers transported back to Hnassumblaw for burial. We want a cemetery for them just as you Prims do for your war heroes."

Gnoorvants dispatched extra shuttle flights to retrieve the dead and wounded troopers. Vasile returned to *Enterprise* on the last flight to discuss the conduct of the battle with the commanders.

While waiting for the briefing, he agreed to an interview with Elinor. Even though it would take weeks before anyone on Earth saw it, he had to convey the importance of freeing more Nameless as well as giving the Biots the chance to prove their abilities.

"Once the troopers adapted to the noise and chaos of battle, nothing rattled them." As he spoke, he noticed Morrow beaming with pride. "Some of the wounded ones need new bodies. While it's never been done before, the Biots think it's possible."

Elinor displayed visuals of laser blasts flashing back and forth and the desperate tactics of the enemy as he recounted the battle. "The troopers methodically worked their way through the buildings around the bunker. The soldiers provided covering fire. While the bunker was better fortified than the previous ones, it couldn't withstand the laser cannons. We benefited from the modifications the mechanics made to them."

Afterwards, Vasile conferred with Gnoorvants, Atdomorsin and Chris in the Conference Room of *Enterprise*. Humbaw, Demmloda and Hector were vislinked into the meeting.

Hector started the session by praising Vasile's handling of the battle. He'd expected criticism from the Beings for allowing the troopers to lead the assault. To his surprise, they only asked about the care of the Nameless.

When the briefing ended, Vasile headed for the cafeteria. His communicator buzzed. He was surprised to see Ruth Huxley's name on the display screen.

"With two exceptions, the troopers have picked names of famous military figures from Earth," she said. "There're obvious ones like Grant, Wellington and Napoleon. However, there're all sorts of names of men that would only be known to students of military history."

"You said two didn't use military names."

"Yes, one goes by Paladin and the other by Hukaru."

"Paladin is another word for a knight. Who's the other one?"

"Nobody. It's a name the Biot made up."

"As in invented?" In his surprise, Vasile spoke the words slowly. "Why do they continue to think they aren't creative?"

Ruth shrugged. "They regard creativity as inventing things like the Beings do. They don't see that adapting the attack craft or the chocolate for the Nameless milkshake is inventive. It must be connected to their programming and training. I need to discuss the issue further with Hton and Dton to understand what it will take to convince them they already have this cherished talent."

"Humbaw wants to keep searching for the main Renegade base and look for a planet to settle the Nameless on," Vasile said. "The latest estimates are that we have more than two hundred thousands of them on the three bases plus the nine hundred at Marlabant. None of the planets we've found are really suitable for them and Kendo is far too remote to provide the assistance these people require. We are slowly running out of food and I don't know how much longer the supplies we have will last. We have to find them a new home. Really soon."

"Micheline Azwatta has a planet in mind," she said. "We will hear about it at the morning briefing."

Chapter 19
The Renegades Revealed

Hector opened the morning briefing in *Alliance's* conference room with a cheery greeting. "We have lots of news for everyone. You're expecting to hear about a home for the Nameless, but Humbaw wants to speak first about the Renegades."

He, Demmloda and Humbaw were vislinked with Gnoorvants, Atdomorsin and Fassad on *Enterprise*.

"We have found the rest of the Renegade bases," Humbaw said. "All the data from the captured ships was fed into the main Controlling Unit on Hnassumblaw. It pinpointed three bases on the other side of our worlds along with the Renegade home planet. We have captured all the bases in this sector and there are seven more stolen transports that have been ordered to report here."

Hector peered at his analyzer. "It will take a couple of weeks to travel to them and more time beyond that to their home world. Do you think they might surrender if we can capture the three bases?"

Humbaw shook his head. "It is unlikely. After they broke away during Transformation, they vowed to take revenge on us for abandoning our traditional militaristic ways. No one kept track of them and our space monitoring systems never recorded any activity on their part. Until recently, the main Controlling Unit didn't connect them to the attacks on our worlds. You would refer to them as terrorists. As a possible explanation for the condition of the Nameless, there were experiments before Transformation with mind-controlling chemicals."

Then to Hector's surprise, Humbaw walked to the beverage dispenser and refilled his mug rather than pass it to his ton to attend to. The unusual behavior showed how distraught the news about the Renegades had made Humbaw. Just as surprising, Hton hadn't noticed the empty mug.

Humbaw returned to his seat and took a drink. "Meanwhile, the Council has decreed that once the three bases are captured and all the Nameless rescued, we're to obliterate the Renegades."

Hector gasped. "The Council is ordering the kind of barbarous actions that it accused Earth of. Why did they make this decision without consulting us?"

"I have failed to convince the Council you are true partners in this campaign. It has concluded that by the time the remaining bases are captured, Gnoorvants and Atdomorsin, along with the flyers, troopers and Controlling Units, will have learned enough from the Terrans to destroy the Renegades on their own."

Humbaw avoided Hector's gaze. "I knew you would be most displeased by this decision and have asked the Council to reconsider. It is absolutely mortified by the actions of the Renegades, more for what they did to the Nameless than for attacking us. Obliteration seems the only suitable punishment. I suspect most Beings would feel the same way.

"As much as this news upsets you, I am pleased to tell you about Mandela, the name Dr Azwatta has given to the planet we have chosen for the Nameless. The Council wishes to establish them while we find out how they came under the control of the Renegades. We will spare neither effort nor expense in helping them and will gladly compensate Earth for any assistance it can provide them there."

A Renegade supply ship reported its approach to the base three days later. Hector kept an eye on the Command Chamber display of the vessel as he reviewed updates about the Nameless at the captured bases.

He looked up when Nonforense announced, "Control acquired of Renegade vessel. Transport 174 was stolen five years ago. It will go into an orbit that brings it alongside us. Incoming transmission from the Nameless who thinks it is in charge of that ship."

Nonforense was bragging about its accomplishment and the Beings didn't realize it. While Hecton kept a straight face, Hector couldn't help smiling at Nonforense's sarcasm. "Why did you take charge of my Controlling Unit?" the transport's captain asked in a deferential tone.

"I'm the new Commander," Demmloda said. The Nameless didn't respond. "An accident has occurred down here and we have to move the things to a new planet. Prepare to send down your shuttles so the loading can commence. File any of your flight requirements."

"Certainly, Commander."

"We will encode your course and destination in the Controlling Unit shortly. Where are the other transports?"

"They are all en route here as ordered, Commander. They should arrive within a week."

"We will load them all with things and you can travel together to the new planet. You will inform the other ships and help them prepare to receive things."

"I will be pleased to fulfill this order, Commander. It will be three days before the next one arrives." Demmloda terminated the transmission.

"You probably aren't disdainful enough for a real Renegade," Hector teased as they walked to the Conference Room. "While you fooled a Nameless, a Renegade wouldn't have fallen for it."

Humbaw waved when they entered. *"Transformation* has delivered its Nameless to Mandela. Her patients are assisting our helpers to build a hospital, dormitory, and solar complex to power the community. Other dormitories are under construction as are thousands of cottages. Dr Azwatta has asked Earth for more medical assistance. Her report has the full details. The fleet will rendezvous at Mandela."

"We must do some serious thinking about the Renegades," Hector interjected as he snapped out of a daydream about what Mandela might look like. "I communicated the Council's order to obliterate the Renegades to the Secretary General. Hopefully, he will offer suggestions for appealing for clemency for a species that we know nothing more about than those mute brutes we've captured."

Images of Mandela floated in the Conference Room displays at the morning briefing following their arrival at the planet. During the week-long trip, the Beings and Feefers had focused on preparations for attacking the other Renegade bases.

Today, Humbaw grappled with a different problem. "We must resolve a dispute about the color and style of the Nameless homes." He pointed at the main display which showed cottages under construction on Mandela. "The human construction advisers want to alternate the style of them. Our engineers see no point."

"That's easy. Vary the pattern. You don't want everything to look the same."

"Why not?"

Hector wondered how to respond until he thought of his trump card. "Because Azwatta would say so."

"Nonforense, tell the construction team to follow whatever

advice Dr Azwatta has on the color of the homes and on their interiors as well." Humbaw nodded to Hector. "That should forestall any further tempests in our absence." Their discussion returned to military matters.

Two cruisers waited at Mandela for the fleet. *Omanora* had guided the Beings through Transformation. *New Jersey* honored the famous battleship of Earth. Its Controlling Unit had adopted the name Jobs. With them was the shuttle to transport Humbaw and Hector to Hnassumblaw.

The fleet would remain at Mandela until Humbaw and Hector returned from the Being home world. While all the humans looked forward to visiting the planet, Juan Feldez had a mission. He hurried from the shuttle to the three storey hospital to fulfill his most fervent wish. In the excitement of finding Micheline Azwatta and seeing her facilities, he forgot to introduce himself.

"It's unbelievable what you've accomplished," he blurted out. "The energy of the Nameless you've treated is absolutely amazing compared to the state they were in on the Renegade bases. When I saw them trying to figure out what had happened after we captured Liberation, I doubted they could ever become normal." He raced on ignoring her reproachful look. "Look at them. They laugh. I saw a female trying to copy a nurse who sang while she worked. I suppose it's like they're coming out of a long coma."

Micheline's initial annoyance at being interrupted evaporated when Azwattaton told her who Juan was. "Oh, it's you," she said wrapping him in a bear hug. "Good to see you're a Sergeant now. It was so brave what you did to capture that base and it helped us immensely because we learned a lot about the chemicals and the Nameless as a result."

"How are they doing?"

"We're not sure if they'll completely recover," Micheline said. "While they're fine physically, we've no idea whether they'll ever be able to handle more than simple supervised tasks."

Juan excused himself. "I know you've much to do. I'm on a home building team. But when this is over, I'm going back to school to become a doctor like you. How you help people has been a real inspiration to me."

The comment earned him another big hug from Azwatta. "I'm sure you will always help people. Come back before you depart. I would like to hear more about those planets you visited. If there's time, maybe we can give you a head start on your medical training." Her praise on top of recent messages from his family saluting his exploits had Juan beaming for days.

The sojourn on Mandela gave Elinor and Chris a chance to resume their strolls arm in arm through the rapidly growing settlement. They headed toward the hospital to record a feature on Micheline. Morrow and Leprechaun trailed behind them at a discrete distance with the recorder.

"Mandela looks like a large suburban development with row after row of homes steadily advancing from hole in the ground to partly finished shell to completed bungalow," Elinor said to Chris. "The exterior is made of the same fabric as the Being tents and the hospital and it maintains a pleasant interior regardless of the outside temperature."

At the hospital, Azwatta said, "I've no time to preen around for you."

"Well, then get on with it." Elinor spoke in a demure tone while Morrow kept the recorder running. "I won't be in your way. After all you've done, you deserve the praise you're getting. You've inspired your colleagues beyond what any judged themselves capable of. Chris overheard a Being and couple of Biots discussing a problem with communications satellites. They'd no success in trying to isolate the problem when one declared, 'We should approach this in the spirit of Azwatta.'"

Morrow had already recorded the shuttles carrying the Nameless from the transports that landed on pads behind the hospital every few minutes. Medbiots loaded them on floating gurneys and guided them, still in suspended animation, into the hospital for the removal of their controllers.

"There're no old people, not even any middle-aged ones," she observed as the recorder purred. Later, it caught a joyful shriek from a Nameless hugging one as he emerged from the hospital. "I think she said it was her brother."

Medbiots assisted the bewildered and hungry newcomers from the hospital to a long single story building where they were fed and issued new clothing. Before Medbiots had put the Nameless to sleep for the trip to Mandela, they assigned them a tag with an ID number, their name and the names of any known family members. On Mandela, Biots took newcomers with family to waiting relatives. They placed singles in the dormitories.

The Biots stayed with lone individuals until they settled in and checked on them regularly. Doctors, medics and nurses monitored their condition and ensured they drank the Supershake regularly. Pictures and identifying information of these individuals were added to a long wall of blank faces that other Nameless could look through in search for family or friends. Not all survived as could be seen in the daily activity in the cemetery.

Mandela became a training ground for the nearly 5,000 troopers in the Being Defense Force. The soldiers served as officers and instructors. Stepped up flight training for all the new flyers proceeded as the mechs on *Alliance* and *Enterprise* continued overhauling the captured attack craft.

Their counterparts on *Omanora* and *New Jersey* had converted a bay on each ship into a manufacturing facility for building a new fighter. It combined the flying saucer appearance of the Being fighter with the long range capability of the Renegade attack craft. The flyers selected Don and Roo to conduct the first test flights.

After 30 minutes chasing the two Biots, Chris praised the new fighter. "They respond so quickly and cannons sure did a job on those space rocks. All our craft should be upgraded to those capabilities."

As the shuttle sped to Hnassumblaw, Hector worked on an overdue letter to his wife and teenaged sons. "It's hard to explain what it's like to step on an unexplored world. Our surveys determine it's safe or we wouldn't land. It's exciting even in an environment suit seeing sights that as far as we know, no one else has gazed on before. I pick spots where it's unlikely anyone has ever stood just so I could be the first one."

He momentarily paused to think about how his sons would relish a trip of this nature before he continued. "I miss you three beyond any words I know. Not being able to talk with you whenever I want, seeing so many wondrous new sights and not sharing them with you saddens me. I just wish you could see the Nameless go from a state like sleep-walking to alert enough to carry out increasingly complex tasks."

Hector let out a sigh. "Mandela is truly a wonderful place, much like Earth or Kendo. The average surface temperature is about twenty-five Celsius, a perfect summer day. Me, who always complained about the heat, shivered when I first stepped out of the shuttle, because of the contrast to conditions in the ship. There's no escaping the heat even with the environment suits and the areas set aside for us. I've adjusted to it after all these months. I could probably even enjoy a tropical holiday if there're any vacation spots left." He thought of all the popular islands and other holiday centers flooded over as the Earth warmed.

"None of the grasses or trees looks like anything I've seen before. But the breeze stirs them as it does at home. The water rushing over rocks and pebbles in a nearby stream sounds like the brook on Uncle Duncan's property. All the creatures we've found are reptilian. There's a green sheen of a crop just emerging on Mandela's cultivated fields. The gravity is a bit more than on Earth, which is really tiring at first, but it does firm up the muscles. Most of the soldiers are in such good shape I doubt they even notice. That's a good sign considering the battles we face."

For the rest of the trip, Hector studied the history of the nine worlds, ran on a treadmill and took Beingish lessons from Hecton and Hton.

As the craft neared the Being home world, Humbaw said, "You speak well enough to appeal for reconsideration of the High Council's decree."

"As long as they don't mind a lot of simple phrases and bad pronunciation." Hector let out a nervous laugh before turning serious. "What should I expect of the High Council?"

Before Humbaw could speak, Hton whispered in his ear. "Perfect, Humbawton will show you his visual of the session of the High Council at which the Councilors finally agreed to my plan. It will reveal what you need to know."

Hector noted Humbaw still hadn't adopted the short name for his helper although most Beings had.

"The visual will start with Beings and tons entering the chamber. It is a circular room and the benches for the Councilors are arranged in a circle with a small display at the side. There is space at the center of the room for displaying large three-D images."

The visual recording was as clear as being in the chamber. It began with the Councilors gathering in the Conference Room. Just like on the ships, the walls had been painted brown and lacked any artwork. It's what Hector would expect of an austere religious order, not an advanced civilization that had mastered space travel and spanned solar systems.

"Dormmundar is the Speaker," Hecton said of the individual who called the meeting into session. Hector put a translator in his ear to listen.

"How did you discover the Primitives' planet considering its remote location?" she said. The visual panned to Humbaw for his response. Hector had enough trouble distinguishing among the eight Beings on *Alliance*. The 50 of them in the Council Chamber reminded him how closely Beings resembled each other.

"I commanded an exploration ship following a comet that entered the solar system of the planet," Humbaw said. He spoke in his usual flat tone. "The rings around the gas giant in the system attracted us until a survey probe discovered the third planet teemed with life. We were naturally curious."

"Why study an unsuitable and remote planet?" snapped a Councilor who Hecton identified as Bessumma.

Humbaw stiffened and inhaled deeply, yet responded mildly to her sharp tone. "While I felt the same way initially, it was the first time we had encountered sentients in our space exploration."

"I would like to hear more," Dormmundar said, "about the Primitives." She sounded miffed at Bessumma's intervention. When the video panned the room again, Hector thought most Councilors appeared interested in Humbaw's revelation.

"We returned almost twenty-five Earth years later," Humbaw said. "This time we had environment suits that made us look enough like Terrans that we could move about unnoticed. We learned the planet was named Earth and the Terrans called themselves Earthlings or more often humans."

"Why did you decide to continue studying them, then?" asked Dormmundar.

"When I was a student at the University of Bunwadon, I had to take a history course to round out my education in Controlling Units and space navigation. I selected pre-Transformation history because it was mainly about battles on Hnassumblaw. Earth is not unlike our old society. I wanted to see if they would undergo anything like Transformation to ensure their survival. That has not come about yet."

Although Bessumma turned away to signal her lack of interest by looking about the room, other Councilors urged him to continue. "Terrans live about a quarter of our years. The health and education of many of them are appalling. They belong to clans called countries. Some cover vast amounts of territory while others are not much bigger than our cities. Some choose the leaders that govern them, but a lot have no say. There are many governments and all have far more control over their citizens than any of us could imagine. Some individuals have more wealth than they can possibly use while others cannot even afford to feed themselves. There are so many other major differences between our worlds that it is hard to comprehend them all." He inhaled deeply and plunged on.

"In the warmer regions, the facemask of the environment suit can be removed although a breathing tube is still required. I will always remember the first time I went without my mask. The air was so moist and the smells and sounds were unlike anything I had ever encountered. Small flying creatures called insects tried to bite me. I must not taste good for they soon gave up." He snorted.

"Since our first inspection, Terrans have made major advancements and fought many wars. On a visit about ninety years ago, we found a major global conflict including the first use of nuclear weapons had occurred."

The Councilors shuddered. From their expressions, Hector guessed they exchanged uncomplimentary thoughts about humans.

"During that visit, we borrowed a couple of Terrans for close examination of their physical and mental capabilities. We released them after attempting to remove their memories of us. They remembered enough to give wildly inaccurate accounts of extraterrestrial kidnappers and galaxyships. Ever since, there has been a steady stream of reports about unidentified flying objects—they call them UFOs—that have appeared during our visits to Earth. The authorities never accept these claims because they are unsubstantiated. Some sightings involved our craft. The rest were imaginary. Earthlings call them flying saucers. When you put two of their meal holders together, there is a resemblance to our shuttles." Humbaw brought his hands in front of himself to show how plates fit.

"In later years, they developed space radar, which forced us to take more care with the shuttles to avoid detection. Still reports about UFOs filled their information networks."

Bessumma leaned forward on her bench to signal her wish to intervene. "Even if the Primitives could help us, what would stop them from turning our weapons against us? Would they quietly return home if they defeat our enemy? Teaching the Primitives to use our weapons is irresponsible and probably impossible."

Fair points, Hector admitted as he continuing watching the visual.

Instead of answering right away, Humbaw looked about the

room. "Do other Councilors share her misgivings?"

"Why do you think Primitives would be more effective than your defensive tactics?" Ardinabts said.

Dormmundar cut off further comments and nodded at Humbaw. "Terrans would only be trained to use our equipment. Helpers would do all the repair and maintenance. While Earth is backward, our society was once at that level and look at what we've accomplished. Are we to turn away from it because of nightmares about our past? Earth has the potential to become far more advanced and in return for fighting a few battles for us, we could give it a big push forward. Perhaps even save it."

Humbaw paused to survey the chamber. "Better weapons might hold off the Nameless until they become too tired or weakened to continue the war. How much disruption to our lives should we put up with while waiting for that to happen? Even if the Nameless are driven off, there is no guarantee that it would be anything more than a temporary reprieve. What would we do if a stronger adversary came along? We have nothing to lose and our future to gain by enlisting Terrans."

The visual ended and then started again. "This is at a session a few days later than the one we just watched," Hton explained. "A big Nameless raid on one of worlds has occurred."

Dormmundar spoke indignantly. "The colony at Andomar is devastated and we have lost three transports. It is our second major defeat in recent months and the demands for stronger action against the Nameless increase every day."

No one spoke against her. "The Council has to respond to this latest transgression. Most Beings think the Council fails to appreciate the damage to our worlds because they're more concerned with ghosts than stopping our enemies. I move we let Humbaw seek the assistance of the Primitives."

The visual skipped ahead. "It's okay. You just missed a bunch of wrangling," Hton said.

It resumed with Dormmundar calling for a vote. No one opposed Humbaw now.

He bowed his head before gazing about the Council. "This was an agonizing decision for everyone. Now we have to gain the Terrans' assistance."

"Surely all you would have to do is reveal our existence and the warriors will flock to help us," Dormmundar said.

"It will be far more difficult than that. We have to approach the planet cautiously so we do not provoke an attack although their weapons are no threat to a galaxyship. If we create a hostile reaction among Earthlings, then we face a horrendous task to overcome their fears and prejudices."

Looking around the Council, he continued. "They have an old saying about the importance of first impressions and how hard it is to change them. We have to get their attention without frightening them. We must make them curious instead of fearful--willing to talk instead of uttering threats. They will be apprehensive enough once they learn about us. If we treat them like children, they will soon resent us and we will never get their help."

At that point, an image of Earth appeared in the center of the Council chamber. "Revealing our existence will likely create a lot of panic," Humbaw said. "There are paranoid leaders who will refuse to accept a more advanced species. Assuming we are able to overcome these distractions, we have to convince them it is time for them to accept a role in the Galaxy. That will be a big step for them.

"Some of their spiritual leaders may suggest we are the Devil." Humbaw's comment produced puzzled looks. "Like us, most Terrans believe there is a supreme entity in the cosmos. Unlike us, they give it a name." The Councilors made a reverential hum. "However, many Primitives think there is a figure that stands in opposition to..." He hummed. "It is called the Devil or Satan. It is supposed to cause all that is evil and corrupt. Terrans have made many attempts to depict it. Unfortunately, it would not take much imagination for some of them to think that we look like it. About all we lack are horns and a tail." The Councilors snorted almost in unison. "This bizarre belief is just one more example of their inferiority. We all know that evil comes from within us. Our species possessed many strange notions before Transformation."

Humbaw pressed on as if he feared someone would try to derail his plan. "Even if Earth will not help us, we will offer to remove the excess gases from its atmosphere, which will improve its climate. We will also provide the celestial orbits of major asteroids likely to come anywhere near the planet. It is in no immediate danger and a cruiser could easily protect it. If it survives its current problems, Earth might grow up. Its location pretty well assures it will never be a threat to any other planet even if it develops galaxy flight."

The visual jumped again. With no further discussion, the Councilors had approved Humbaw's plan, and then had moved onto a discussion of future space exploration. It really stunned

Hector that no one wondered what it would take to convince the humans to help.

"You are surprised by the sudden decision, General," Humbaw said. "So was I. I have expended a lot of time and energy in trying to determine why ardent opponents shifted their positions so quickly."

Behind the Being, Hton grinned.

Chapter 20
More Surprises

Hector first noticed the brilliance of the stars surrounding Hnassumblaw when the shuttle dropped out of galaxy speed for its approach to the planet. Unlike the specks of light visible from Earth, a shimmering curtain surrounded the Being home world.

From space, the planet appeared as brown as Earth was blue. It had few clouds and although he couldn't see them, its four moons were considerably smaller in total than Earth's solitary satellite.

When Hector stepped onto the planet, he gazed about trying to fix first impressions in his memory. Elinor Brady would certainly question him about them. He now understood Simdar Panamar's comments about the overwhelming emotions he experienced climbing down the ladder from the *Nile* into the Being galaxyship.

The environment suit sheltered him from the planet's hot and dry climate. Looking at the light grays and sandy browns around him, he appreciated why all the color and wildlife of Earth had intrigued the Beings.

The squat, sand colored Navigation Center and Space Port didn't look like the welcoming point of a great civilization. The names of the cities on Hnassumblaw, mostly abandoned because of nuclear contamination, were numeral derivatives of the planet's name. They'd landed at Hnassumblawprime, the biggest and home of the High Council.

More than 100 Beings, all dressed in light-colored togas, formed a welcoming party. "There're so many here," Hector said. Then he remembered the crowds that greeted Humbaw in New York.

Humbaw steered Hector toward the welcoming party. "By their presence they wish to make you feel welcome."

Not knowing what else to do, Hector thanked them in Beingish. "It's most kind of you to greet me. Humbaw has told me a great deal about your worlds and I welcome the opportunity to see them firsthand." With that, he bowed. The Beings seemed unprepared for the gesture and made awkward efforts at copying it.

A smile flickered across Humbaw's face. "So, they wish to

demonstrate the importance of our ties with Earth and apologize for originally underestimating Terrans."

"Is this a normal welcome? I mean Beings usually are so reserved," Hector said. Humbaw nodded. "So you really had to step out of character to deal with us?"

There was another nod, then a snort. "Except for Gnoorvants and Atdomorsin," Humbaw pointed at a low slung, open box. "This will transport us to my residence." With that, Humbaw steered Hector toward his conveyance.

Hector caught a glimpse of Hton and Hecton shaking hands with the other tons. Ruth said the Biots had adopted the custom as a way to recognize themselves as individuals. The Biots snapped to attention, saluted and called out in English, "Welcome General." While he felt odd saluting civilians, Hector stopped and brought his right hand to his forehead.

The sides of the vehicle folded down to form entry ramps. As soon as they sat, the motor hissed lifting it a few centimeters into the air and they floated soundlessly forward. Hector couldn't take his eyes off the passing city. The structures, at the most four stories high, had been constructed in the same style and material as the SpacePort. "Were the buildings grown?"

"No, there was too much radiation for that," Hecton said. "They're built by us, much like stone buildings on Earth." The structures had few windows and doors. The sparse sandy brown vegetation surrounding them made the city look camouflaged.

Humbaw had his own distraction. "There are thousands of helpers on the street."

"What's unusual about that? It's like on board *Alliance*."

"Normally, you see few of them about the city. Not only that, these are mainly old ones!"

"They all appear the same to me."

"Look closely and you'll see the color in their skin is much lighter than among the helpers on *Alliance*. Age and exposure to sunlight fades the color." Humbaw turned to his ton. "What is going on?"

"All the Biobots know we're involved in defending the nine worlds." His voice sounded unusually heavy. "It's the opportunity to prove ourselves, which we've always wanted. For that, we have the Terrans to thank. As the General is the only one many will ever see, they want to show their appreciation so he can convey it to Earth."

Humbaw's frown indicated the Biot had only partly answered

the question, yet he didn't press his query further. The Beings still didn't understand the helpers had their own plan.

Humbaw's residence consisted of a series of one-storey buildings that resembled all the others Hector had seen. Spread over several hectares of what looked like a giant sandbox, covered walkways connected the homes of several generations of Humbaw's family. There were grandparents, in-laws, a brother and sister and their families, his wife and five children—three female, two male—their families and other Beings whose status Hector never did figure out.

In honor of their special guest, the whole clan assembled for the evening meal on an open air deck in the middle of the buildings. Although it was dusk, only a few lights glowed leaving the gathering in shadows. Hector counted more than 50 Beings seated in small groups, with their tons nearby. Most wore robes although a few dressed in the pullover top and pants style of Gnoorvants.

The low light made the physical similarity of the Beings even more striking. As the young were full grown within two to three years, Hector couldn't guess who they were except for a couple of obvious infants. The size of the gathering should have made Beings feel uncomfortable although they showed no signs of it.

The food, prepared and served by a squad of helpers, came in large bowls that were placed on low tables. The tons served the Beings. Humbaw and Hector had their own bench.

By the silence, Hector assumed that the Beings were communicating telepathically as if it were impolite to speak directly to their guest. "My family has many questions for you," Humbaw said. "While they have learned much about your species from Ms Brady's visuals, there are many personal matters that interest them. They want to touch your skin to know what it feels like. I have explained your custom of shaking hands and told them to do that before they retire tonight."

At first, the Beings sent their questions to Humbaw to pose to Hector. After a while, a few spoke. While he understood some comments, he waited for Hecton to translate before he replied. In between answers, he nibbled at the stews and salads in front of him and gulped air from his breather. The food was bland, almost tasteless, just like on the galaxyships. These people would love cafeterias except for the crowds.

As questions about raising young, family structures and the origin of the Nameless showed no signs of running out, Humbaw said, "I have told them no more until you and I have finished our meals. Afterwards, you will answer more queries."

Hector went back to tasting the various dishes before him. A Being sat beside him and put ingredients from several dishes on his plate before speaking in halting English. "Try together."

Her words silenced the others. She smiled at them, and then at Hector while Humbaw hushed criticisms of her boldness.

"What's your name?" Hector said.

"Humbawloda." She pointed at Humbaw.

"She's Humbaw's granddaughter," Hecton said.

She nodded her head vigorously. "I want visit Earth. Talk Huxley."

"I would like to invite you to my home to meet my two sons just as you've received me here today."

Humbawloda gave her grandfather a quizzical look until her ton translated. She smiled at Hector. "Sorry. Now understand. Accept invitation. Hope behave better than brothers." She pointed at two Beings who stared back at her.

Hector turned to Humbaw with a puzzled look on his face. "What's your family upset about?"

"They disapprove of my granddaughter's criticism of her siblings and the looks on her face. Many youngsters use facial expressions now. My wife says they learned it from Ms Brady's visuals and are quite impressed with how much Earthlings say with looks and gestures instead of words. Traditionally Beings consider that impolite."

"I learn Nglis too." This time it was a young male, another of Humbaw's grandchildren. "I want visit Earth see oceans." He beamed with pride and smiled at Humbawloda.

"Their tons taught them English, but weren't sure if they should encourage them to speak to each other," Hecton said. He had to raise his voice over the buzz of conversation among Beings and their tons. "Maybe they all want to learn Primtalk."

Humbaw beamed with the biggest smile Hector had seen on his usually somber face. "Tonight I hear two grandchildren speaking your language. They want to visit your world and open themselves to new experiences. As much as stopping the attacks, this is what I wanted from interacting with humans. To see my species start to grow again, to reach out. Your technology is well behind ours, but your spirit isn't."

Hector spent the rest of the evening fielding questions from dinosaurs to how humans regarded the physical appearance of the Beings especially as they attached so much importance to their own looks. Answering became easier as he adjusted to the breather. The Beings always waited patiently for him to regain his breath if he overextended himself. When he explained that to humans, Beings looked virtually identical, the Beings peered at each other as if they had never noticed it before.

The next day held even more surprises. The High Council building was just as bland as it had appeared in the visual. Hector wondered why the Beings lived in such uninspired surroundings. Considering their technological accomplishments, he'd expected more.

Humbaw took him for a tour introducing him to every Being as well as their tons and the Council helpers. Underneath their Beingish symbols, the helpers had the same identification information in English.

In addition to the benches for the 30 Councilors, additional seating had been added for tons and spectators. The walls and furnishings were sandy brown with few windows. "There're a lot of Beings and Biobots here," Hector said.

"They're making amends while we're saying thanks," Hecton said.

After losing his breath so often the previous evening while speaking, Hector felt increasingly anxious about addressing the High Council. His disappointment with the Chamber ended when he looked upwards after noticing the Beings and tons glancing at the ceiling before taking their places for the start of the meeting. The giant star map in the ceiling radiated light through the whole room. The more he looked at it, the more inspired he felt. The Beings and helpers frequently glanced at it. Perhaps seeing so many stars provided an infusion of hope. Maybe the magnitude of the Universe brought context to their concerns.

"Humbaw has explained why you do not want the Renegades destroyed for what they did to the Nameless," Dormmundar said.

Hector had decided to skip pleasantries and get to the point while he still had control of his emotions. "Although their conduct is despicable, at least allow us to try to deal with them." He stopped to catch his breath.

He recalled how Kendo looked about the room when he addressed the Security Council to make sure everyone got his message. However, with speaking Beingish and keeping his breathing regular, it was hard to raise his eyes from his speaking notes he had prepared with Hecton's help. "We want to capture the other bases and finish relocating the Nameless to Mandela. Then we could capture the Renegade home planet to see if a peaceful government is possible." Again, he stopped to gulp oxygen.

Dormmundar spared him any further argument. "Humbaw has already presented us with an explanation of your views. The brilliant Dr Azwatta has sent us a document. We are impressed by your willingness to come here, which must be uncomfortable, to seek a reprieve for our enemy. We have decided to rescind our order to obliterate them. However, the leaders and other criminals in that society must be destroyed. We will closely monitor a new government to ensure no bad elements resurface. If possible, the Renegades must learn to live as proper Beings. We will have to help them or they will not escape their lamentable state."

She tipped her head to Humbaw. "Terrans are more thoughtful and resourceful than most of us thought possible." He returned the gesture. "Humbaw has long contended our culture needed a shake up," Dormmundar said. "Our association with Earth certainly has done that. We wish you well in your final campaign. This part will be far more dangerous even though you have learned a great deal about the enemy."

"There is one other matter, Councilors," Humbaw said. "I ask you to listen." With that he motioned Hton forward.

"I bring a gift from your helpers," the ton said. "Yesterday, thousands of the old ones came to greet General Davis. It was an act of gratitude, but also relief. For the last several hundred years, all the tons that were scheduled for decommissioning after their Being died instead went to work on our special project.

"Those tons and other helpers have restored the badlands, even the old cities, so they are fit to live in. That is our gift to you. You gave us life. We give you back all of Hnassumblaw. The radiation from the Time of Horrors is buried and the land rehabilitated." The displays showed vast stretches of brown plants and herds of grazing creatures.

When the Beings recovered from their surprise, they spoke in hushed voices with their tons. Not able to appreciate the change in the Being countryside, Hector leaned back to admire the star map. To his amazement, he recognized the constellations and stars visible from Earth. The Beings had changed it to mark his visit. Many Beings were seeing Earth's region of space for the first time. He sat watching, wishing he could have recorded the moment.

He recalled a university professor lecturing about the gift of witnessing history happen. Finally he understood.

The UN released Elinor's report on FEEF reaching Mandela to the comnets and they broadcasted it immediately. Even though the news was almost two months old, the networks played it over and over. It was about the only topic in conversations in coffee shops and meeting halls and on open line shows for weeks.

"I'm sure it got the same reception in our worlds," Bemmonloda assured Kendo. "It has been a remarkable six months."

"Every time I watch it, I keep wondering what FEEF is doing right now," Kendo told his wife as they relaxed in their UN apartment. "You know, if all goes well and with the communications time lag, they could return home before we could get the final reports of what they did out there."

Stroking her leg, he continued, "It was a most clever idea of yours to ask Bemmonloda to act as a mediator in northern Africa and central Asia. There's no way any side can question his impartiality."

"Or withstand for long his criticisms of the positions combatants always take in these wars," she said. "While I should know better after all these years, it still angers me to hear the nonsense that's advanced by tin-pot dictators for slaughtering their own people or neighbors. I thought of the ambassador after listening to some acidic comments from him about the stupidity of our wars especially in contrast to the exploits of the Feefers."

Humanity's Saving Grace

Chapter 21
A Second Chance for the Bad Guys

An ancient Being named Cubunowres had joined Humbaw and Hector on the flight back to Mandela. Before retiring to his quarters he spoke briefly to Humbaw. "He considers his English too poor to speak with you."

"Compared to my Beingish!"

"You're a Primitive so he wouldn't expect anything else," Humbaw said with a straight face before snorting. "He knows much about the old days. We may need him before we are done."

As the shuttle neared Mandela, Humbaw and Hector held a vislink briefing for the fleet on the Council's decision. When they finished, Gnoorvants outlined the plan to attack the other Renegade bases.

"They're in neighboring star systems. The closest, which we call Alpha and Beta, are heavily fortified while Charlie is lightly defended. It appears to be mainly a breeding world for the Nameless and a repair center for the attack craft. It is about the size of Mars.

"We will attack Charlie first to see if we can force the other bases to come to its defense. We will either face Renegade pilots or Nameless crews that we can collect as we did at Marlabant. Our flyers can handle either. That will eliminate some enemy craft and might even draw out their galaxyships."

"Plus we will have the main collection of Nameless under our control," Atdomorsin added. "As our primary mission is to liberate them, it is a good place to start. We could transfer them to Mandela while we attack the other two bases."

Gnoorvants selected *Enterprise, New Jersey, Temeraire, Mesopotamia* and *Hercules* for the attack. *Alliance, Omanora, Yamoto, Ting Yuen, Constitution* and *Oriol* would prepare to intercept attack craft sent to relieve Charlie. Each pilot was assigned five flyers as wing mates while every soldier led a platoon of 10 troopers.

The Being ships appeared out of galaxy flight on the far side of the planet from the base. When there was no reaction to their presence, *New Jersey* launched its jets and fighters to reconnoiter the planet for settlements or defensive installations.

"The pilots are checking out the three continents and a chain of islands," Atdomorsin told the morning briefing. "The base is on the middle continent. While there are several hilly areas, the terrain is mostly plains covered in brown vegetation. There's some small wildlife. While the daytime temperatures are close to forty degrees Celsius, the oxygen levels are adequate."

That evening, Chris reported that other than a couple of old wrecks of crashed attack craft, the pilots had found no evidence the Renegades had installations on the other continents. As he spoke, displays in the Conference Rooms of the ships played visuals gathered during the reconnaissance.

"Surely they've got to know by now they face an attack," Hector said. "We will send scouting parties at first light."

Smiling broadly, Gnoorvants leaned toward him. "Why, even a peaceful, non-combative soul such as me would set up defenses or send some Nameless on patrol."

Enterprise dispatched three shuttles, each carrying a soldier and his platoon, to the surface with orders to scout around the base. Sergeant Juan Feldez's group was first to land.

Using a tall hill with a badly cracked ridge of rock as a reference point, they started toward the base. "We're working our way through an area of thick vegetation," he reported to *Enterprise*. "It's more jungle than forest." He took the lead so his inexperienced troopers could learn by following him. His environment suit provided welcome relief from the heat that he could feel on his bare face.

About 300 meters from the landing site, he passed a stand of plants, covered in pale yellow flowers. While he admired the blossoms, armed figures slipped out of the undergrowth right into his path. By reflex, he raised his rifle until he saw their weapons remained slung on their backs. He counted 11 men and two women, in well-worn sleeveless tops and pants that ended just below their knees. He couldn't determine if their skin was dark or dirty.

While they had to be Nameless, they stood fully alert rather than peering at him with the puzzled expression of the usual Nameless waiting for a command. To compound his confusion, the figures peppered him with questions as soon as he barked at the patrol to halt. His hesitant replies to who was and where he came from produced more queries. The newcomers were every bit as he puzzled as him.

He called over his communicator for his ton Hukaru. The arrival of the fully-armed trooper produced gasps that grew louder when he spoke in Beingish.

After several minutes of animated conversation with the strangers, who barely took their eyes off Juan, Hukaru switched to English. "We have a mystery here, Sarge," he said in a cowboy style drawl. "Even though their ancestors came from the base, they seem more like Terrans than Nameless."

"*Enterprise*, can you see the Nameless we've encountered on Bolivar's visual?" Juan said. "I am going to get him to question them further." The trooper handed his weapon to Juan and raised his arms at his sides before advancing slowly toward them.

Over his helmet receiver, Juan heard Gnoorvants speaking to Hukaru. "Put your communicator at maximum so we can hear clearly."

A dark haired male passed his weapon to a member of his group before approaching Hukaru. They talked too fast for Juan to understand so he turned on his translator. Hukaru pointed at him. "Juan is one of many Terrans who have come to rescue your kind at the base."

Gnoorvants spoke over the communicator. "In your language, the name of these people is the heart or core of the planet and you would likely call them the Core or Corens."

"We saw strange flying machines yesterday that were obviously trying to hide from the Masters," the Coren said. "Today we saw you leave the carrying machines and knew you had come to attack the base because of your weapons."

"The Corens don't understand where you come from," Hukaru said.

"Where to begin?" Juan peered at the Corens contemplating his next move. Finally an answer became obvious. "We'll take them to the shuttle and show them images of the other bases and Mandela."

"I told them about how you saved their people at the first base and that Terrans welcome strangers with a handshake. Perhaps you should do that now."

Juan stepped forward and extended his right hand toward the talkative Coren. "Juan Feldez," he said.

The Coren stared at his hand, and then realized Juan was extending a symbol of peace, he stuck out his hand. "Sinomla."

While rough, his hand felt like any human's. Juan went to the second Coren and shook his. Soon, the troopers joined the greeting. The second Coren female, who was the same height as Juan, smiled and spoke a traditional Being greeting for a stranger. He didn't understand what else she said. Her name sounded like Umet. He looked into her dark eyes, she smiled and he smiled.

Juan led the Corens to the shuttle. "Hukaru, explain what we're doing. We'll play some of the encounter with them first." With that, a dark rectangle appeared in the air displaying the visual of the Corens talking with Juan and Bolivar. Initially startled, the newcomers soon chuckled about their appearance.

"We've never seen ourselves before," Sinomla said.

Enterprise transmitted visuals of the capture of the Nameless craft at Marlabant and the attacks on the three bases while Bolivar explained the scenes.

"You call us Nameless," Sinomla said. He repeated the word gruffly several times. "That's a good description for us. We have no idea of who we are."

When the visual advanced to scenes of soldiers and Biots tending the Nameless, the Corens spoke among themselves. Next came images of doctors removing controllers and the weaning off the chemicals. "It can be done," Sinomla said as the others cheered. "We always hoped it could."

As the Corens babbled, Hukaru moved beside Juan. "You don't need translation to know we've shown them their fondest dream. They're like Terrans in the way they show their excitement."

"This is nothing. You should see and hear my family. It's nonstop talking."

The Corens fell silent at the images of Biots and Terrans building Mandela and the arrival of its first inhabitants. Again, Hukaru didn't bother to translate the whispered comments.

"Where is Earth?" Sinomla said.

Pointing skywards, Bolivar said, "It's in that direction."

The Corens looked up skeptically. "Terrans are not of this world?"

"You cannot see the light of their sun from here. We recruited them to stop the Nameless from attacking us." Hukaru recounted the plan to capture the remaining bases and the Renegade home world although frowns suggested the Corens didn't comprehend much of it.

Sinomla appeared to be in his thirties and had the leathery countenance of someone who had spent most of his life in the sun. "A long time ago, an explosion destroyed the base. While all the Masters died, many Nameless survived. They ventured into the surrounding territory and found enough to eat. A few of them overcame their dependence on the chemicals. The rest died. When the Masters returned, the survivors stayed hidden. My parents were the offspring of these survivors. The Masters brought more of us to the planet."

Sinomla's tone rose steadily and he jabbed the air with his arms to emphasize his statements. "We want to drive the Masters away. They have many weapons and kill our people for simply looking at them the wrong way. Any action on our part would cause many deaths. The Masters pay little attention to the Nameless outside of those trained to do particular jobs such as repairing the flying craft or machinery. The females are kept to produce young."

Sinomla momentarily stood silent, his shoulders and face sagging, before he continued with his story. "For all their control over our kind, the Masters don't know how many Nameless there are. Until they became too old, our parents and others of their age could enter the base. Most of their children were not pale enough to dare go there. There are still some who can. The Nameless are too terrified of the Masters to tell them about us and the Masters regard our people as too stupid to question them about anything. There're no defenses or guards, which makes our coming and going much easier. We will show you."

The base sprawled over 50 hectares with a towering bunker in the middle surrounded by smaller structures and thousands of Nameless huts. "There are more than three thousand Masters," Sinomla said.

Vasile had come to Charlie to direct the assault. Although he spoke to the Corens in Beingish, he often needed Whiz to translate their comments. "Don't feel bad Captain, I have trouble with them as well. They use a lot of words and expressions they've developed. But they understand our plan."

The Corens took Vasile and Juan to a spot where they could view the bunker. After studying it with his binoculars, he said, "It'll be a tougher fight than at the previous bases."

Sinomla shook his head. "The Masters prepare very little. If their commanders are coming for an inspection, they make our people do extra work to get ready."

"Can you get the Nameless out of the base before the shooting starts so they don't get hurt?" Vasile asked.

Sinomla looked at the others before answering. "Where would they go?"

Juan pointed to stand of trees 500 meters away from the

bunker. "At least past them."

"They're afraid of the dark and the woods."

"Persuade them."

"We'll see what we can arrange." Sinomla looked perplexed.

"Once they're safe, we'll surround the bunker," Vasile said. "We want to make sure the attack is noisy and effective. The visuals of it must alarm the Renegades at the other bases." By the surprised looks from the Corens, they knew nothing about Alpha and Beta. Whiz filled them in.

That afternoon, Hukaru reported that troopers had marked 17 landing areas with location beacons. Some were big enough for two shuttles.

Sinomla returned. "Many will leave when told. If enough start moving, the rest will follow. The Masters are planning a big celebration tomorrow night. Some Nameless have to help with it. We'll slip in to open the doors for your soldiers."

"That will help." The suggestion startled Juan. He had to remember that Corens could think for themselves.

"There's something else you should know about the Masters." Sinomla stared for a moment, seemingly wrestling for words. "I don't know if you can understand my explanation." He looked about. "Where is your Biot? It would be easier to tell him."

Juan called over Hukaru. Sinomla cleared his throat and then hummed and hawed his way through his problem. "We talked about this amongst ourselves trying to decide what to tell you. Only some Masters mistreat the Nameless. Most try not to hurt them. Those ones are belittled by their leaders for any kindness they show. The life of these Masters is not much better than our people. The vicious ones kill and abuse them just like they do our people. You should try to spare them if you can. About the only way to tell them apart is the bad ones wear fancy uniforms. We should go with you to pick out the good ones."

"Talk about turning the other cheek," Juan said. "After what the Renegades have done, I would expect you would want them all dead."

Sinomla stared at the ground as if it would supply an answer. "None of us know how it started. We just want it to end. You should only punish the bad ones."

"We'll do our best. I'll order my troops to kill only Renegades that fight and wear fancy uniforms." Juan found some strange humor in what he was saying.

"Sinomla can prepare a message for us to broadcast to the not-so-bad Renegades," Hukaru said.

Just before midnight the next day, 500 troopers and soldiers slipped into the base. The tanks remained close by.

The troops advanced cautiously in the gloom cast by the bunker's exterior lighting waiting for the signal that its defenses were disabled. Nameless shuffled past them shepherded by Corens. Umet waved when she spotted Juan and he waved back.

"Is she your sweetheart?" asked Hukaru. "You manage to spend time with her."

"We'll see some day." Juan was sure the question had made him blush. "Come on, we have work to do."

The troops took positions behind outbuildings and raised their rifles when an entrance to the bunker flew open with a resounding clang. Two Nameless raced out of the building. Several armed Renegades stumbled after them until they discovered red dots from hundreds of lasers covered them. They crumpled under laser blasts.

Juan, Hukaru and Simon Bolivar sprinted forward. As the entrance door closed, Juan fired his laser rifle at it. It clattered off the bunker wall and smashed to the ground.

Without breaking stride, Bolivar and Hukaru leapt effortlessly through the entrance and fired their weapons. When Juan reached them, four Renegades lay on the control room floor.

Between gasps of breath, Juan heard Renegades thumping down the stairs. "Short bursts," he barked. "Keep them up there."

The Renegades halted and fired back, wounding a soldier and leaving a black smear on Bolivar's chest. The trooper looked at the smudge. "That's why we should be in the lead. They can't wound us as easily." Hukaru nodded.

More soldiers and troopers poured through the entrance. Juan sent them to guard the first two stairways and the elevators, and directed the others to protect the stairways at the opposite end of the main corridor. Firefights broke out at each one.

Troopers began creeping up the stairs until Juan called them back. "We've gained the main floor, which was our objective, and it's time to let the tanks go to work. Meanwhile, move these Renegades and our wounded out of here. Those two will have to be sent to *Enterprise*. The others can be patched up back at the field hospital." Troopers hurried to act on his orders.

Three laser cannons on top of the bunker fired off several rounds before one was blown away by a blast from a tank that rocked the entire structure. Troopers shot at Renegades trying to fire missiles and rifles from the windows. The thump of laser cannons and the sizzle of rifles filled the air. Additional tanks pummeled the bunker. Renegade cannons destroyed two of them before they were blown away. A steady stream of concrete chunks fell to the ground.

The assault went on for 20 minutes until Juan ordered a halt. Bolivar's amplified voice called on the Renegades to surrender. "There is no shame. Give up your arms."

From the upper floors, the steady pattern of thump and sizzle continued. At the same time, Renegades called out as they descended the stairs, their weapons held over their heads. Bolivar repeated the offer of surrender. Even more Renegades rushed down the stairs.

"We've destroyed the exterior of the bunker, but it's likely that much of the interior is intact," Juan told the ships. "We'll get the tanks to cover out retreat. There're lots of hostiles in the upper floors. Once we're clear, we'll give them another chance to surrender. If that doesn't work, we should move the soldiers back and let the ships finish this place."

Gnoorvants responded almost immediately. "Let me know when you are ready for our contribution."

"I'll leave recorders so you can see what your firepower does to targets on the ground."

Just as the withdrawal of the warriors and tanks started, a large band of unarmed Renegades slipped out of the bunker. "Hold your fire *Enterprise*; we got Renegades on the run." More appeared, weaponless and limping or assisting others. Renegades leaned out of upper level windows to shoot them. Lasers crackled as troopers returned the fire. Swarms of unarmed figures streamed out of the bunker to make a wild dash for safety.

Juan figured they'd collected close to 2,000 prisoners. "There could be more than five hundred Renegades still in there."

Juan called for Sinomla and Hukaru to interrogate the prisoners and bring the Corens who fled the building at the start of the attack to him.

"We've a problem," Hukaru said as he returned with Sinomla and another Coren. "They don't seem to hear us. They're in shock from the noise of the battle."

Not having any time for niceties, Juan yelled at the Corens. "If this many have given up, will any more of them in there want to surrender?"

Sinomla snapped out of his stupor and spoke with the man beside him. "It seems quite likely."

"Get a couple of your people and we'll go back to the bunker," Juan said, lowering his tone.

"Do you need additional time or shall we fire now?" interjected Gnoorvants.

"We don't know yet."

"*Alliance* reports attack craft are headed here," the Commander said. "I want our ships in space rather than in orbit when they arrive."

"I'll update you in an hour." Juan hated guessing how long an operation would take but there were so many uncertainties.

"I can't wait that long. We should just blast the bunker and be done with them."

"There're probably Renegades in there that want to get out." Juan now understood Gnoorvants' determination to prove that Beings could protect themselves. He didn't want to miss the space battle.

Sinomla and Norcel, the other Coren, accompanied Juan back to the bunker, which was illuminated by the lights of the tanks and surrounded by marksmen. Just as they prepared to enter, a large group of Renegades appeared, their arms in front of them. One of them shouted.

"Nardum says there's a bunch more in the jail on the main floor," Hukaru said. "There're several hundred armed, he calls them Rulers, left upstairs that will not surrender. There're others who would flee, but they're afraid to come out. He says he will help us find them."

"Tell the ones with him to walk slowly with their hands over their heads toward the trees where they'll be taken care of," Juan snapped. "If they don't, they'll be shot."

A faint glow from the spotlights of the tanks slipped through the entrance and holes in the walls. The air in the bunker was thick with dust and the floor littered with chunks of broken ceiling and wall. His troops faced a daunting rescue mission.

"We'll kill ourselves trying to get through all that to the jail," grumbled Nardum as he climbed over rubble at the entrance.

"Permit us to remedy the situation somewhat," Bolivar said. Simultaneously, he and several other troopers turned on lights they had drawn from their packs.

Shielding his eyes, Nardum said, "That's a lot better. Let's get the prisoners." Even with light, moving over and around the debris made for slow progress and the dust soon had everyone but the Biots coughing.

Nardum stopped to mutter a brief phrase over the bodies of several Renegades sprawled in awkward contortions on the floor. The Corens repeated it. The delay for each blessing made Juan more anxious. "He's requesting a better life for them in the next world," Hukaru whispered.

Juan stationed guards at the staircases to prevent a surprise attack. Suddenly, Nardum rushed ahead and pressed his ear against the wall. When the troopers shone their lights on him, the faint outline of a door appeared.

"There are sounds in there so somebody is alive," Nardum shouted. "Although the door has a motorized slider, without power it will be difficult to shift it out of the way because it's heavy and there's nothing to grip."

The rest of the group joined him and Juan checked the door. "It's recessed too far into the wall to pry open."

"Our turn," Bolivar said stepping up to the entrance accompanied by two other troopers. Passing their lights to others, they pulled drills from their packs and pressed the bits against the door.

"Alert the guards at the staircases," Juan barked. "Once they start drilling, the Rulers will know we're here." After a pause, he added, "Unless we can distract them."

The tank operators already had their cannons trained on the bunker. "As soon as they start firing, you guys can begin." Pointing at Nardum, he said, "Tell your fellows inside what's happening and that we've got to get out of here as fast as we can."

The bunker trembled when the tanks opened fire. Their salvos were at half power to create more racket than damage. The drills added to the cacophony as they bit into the door. After a couple of minutes, the troopers stopped to extract round pieces of metal from side pockets on their packs and shove them into the holes. Grasping them, they began pushing the entrance sideways. When it cracked open and light spilled into the jail, hands from inside and outside joined the effort. The grunting and straining of Renegade, Coren and human all sounded the same.

With an eerie creak like a rusty old hinge slowly letting go, the door rollers shifted. Once the door opened wide enough for them, prisoners slowly stumbled out. Shielding their eyes from the sudden light, they shuffled forward staring at their rescuers.

"Collect the wounded," Nardum bellowed. Looking at the prisoners, he pointed toward the outside door. "Get moving through that entrance. Once you are outside, head for the trees with your arms up. Do exactly as you are told and no one will be hurt."

Nardum and Norcel found no one else alive in the jail. Juan counted 93 prisoners before the exodus stopped.

Tank salvos rocked the bunker. "Now what?" Norcel said while Nardum performed the departure rites over several bodies.

"Find out whether there're any other Renegades willing to surrender," Juan said. "We have to get out before this building falls on us."

Genghis called, "There's a group coming down the first stairway slowly."

Nardum rushed off yelling, "Drop your weapons and raise your arms."

"They're pleading to be spared," Hukaru said.

"Tell them to hurry," Juan snapped.

The ton ratcheted up his voice. "This is your last chance to escape."

As more Renegades rushed down the stairs, Juan activated his communicator, ordering the soldiers and troopers to withdraw.

"*Enterprise*, we're vacating the bunker. There're still hostiles in it. Give us three minutes and it's all yours. Also, for the record, I'm recommending Bolivar and Genghis Khan for promotion to corporal."

Gnoorvants muttered incomprehensibly. "Three minutes and counting, Sergeant."

Juan glanced about to make sure his troops had left, and then dashed for the tree.

His hands on his knees as he gulped down air, Juan kept his eyes on the bunker expecting to see the building blown to smithereens. There was no explosion or boom. The building disappeared in a thick swirling cloud of dust and its debris dissipated in the breeze. Without looking, he knew all that remained was a blackened swath of ground that in time would succumb to the surrounding vegetation. He shook his head in admiration at the destructive power of the upgraded laser cannon.

"If anyone ever wants to debate on the ultimate weapon, the

mechanics' laser cannon would have to be considered," Vasile said when he reached Juan's position.

From muttered comments nearby, the Corens and Renegades agreed. "We've seen no sign the Rulers can match the technology of the Beings and the Biots," Vasile said. "Do we just have to wear them down or will there be more surprises like the Corens and Renegades who oppose the Rulers?"

No one had an answer. "Maybe we just need to weed out the Rulers." Vasile watched the Renegades hobbling and limping under guard toward the field hospitals. They'd joined the cheering when the bunker vaporized.

"Do the Beings even need us any longer?" Juan asked.

Before Vasile could reply, the tons in unison said, "Yes." Hukaru took over. "We cannot finish this by ourselves. You remain as important as ever."

"*Enterprise* to Captain Vasile. You'll have to remain on the ground as we are leaving to deal with the incoming attackers."

"Good hunting *Enterprise*," he responded. "We've got plenty to do here with wounded soldiers and Renegades to attend to."

Chapter 22
Fish in a Barrel

Hector turned his attention to 200 Renegade attack craft hurtling toward the galaxyships. The commanding officers of the four cruisers were vizlinked in from their Command Chambers for a conference.

"We will let a few of them reach Charlie so they can report the destruction of the base," he said. "Hopefully, this will draw more craft from the other two bases."

Hton had a front row seat and at the first opportunity advanced his plan for expanding the Being Air Force. "All the attack craft we capture could be upgraded. We can do the same with the ones on Charlie. The flyer trainees can bring them up here as those guys are always looking for a chance to spend time in a cockpit. That would give us several hundred more fighters."

"Of course," Humbaw gasped. The other Beings leaned forward their seats holding their heads and moaning.

Hton glanced between them and the Terrans. "It didn't strike them before that they're in combat. Now they know what's happening, their anti-combativeness conditioning is taking over. We should adjourn this conference."

"Agreed," Gnoorvants said in a loud voice before standing up.

"You're not affected." Hector stared in surprise as he compared Gnoorvants to the hunched over Beings on *Alliance*.

"Except for Gnoorvants and Atdomorsin, I would suggest that all the Beings move to the back rows of the chambers," Hton said. "They'll be a lot more comfortable and able to follow what we're doing. Their tons can take over their functions."

With Humbaw incapacitated, command of the mission should fall to Gnoorvants. Hector wondered if the Beings would follow him as many of them still considered him as a maverick. However, they were even less likely to take orders from Hton.

"The attack craft will appear in fifteen minutes and we must have the jets ready to intercept them," Hton said. "We'll maintain a constant link with the Command Chambers of the other cruisers so we can be aware of what's happening on each vessel."

"BAF has already shown its mettle," Gnoorvants said. "The flyers can take them on. Keep the pilots in reserve."

Hector relaxed. Hton and Gnoorvants had settled on a shared

leadership without any discussion. Even incapacitated, Humbaw had shown the Beings their future. Once again, he'd witnessed history. Hopefully, Ruth would see this scene because it was her research that had unveiled the real story of the Biobots.

Hton broke any lingering tension in the wait for the attack craft to arrive. "The Navigation Directorate reports the transfer of the Nameless from the other side is complete. There are about two hundred and seventy thousands of them at Mandela. The transports will report here as soon as they can. Dr Azwatta's team has made more improvements to the recovery process and she's anxious to get the Corens there so they can help. Also the first Nameless babies have been born on Mandela. They will undergo a life free of chemical manipulation."

At the back, Humbaw beamed like a new grandfather. "Pass this good news to Sinomla and Norcel."

Hector didn't feel cheered by it.

"What troubles you?" Hton said.

"Sooner or later the Renegades will throw something at us we aren't prepared for. We've outmatched them all along. Could they have so seriously underestimated you?"

"They don't have our Primitive advantage."

Hector peered at the ton until he saw it was struggling to remain straight faced. "It's possible they simply miscalculated their strength and our weaknesses." On the screen, Gnoorvants nodded.

The discussion ended as Nonforense reported the fighters moving to intercept the attack craft. "In response, they broke into seven groups flying on different trajectories toward Charlie."

"They're Nameless pilots like at Marlabant," Mig reported as his squad descended on an attack craft group. "They won't engage us and are trying all sorts of evasive moves. The new electronic pulse shuts them down almost instantaneously."

Although 14 attack craft reached Charlie, with the base destroyed and the troops, Nameless and prisoners hiding in caves and dense forests, the visuals from the craft showed only a few damaged small buildings and the Nameless huts. All that remained of the gigantic bunker was a black smudge.

"Imagine the Renegades poring over these images and realizing the bunker is gone." Hector scrolled through the images on his analyzer screen. "This should make them desperate."

Temeraire and *Yamoto* remained behind to protect Charlie until the transports arrived. Shuttles removed most soldiers and troopers along with Sinomla and several other Corens to join the attack on Alpha and Beta.

On board the cruisers, mechanics worked steadily to upgrade the captured attack craft. Ruth entered Bay 3 of *Alliance* every day to observe them disassembling and rebuilding the craft. She noted they'd cut in half the time required to turn an attack craft into a fighter. A melody she didn't recognize boomed through the bay.

"It's an aria by Antonin Dvorak called a *Song for the Moon*," Huxton said. "It has become our anthem although we will write our own lyrics in Beingish."

The ton recorded the rebuilding of the fighters for Elinor Brady. By the flair in her commentary, Ruth figured Huxton had a future as comnet correspondent or in advertising.

As entertaining as her ton's style was, Ruth's main interest at the moment was a conversation she had with Hector a few hours earlier. After sending their tons on errands, he'd asked for her observations on how the helpers worked together on the craft.

"When they started, they only talked about matters pertaining to the overhaul," she said. "Now they chatter on about all sorts of issues like where the Nameless came from Earth, what the Renegade home world must be like and our physical and classroom training. While they work effectively as a team, they have distinct personalities and interests. Some have a natural aptitude for flying while others adapt to medical tasks with ease."

"Some like Hton and Gnoorton are true leaders," Hector said. "Is that the result of being associated with their particular Beings? On the other hand, how to explain the development of Genghis and Bolivar? They were just regular helpers, yet the others follow them readily. I'm sure more troopers will show leadership ability when the opportunity presents itself."

Ruth looked at him. "You haven't noticed?" Hector shrugged. "There's tension between the tons and some Biots especially when they think you're not paying attention. They're unhappy or possibly jealous of the leadership role of the tons. I have yet to get to the bottom of it." She couldn't keep the uncertainty out of her voice.

"My tons rarely leave me alone long enough to have a conversation with Hton or Dton so I'm just going on observation."

Humbaw and Hector conducted a tour of *Alliance* for the Renegades and Corens that concluded in the Conference Room. "If we don't show it to them beforehand, they'll be too distracted by the novelty of their surroundings to concentrate during the conference," Hector had said. Elinor had joined the tour to observe the newcomers up close.

Nardum and Pqwnrx spent the tour trying to figure out the function of equipment they hadn't seen before.

"It is so clean and comfortable," Nardum said. "The ones we captured from you were a mess and nothing functioned well. It took a lot of work to make them fit for service, but they were never anything like this."

Sinomla looked about in wide-eyed wonderment. "This ship is simply beyond our comprehension. We lived in primitive conditions on Charlie compared to this." He looked around in bewilderment at the laughs his remark drew. "We regarded the bunker as a marvel. We didn't know the craft the Masters used to supply the bunker came from other worlds."

He stopped speaking when Norcel whispered to him. He nodded. "We should call everyone recovered from the chemicals a Coren. Then before long there won't be any Nameless."

Everyone agreed, which brought Nardum into the conversation. "Please start calling us citizens as the Rulers do or Pozzens as we call ourselves." He looked about the room anxiously after his outburst.

"All you have to do is defeat the Rulers. They caused all the trouble for the things and as you can tell from what happened on the base, we'll help." He stopped to catch his breath. "What do you plan to do with the Rulers?"

"We're under orders to destroy them," Humbaw said flatly.

"That would be fitting," Nardum said.

"We did not know about Pozzens when we first made our plans. We will help establish a new government on the condition the Nameless are freed, and your ability to attack other planets is destroyed."

Nardum looked at Pqwnrx who nodded. "I'm sure the Pozzens will accept your offer. Getting rid of the Rulers has long been our fondest desire. Once done it will be a wish fulfilled. Without the Rulers, Pozzens will not cause trouble. I must warn you the Rulers have plenty of weapons and will fight to the end. There're armed citizens called defenders who will assist you."

Hector interjected with a question he had been pondering,

"What's the difference between Ruler and citizen?"

"Birth and attitude," Nardum said. "The Rulers come from a group of families. We don't know how they gained control of our society or the Corens. They certainly treat both of us badly. If a citizen gets too ambitious, he or she simply disappears or is murdered. So we keep our heads down." Sinomla nodded in agreement.

While he didn't want to say more, Hector kept prying. "The prisoners we captured at the earlier bases were completely uncooperative until you talked to them."

"They believed all the claptrap about evil Beings. When you defeated the Rulers, we knew there was hope for us. Now, how are you going to attack those bases?"

"The plan is quite straightforward." An image of the bunker on Beta appeared on the main display. "Both bases are protected by an energy wall. Hopefully, the Rulers will think they're impregnable and remain inside. Otherwise, we'll have to hunt them down on the planet."

The image changed to show the energy pattern of the wall covering the base on Beta and then a simulated laser cannon blast striking it. "We want to pin the Rulers in the base while we dispatch the soldiers and troopers to the surface. We'll need some Corens and citizens to go with them. After we knock out the wall, we'll attack the base. Before we start the bombardment, we'll broadcast a call to the Nameless and citizens to flee. We need Corens and Pozzens to help with the ones that do."

Nardum was shaking his head. "The Rulers worked for ages to destroy the Beings. In a matter of months, you have run them out of their bases and taken away the advantage of the Nameless. It looked so easy."

"It was just a matter of becoming properly prepared," said Humbaw.

A couple of days later, *Enterprise* and *New Jersey* moved into orbit around Beta and began pummeling the protective energy wall of its base as shuttles transported tanks and troops to the surface. Nardum's recorded plea to prepare to flee was broadcast repeatedly.

"It's quite the pyrotechnic show when the laser blasts hit the energy wall," Vasile Stocia, the on-the-ground commander, reported to the ships. "It is an orangey-yellow color. Every strike drains the color from the surrounding part of it. While it reforms, the color isn't as bright. The power for it comes through underground conduits. We'll deploy the tanks to concentrate on destroying them."

"We'll keep pummeling the wall," Hton said.

Three tanks surged forward, their cannons firing in quick succession at the same spot on the wall. "There's a hole in the energy field. We're sending a tank inside," Vasile said.

It passed through the wall and advanced for a couple of minutes under withering fire from the Rulers, which flared off the machine like mini rainbows. Finally, its propulsion system gave out.

"Blow it up," Vasile barked to its operator. Although the wall appeared to buckle outwards from the blast, it held, rebounding the force of the explosion over the base with a deafening roar. Two more tanks headed through the opening while a third approached a smaller break and opened fire.

Vasile surveyed the row of soldiers and troopers stretched out on the ground beside him. At this distance, they couldn't pick out any targets and it would be suicidal to move closer.

Laser blasts from the ships rained down on the screen. On the inside, another heavily-damaged tank was blown up and more entered the base firing in all directions. Additional gaps opened in the wall.

Vasile's communicator beeped. "The power station for the wall is near the center of the base," Norcel reported.

The generator's location was sheltered from the tank lasers by tall structures. "Launch missiles at the spot," Vasile ordered. They streaked into the base followed by loud explosions as they struck. Clouds of debris and smoke rose from the area and the scream of a loud siren filled the air.

"That's a warning the generator is shut down," Nardum said.

The wall crackled and roiled before flaring in a brilliant yellow. With a final sizzle, it disappeared. Its incessant hum was replaced by more alarms.

Hundreds of attack craft rose into the sky from the base. The jets went after the ones headed for orbit while the fighters engaged the rest as they lined up to strafe and bomb the troopers and soldiers. They couldn't fire their rifles at the Ruler craft because it was hard to distinguish them from the fighters as they dueled overhead.

Citizens in tattered clothes sifted out of the base. Although the trickle soon became a torrent, Nardum stopped Vasile from sending troops to rescue them. "They have to make the first steps themselves. And the Rulers must see it."

Troopers guided them to an area well away from the Nameless. "They say there're several hundred Rulers left in the base," Nardum reported to Vasile.

When the flight of Pozzens had slowed to a trickle, Vasile ordered the troopers forward. "Corporals Bolivar and Genghis, you are in charge. We can't use the tanks because all the grit in the air might damage their motors. You're taking the lead because you can talk with the Pozzens and you're always looking for ways to prove yourselves."

While the corporals snapped salutes, they didn't rush away.

"Sergeant Feldez and his soldiers will be right behind you," Vasile said.

"We'll make him proud of us," Bolivar said.

The battle raged from building to building in swirling clouds of dust and deafening blasts. The troopers mimicked Nardum's voice to coax terrified citizens into fleeing and cajole Rulers into fighting. When the troopers called for an air strike, the flyers delivered the blow.

The Rulers fought doggedly to the end. They launched furious barrages at the troopers and tanks and left booby traps and mines everywhere. After several hours, the fighting subsided. Gradually, the thick smoke and dust drifted away to reveal a scene of utter devastation.

Bolivar reported over his communicator. "We've combed every building and we can't find any more Rulers. We could use some help moving our casualties."

Tanks surged into the center of the base to assist with the removal of the damaged troopers. Soldiers and troopers helped the wounded from the battlefield. Vasile spotted a soldier supporting an injured trooper while carrying the Biot's arm in his other hand. More than 50 Biots were destroyed and close to 100 others would require major repairs. Many others would wait for cosmetic fixes.

A few citizens appeared from hiding places. While they were moved to safety, Nardum kept busy performing the departure rite for the dead.

"*Enterprise*, we'll get you a complete count of Nameless and Pozzens as soon as everyone is patched up," Vasile reported.

"You can start hauling up the tanks and the soldiers and troopers whenever you're ready."

"That will have to wait." Gnoorvants sounded highly agitated. "We've detected galaxyships heading to Beta from Pozzen. *New Jersey* and the freighters will remain here to protect you."

Chapter 23
The Big Boys Duel

Nonforense reported that the trajectory of the Ruler ships would bring them to Alpha, and sounded the alarm for battle stations throughout the fleet. *Alliance* and *Omanora* halted their bombardment to prepare for the engagement.

"How many are we facing?" Hector said.

"The ships are too distant to make an accurate determination," Nonforense responded. "They will have to come out of galaxy flight soon or they'll shoot past the planet."

"Nonforense, order all squadrons to take up protective stations around our ships," Hector commanded.

"*Enterprise* is on course to intercept the Ruler ships!" shrieked Connun.

Suspecting the anti-combative conditioning had finally influenced the normally soft-spoken Being, Hector said, "Let your ton take over." Connton stood right behind her.

Gnoorvants' voice boomed through the Command Chamber. "We have a side view of the column and there are seven stolen transports plus five bigger ships behind them."

"*Enterprise* will intercept the vessels at the rear of the column." Her hands trembling, Connun remained at her post.

Hector marveled at Connun's willpower as the other Beings huddled at the back of the Chamber in obvious distress. She seemed to have found the same inner strength as Gnoorvants and Atdomorsin.

"They're splitting up!" The alarm in Connun's voice rang through the Chamber. "Our former ships are moving toward the freighters. The larger ones are coming for *Omanora* and us!"

"Either the stolen ones have a new weapon or they're just a distraction," Hton added.

"The Rulers probably don't know how heavily armed the transports are," Hector said.

"Precisely, they would be no match for them unless the Rulers have made major improvements," Hton said. "Based on what we've seen so far, that seems unlikely." He sat at the center of the command bench, his eyes darting from display to display. The ton was clearly in command.

"Nonforense, report any evidence you see of modifications to the stolen ships." Hector paced while he considered strategies and studied the data flashing on the displays they monitored.

"None detected."

"How do the Ruler vessels compare to the cruisers?"

"Weaponry not determined."

Hector's face lit up. "Maybe we should try to capture your former ships as we did with the other transports. Prepare boarding parties to protect them from sabotage."

As soon as he finished outlining his plan, Dton and Nonforense assigned soldiers and troopers to shuttles.

"If we can't get on board the transports, then we'll have to attack them," Hector said. "I would rather save them to move Corens and Pozzens."

The Ruler warships, rounded at the bow and stern, were about two-thirds the size of the cruisers and bristled with menacing looking weapons pods. Hector chuckled until he saw the tons watching him. "The Ruler ships look like what Ambassador Vladmitz expected of *Alliance*." The tons continued to stare in puzzlement.

"*Enterprise* will be in firing range in three minutes," Connun said. Calm had returned to her voice.

"All laser cannons power up," Hector said. Although he delivered the command with quiet authority, he doubted it mattered to the tons. They worked the displays with a minimum of comments.

"Atdomorsin asks if the citizens have any insight into the Ruler tactics," Hton said.

Nardum shook his head. "The warships are new. The Rulers must have built them in secret."

"Order the transports not to let the attackers get too close," Hector said. "Are the boarding parties ready?"

"The last of the shuttles carrying them has launched," Hton said. "It appears *Enterprise* intends to attack before the warships can engage us." A smile spread across the ton's face. "General and Humbaw, Gnoorvants wants to be as bold and cunning as the brave captains of the *Enterprise*."

"There're just stories," Hector said. "Gnoorvants and Atdomorsin are unusually assertive and aggressive for Beings." Afraid he'd gone too far, he instantly added, "That's said with great respect."

Connun glared at Hector.

"It's just as well you cannot hear what Connun is thinking

right now." Humbaw spoke barely above a whisper. "She'll join with Atdomorsin when their time comes. She didn't appreciate your comment, but she did not hear the second part of it. She worries about him."

"*Oriol* has closed on its target and a boarding party is about to land." Connun rocked back and forth as her eyes flitted about the data streams on her display. "*Enterprise* will be in firing range of the first Ruler ship in thirty seconds."

Alliance would soon face its own foe, which would present Connun with a real test in handling this ship and also tracking *Enterprise*.

Gnoorvants and Atdomorsin sat beside each other on the command bench of *Enterprise*. "Turing, when we are in range, fire on the closest ship at maximum power. As soon as the other ships target us, shift the wall around to protect our exposed sections!"

"Five seconds." Then without any change in its somber tone, Turing declared, "Implementing turn and wall rotation to counter incoming strikes from enemy ships." Alarms hooted throughout the vessel as it heeled into as sharp a course change as such a mammoth vessel traveling at half of the speed of light could manage in the vacuum of space.

"Commence firing," Hurandi said. A box appeared on the weapons display showing the order in which the cannons fired and anticipated time of impact.

"Five strikes coming," Turing said. "All on the wall."

Enterprise lurched from the impact and fired. Its opponent still reeled from the first strikes when the second round flared over its wall. "Forty per cent reduction in enemy ship's protection."

The second and third Ruler warships fired at *Enterprise* as it continued to pummel the first one. "Ten strikes coming," Turing said. The ship shuddered under the blows. "Minimal damage. The first ship has ceased firing and is losing speed. Adjusting course projection to match."

"The enemy ship's wall is gone," Fassad shouted. "Our blasts are punching huge openings in the vessel."

"Second attacker is obscured by the first ship," Turing said. "Third attacker can't fire at us because it's behind the second one."

"Take us over top of the first ship," Gnoorvants ordered. "By the amount of debris, it's venting its atmosphere. It'll not last much longer. Major, when we're in position, fire at the second one."

"Reinforce the sections of the wall closest to the first ship," Atdomorsin added. "Distance to second target?"

"Half a kilometer," Turing said. "The third one is a kilometer away."

Enterprise soared past its first opponent like a giant beast seeking its next prey. The forward cannons pounded the second vessel as it closed. "Fire as much as you can at it," Atdomorsin barked. The Controlling Unit shifted the wall to counter the blasts from the second attacker while protecting *Enterprise's* stern from explosions on the first one.

"How soon do we pass the second ship?" Gnoorvants roared. They were almost alongside and energy beams slashed the distance between the space heavyweights.

"Ten seconds."

"As soon as we do, make a brief shift to galaxy flight to put us behind the third vessel. When we are there, concentrate all weapons on it."

"Confirmed, seven strikes coming."

Gnoorvants gripped his seat again as the ship recoiled from the blows. Alarms blared.

"Prepare for transition to galaxy flight." A hint of excitement had crept into Turing's voice.

Although it was too short a burst to propel the huge vessel to the speed of light, it shot *Enterprise* behind the third attacker. The energy discharge from the maneuver shoved the second warship into the remnants of the first one. They exploded in a gigantic white ball of light.

Alliance dueled with another Ruler warship although their distance apart and walls kept the blasts from doing more than shaking both vessels. As the flash engulfed *Enterprise*, Connun's shriek startled Hector.

"Fifteen seconds to next firing," Nonforense said.

"All squadrons, watch for craft going to or coming from the surface," Hector ordered.

"Hton, General Davis. *Omanora* reports the third Ruler warship is under attack," Hanasston called.

"*New Jersey* was supposed to stay at the other base." Hton looked intently at the center display.

"It did."

"Oww!" exclaimed Connun, pumping her fists in the air as the main display showed *Enterprise* unleashing a broadside at its new opponent.

Vasile Stocia was packed in a shuttle with two sergeants and 15 troopers. They carried laser pistols and stun guns. They wore infrared glasses to pick out body heat or movement as well as electronic detection signals. The glasses also protected them from blinding by flashes of light.

"We're waiting for conformation *Oriol* has control of our target," Vasile explained to the others. "If the Rulers haven't made any modifications, it'll switch the transport to maintenance mode until we take over and then our buddies will run the ships." He nodded toward the troopers.

"Actually, we'll restore the crew to operate it," Whiz said.

"Just in case there're problems, remember the stun gun will knock out the Nameless if needed." Vasile held up his pistol. "This is for the Rulers. We don't know if there're any on the transport so don't take chances."

In recognition of his experiences exploring planets, Elinor had recorded a documentary on Vasile. While it described his discoveries in the abandoned bases, it said nothing about his lack of direct involvement in any fighting. Having not proved himself, he worried about how well he would cope in battle. A naturally cautious person, he climbed mountains to test his courage but never took reckless chances. He'd wondered since he was a kid whether fear or just a healthy respect for his surroundings drove him. The wait in the shuttle made him increasingly agitated. He hoped it was just from being cooped up in the windowless craft.

Do something. He instantly focused on a deep breathing technique he had learned in Tae Kwon Do training. It calmed him although it was hard to ignore the regular buffeting of the shuttle by the laser blasts of the Ruler ship. He looked around hoping to garner some strength from his comrades. The Sergeants appeared relaxed while the troopers bore their customary blank expressions. He scanned their chests trying to memorize names to diffuse his nervousness.

"We're still trying to complete the takeover procedure," *Oriol* called to the boarding parties. The rocking continued.

"There's something else we never told the Beings," Whiz said in a conspiratorial whisper. "We've modified the transports so they can be operated from various locations including the bays. We could fly in and take control of the ship."

"Won't they blast us?"

"They'd have done that already if they regarded us as a threat."

"There's no point floating around out here waiting to get hit by accident," Vasile said. "Let's go in."

"Once we gain control, we should follow your plan for seizing the ship," the ton said. "Each of us carries a recording from Nardum that explains to citizens what's happening."

The shuttle's interior lights dimmed to warn them their craft was on final approach to the transport. "All we have to do is secure the docking bay," Vasile said between deep breaths. "Another shuttle is following us with reinforcements." He glanced ahead at the hiss of the ship's protective atmosphere forming around the craft. As soon as its hatch opened, Shaka jumped from the shuttle and sprinted toward the control panel that controlled access to the bay.

"Hate it when I can't see what's outside," grunted French Sergeant Frederique Mazue.

"We're in an empty bay like on the *Alliance*," the shuttle nanalyzer said. "Get ready. Shaka has reached the access chamber."

Seconds later, the trooper called. "Get a move on in there. I've control of the ship, but we haven't got all day. There're Renegades and Nameless on board. I've shut down the weapons and told the Controlling Unit to await further orders from us." He sounded positively boastful.

Troopers and soldiers poured out of the shuttle into the access chamber. As soon as they arrived, Shaka closed the hatch and began raising the air pressure to the level inside the transport. Once it was equal, they entered a shabby-looking corridor.

"How's the air?" Frederique said.

"Safe enough, but..." Vasile gagged. "Leave your breathers on, the ship stinks big time."

"That means the crew is in hiding and the atmosphere recyclers aren't in service," Whiz gloated.

Frederique and Yamashita sprinted to the first intersection of corridors to stand guard while two troopers lifted a third one to remove the ceiling cover to the service conduit. Vasile, Whiz and Dumont were hefted into it and started on the overhead route to the Command Chamber. The other soldiers and the rest of the troopers secured the ship. Shaka, Lancelot and Spartacus left to search for the Biobot crew. Marlborough remained behind to hold the entry chamber for the next shuttle.

Dumont led the way to the Command Chamber turning right and left and climbing ladders so quickly that Vasile could only retrace the route by the boot marks they'd created in the dust that had collected because of the shutdown crew.

Without warning, Dumont knelt to peer through an access cover. He moved back and signaled for Vasile to look. "Nothing's been changed in the Command Chamber since it was stolen," he whispered.

Two Nameless sat on the Command Bench waiting for the displays to return to service.

They've no idea what's happened, Vasile thought. He pulled out the stun gun, reduced the power setting, and signaled for Dumont to remove the access panel. With Whiz holding his legs Dumont leaned into the chamber.

As he aimed at the Nameless, Vasile recalled an earlier conversation with Gsolghwan, who helped organize the boarding parties. He had said there were unofficial bonuses for anyone who killed a Ruler. "They would be good target practice. Citizens should be spared."

"I thought you guys aren't in favor of killing," Vasile had said, hiding his doubts.

"Oh, we are not," Gsolghwan replied completely straight faced.

"So you want us to do the dirty work?" Vasile asked.

"Something like that."

The Being's frankness had surprised Vasile. It was usually hard to get anything straight with Beings because they could talk about the most trivial and most complex issues without any expression on their faces or emphasis in their voices.

"Don't tell Councilor Humbaw or General Davis about this deal," Gsolghwan said. "This is Commander Gnoorvants' idea. He'll pay. He says that Beings are all talk while Earthlings get things done."

"He might be disappointed if he ever comes to Earth." Vasile remained dubious about the deal although Gsolghwan and Gnoorvants were from the same world. "So how can the soldiers who kill a Ruler take the bonus home?"

"They will be paid as gambling winnings. Gnoorvants wants to make sure we get every one of the Rulers."

Vasile had laughed. Beings were terrible gamblers. They could be easily bluffed when they used telepathy on humans who imagined a different hand than the one they held.

Suspended from the ceiling of the chamber, Vasile fired at the Nameless who slumped in their seats. Dumont and Whiz pulled him back into the conduit, and then they dropped into the chamber. His ton caught Vasile as he let go of the edge of the access panel while Dumont opened a panel behind the command bench and punched a sequence of symbols. The displays came on showing scenes in and outside the ship.

"Controlling Unit, acknowledge the change in command and provide a status report," Dumont snapped.

"Confirmed. All systems online and overdue for service. Displaying location of unauthorized personnel. There're three new ones of unknown origin including one standing beside you. Status of crew cannot be determined."

"The new ones are on our side," Dumont said. Keying his radio, he said, "*Oriol*, we have control of 147." Just then, they heard laser fire.

"We've run into Rulers about half way to the Command Chamber," Frederique reported over the communicator. "They're headed toward you, can't tell how many. We've sent a bunch of citizens and Nameless to No. 1 bay."

"There're thirty-nine Renegades on the ship," Dumont said without taking his eyes off the display. "The images keep shifting. Here we go, there're eleven headed toward us. The rest of them and the Nameless are going to the bay. Nardum's message worked."

"We'll move into the corridor and set up a defense against them," Whiz said. The laser fire sounded closer.

"Why wouldn't they escape in a shuttle?" Vasile asked. "There're plenty on board."

"The ship's destruct mechanism is here," Dumont said. "They probably want to trigger it. At this range, it would cause a lot of damage to our ships."

"Can we disable it?" Vasile said.

"You'll have to keep the Rulers out of here to give me time to disarm it," Dumont said.

In the corridor, Vasile and his ton spotted two rulers backing into the corridor about 15 meters away. Whiz bagged both before they could look around.

"Should've waited a bit longer," Vasile said. His anxiety flared. "The second body is visible from the other corridor."

"Still it was good shooting, Captain," the ton replied with a grin. "That's two for you. We'll make you rich yet."

Vasile looked at him in amazement. "How do you know about the bonuses?"

"I'll tell you later. For now, get down and cover your ears."

A concussion grenade rolled down the corridor. While it exploded with a roar, it caused little damage other than loosening chunks of the ceiling. A section swung down cracking the skull of an advancing Ruler. Vasile's pistol blew a hole in its chest and it dropped with a loud thud. The remaining Rulers charged.

Vasile dove at the legs of the first one who fell on top of him. The other Rulers tripped over them creating a heap of bodies. The pile got bigger as Whiz jumped on followed by Shaka, Lancelot and Spartacus, who'd dropped out of an overhead access.

Vasile was on the bottom of the seething mass, his arm part way around a Ruler's neck. He couldn't tighten his grip. The Rulers grunted and cursed as troopers pulled them from the pile and slammed them into the walls. Laser pistols discharged. He'd ended up in the worst position in the brawl. When the Ruler tried to roll away and aim his weapon, Vasile grabbed his arm and the discharge smacked into the ceiling. Then his arm snaked around the Ruler's neck and he twisted sharply. His opponent went limp.

"That's number seven for you, Captain," Whiz said as he pulled Vasile to his feet.

Dead Rulers lay scattered about him. Although he ached in several places, an immense sense of relief swept over Vasile. "Thanks guys, they were crushing me."

The troopers shook his hand and slapped his back in celebration. "When we saw you tackle that Ruler, we understood the bravery of a real soldier," Shaka said.

They saluted Vasile as Frederique's unit advanced up the corridor and the revived crew came out of the Command Chamber. They'd dropped into it through the same access as Vasile and the troopers.

"The crew is glad to be back in operation," Dumont said. "Let them fix up the Command Chamber and take control of the ship.

We'll go to the bay and report to *Oriol* from there."

"You guys all seem okay," Vasile said. The troopers nodded their heads.

"The first Ruler I pulled away from you made a particularly vulgar response when I ordered him to surrender so I shot him," Lancelot said. "I considered the dictates of the Code and concluded I was justified in killing him because of the threat his kind pose to the Beings and us."

"I'm sure your reports on this fracas will reflect well on us," Shaka said.

"I will recommend citations for all of you," Vasile said.

"Will that get us medals?" several troopers responded quickly in unison.

Chapter 24
On to Pozzen

*A*lliance continued its pursuit of the fourth Ruler warship, pummeling it with cannon blasts. "It's probably preparing to go to galaxy flight," Hector said. "We need to at least damage it so it can't."

The Ruler ship grazed the planet's atmosphere to slingshot its escape. It looked like a successful move until *Temeraire* and *Oriol* appeared over the horizon. The fleeing ship had put up energy walls to protect its belly and stern. Cannon blasts from the transports chewed up its unprotected bow and debris poured from it. The stricken ship tumbled toward the planet becoming a glowing mass that hurtled into a mountain with a tremendous explosion.

Meanwhile, *Omanora* chased the final one around Alpha until repeated laser blasts caused its drive to flare out like an old-fashioned rocket, propelling it at the planet. It transformed into a giant fireball when it struck the atmosphere.

The Biots on *Alliance* cheered and hugged each other in celebration of the victory while Humbaw watched intently. Hector couldn't tell whether he was angry, pleased or simply surprised. "I guess we're just a bad influence."

"This is nothing. What to do about Gnoorvants."

"On Earth, there will be lots of talk about *Enterprise's* new captain. In the comnet shows and visuals over the years, *Enterprise* had four brave captains. Now there's a fifth. They couldn't have written a better script for him."

Covered in dark smudges, *Enterprise* pulled alongside *Alliance*. Gnoorvants and Atdomorsin shuttled over for a conference with Humbaw.

"Come to the Command Chamber," Humbaw said. "There is someone who wants to see that you two really are alive." Connun's shoulders straightened. "Perhaps you would join us, General, to keep them or me from saying something rash."

An excited clamor accompanied Gnoorvants, Atdomorsin and their tons as they proceeded from the bay through the ship to the Command Chamber. Throngs of Biots lined the corridors flashing fingers to the tons.

For all the accolades, Gnoorvants and Atdomorsin looked like a couple of sheepish boys rather than two conquering heroes.

Humbaw led them to Connun's station. "As busy as it was on this ship, our communications officer kept us informed of your actions. You should express your gratitude to her," he commanded in a most formal voice.

The aquamarine color didn't hide Connun and Atdomorsin's blushes. "Ummm," Atdomorsin managed before the Command Chamber erupted in snorts and laughter. Humor was a rare among Beings and showing affection in public even less so. Atdomorsin and Connun obviously didn't know how to react to each other. She hid her face in her hands. Atdomorsin pulled her from the bench and put his arm around her. In an effort to provide the pair some privacy, the Beings turned away.

When Atdomorsin reached the Conference Room a couple of minutes later, Humbaw said, "For what purpose did you request this session?"

"We have exceeded the proper conduct of Beings and should be relieved of our positions and sent home," Gnoorvants said.

Humbaw leaned back in his chair looking grave and stern. His voice almost matched his face. "It's true you have violated traditional Being behavior. At least it has been traditional for the last millennium. I'd hoped recruiting humans would extract us from the binds of that tradition so we would never again tolerate attacks like the Nameless ones. The only thing you two are guilty of is pushing our society ahead. General Davis says your actions gave us a major victory and saved many Being and Terran lives. That'll probably accord the both of you the status of honored citizens on our worlds. Obviously from the reaction on this ship, you're already regarded that way."

He rubbed his chin a few times. A smile flittered across his face. "So I reject your request and order you to return to *Enterprise* to resume your duties. We still have to capture the base on Alpha and finish the evacuation of the Nameless."

Humbaw paused to look at his display. "Actually, I have a better assignment for you. Take half the ships along with Captain Donohue and Jiabao's squadrons and half the soldiers and troopers and lay siege to Pozzen. Nardum and some other citizens should also accompany you. The rest of the fleet will join you as soon as possible."

Humbaw had delivered his orders telepathically as well because the Beings in the Command Chamber waved cheerily to Gnoorvants and Atdomorsin as they returned to their shuttle.

Later, Hector related the event to Elinor. "It was the first time

Humbaw gave orders without discussing them with us in advance. Perhaps Gnoorvants' exploits have affected even him. Or Hton and Dton have even more influence than we realize."

After a hasty review of the space battle, the next morning's briefing focused on what resources the ships needed for the attack on Pozzen. Hector wanted to know how best to counter the Ruler ground attack vehicles discovered during the inspection of the reclaimed transports. Painted in soot black that enhanced their sinister appearance, they resembled an armored personnel carrier. They moved on large spoke wheels and each carried four laser guns.

"The Rulers will attack your troops with these machines," Nardum said. "They use them on Pozzen to terrorize my people. They have bigger versions that can easily destroy buildings."

"The Terran name closest to their Ruler term is Marauder," Nonforense said. "It sounds nasty."

The comnets marked the six months since FEEF's departure with special features and hours of speculation by scientific and military commentators on how the soldiers and pilots would mark the occasion.

Benjamin Kendo organized a ceremony at the UN to honor the Feefers. He unveiled a monument commemorating the thousands of soldiers who served as international peacekeepers during the last century.

Meanwhile, the Being embassy Terraumblaw invited representatives of all the countries that had contributed to FEEF to an outdoor open house to meet a newly-arrived team of Being scientists. They explained their techniques to further cleanse Earth's atmosphere as well as how to build more effective solar and wind power systems.

To answer a question about the current location of FEEF, Ambassador Bemmonloda did quick calculations on a small analyzer. "This is just a guess, but unless some major complications have developed, they should at least have reached the Nameless bases on the other side of our worlds. We all hope it goes as well as it did in the first part of the mission."

The next question dealing with Pozzen posed a more difficult answer for him. "I don't know what will happen when they reach Pozzen. While our technology seems far superior, your own history shows the toughest battles often occur on the home territory of a combatant. Remember I have no training or inclination to be a warrior so you would probably be in a better position to answer that question than I."

None of the speculation about FEEF concerned Kendo who left New York right after the ceremony for his first real holiday in years. Sitting in the shade at an ocean side resort in South Africa, he stared at the ocean. Wave watching had always brought him hours of contentment as the rhythmic sounds of water lulled him into a somewhat meditative trance.

While it was too soon to say Earth's atmosphere and weather had improved because of the Being cleanup, Benjamin didn't disagree with anyone giving the aliens and the UN credit. He pondered ways to lever the accolades into a bigger role for the organization in Earth's future. That success allowed him to forget at least temporarily the nagging uncertainty of not knowing what dangers Earth's soldiers and pilots faced.

Later in the holiday, Benjamin's tranquility would be interrupted by requests from Bemmonloda for more medical, agricultural, educational and police personnel for Mandela.

With the pay and other rewards the Beings were offering, Benjamin had anticipated there would be a significant migration of people to Mandela. He saw no point in disputing the Being decision to ban religious missionaries on Mandela even though many groups on Earth would have lots to say about it. He figured if they didn't like it, they could take up the matter with Bemmonloda.

One issue he hadn't discussed with the Ambassador was whether Earth should shift some of its population to Mandela. Although a Being cruiser could protect Earth, the Stephen Hawking Institute had gained a lot of support for its plan to move millions of humans to Mandela. Under the Institute's plan, there would initially be no integration with the Corens until they were ready for contact with the newcomers.

Benjamin's thoughts strayed from the issues of Mandela to the planet Kendo and the pilots and soldiers who'd seen it. That led him to wonder about their current whereabouts. He stopped himself. That was a path he didn't want to venture down. He focused again on the caressing motions of the dancing turquoise waters.

Alliance and *New Jersey* pounded Alpha's protective wall while troops and tanks took up position around the base. Soldiers and troopers advanced toward it through rolling plains of short grass that released a stomach-churning odor when stepped on.

Nonforense had calculated a bombardment pattern to wear down the wall faster than the random blasts of the first attack. "Even with the tanks chipping in, this is going to take a while," Vasile told Whiz. They crouched close to the front line hidden behind a low hill. "If it weren't for this stinking grass, the troops could stand down for a while. I am not sure how much longer we can withstand this smell."

When the patterned pummeling finally took its toll creating large gaps in the screen, Whiz transmitted Nardum's message to the base.

The response came in the ear-splitting roar of a convoy of Marauders and other wheeled vehicles surging from the base, lasers spitting in every direction. Ruler aircraft soared into the skies to challenge the jets and fighters.

"They're too close to our lines to use the laser cannons on them," Vasile said. He ordered a fallback to enable the troops to regroup against the assault. Marauders attacked with wild abandon and the tanks fought back. Clouds of fine soil interspersed with acrid smoke from burning machines filled the air. The whine of dueling aircraft added to the cacophony.

Vasile peered over his shoulder at approaching footsteps. Pqwnrx was in charge of questioning citizens since Nardum had departed on *Enterprise*. "We have determined the location of the Nameless and Pozzens inside the base. I'll gather other citizens to come with me to collect them."

"We'll send some troopers to help you and monitor your movements to make sure you find them all," Vasile replied. "They have location transmitters. As soon as we can, we'll start removing the Nameless and Pozzens to the transport ships." Before he could explain further, his communicator beeped.

"All the Nameless have been removed from Beta," Demmloda said. "The transports have room for some from Alpha."

"We'll have to wait until after the battle to organize their departure," he replied. "Also we're going to need more medical help because we've lots of wounded down here." He followed the rapidly-shifting battle on his communicator screen as tanks rumbled past his position to enter the fray, their operators riding on them until they got closer to the fighting.

The soldiers and troopers trying to contain the Ruler breakout had regrouped at an area of huge rocks and boulders. While the Marauders wouldn't get far in the jungle surrounding the base, Juan didn't relish trying to track down any Rulers who escaped into the thick growth.

Shielded by the rocks, the soldiers and troopers, backed up by the tanks as they arrived, laid down a devastating barrage. Fighters joined in the assault on the Marauders. As the vehicles were knocked out of action, Rulers sprang from them and continued the fight.

A Marauder made a dash for the jungle until repeated laser strikes brought it to a halt. Its back doors popped open and four Rulers sprinted for cover among the rocks, their lasers blazing. More machines followed attempting to reach the forest.

The closest a Ruler made it was about 150 meters.

The Being fleet had dropped out of galaxy speed close to Pozzen. "The view is almost romantic, my dear." Chris Donohue had his arm around Elinor Brady as they watched a three-D display of the planet that filled a corner of the *Enterprise* Conference Room. "I keep hoping we'll find more planets comparable to Earth instead of ones suited for the Beings. So far we've only got Kendo and Mandela and the ones with ruins on them."

She leaned into him. "Maybe I'll get to visit this one." Her time on Mandela and Kendo made her wish she'd toured the other planets.

"Nardum hasn't succeeded in contacting any defenders yet," Chris said. "There're about seventeen million citizens down there, most of who live in the five cities. Much of the planet is desert or scrub forest, although there're large tracts of land reserved for the Rulers."

"Pozzen sounds like a feudal society," she said. "The Rulers tend to live apart from the others. Nardum has risen about as high as a citizen can. It's a crime for them to possess a weapon and they must do anything a Ruler commands or be executed. The Rulers keep them disorganized, mainly by killing anyone who shows leadership ability."

Chris didn't reply as he wanted to enjoy the time with her. He squeezed a bit tighter.

On the Command Chamber's main display Nardum stared at an image of Pozzen as he worked with the Controlling Unit to contact the defenders. While it had discovered a lot of activity on the surface, Turing couldn't provide any details, which had made him anxious about the fate of his family.

The frequencies used by the defenders hummed with warnings about roving Marauders and Rulers. Finally, Turing reached a harried operator who sounded dubious about Nardum's claim to have warriors to fight the Rulers.

Able to understand only snatches of the frantic communications, Fassad Hurandi had called to Atdomorsin. "Does Nardum know what's happening down there?"

"It must not be good because he's very agitated by the chaotic state of the defenders."

With an exasperated grunt, Nardum ended the transmission and spoke in a rapid-fire voice. "The Rulers have fled the cities. We do not know where they are, but they've launched relentless attacks, striking wherever we gather. Thousands are dead already while the rest hide from the aircraft and Marauders, which destroy any building they suspect citizens are in."

He raised his arms, palms up. "Their machines will just keep on slaughtering my people. We mean nothing to the Rulers."

"We'll launch jets and fighters as soon as we're in range so we can reconnoiter the planet," Fassad said.

Atdomorsin peered at him. "Aren't you worried that your plan is close to the Council's plan to obliterate the Renegades?"

"We're trying to save most of them. What happens to the Rulers is another matter." His voice gaining certainty with every word, Fassad said, "Captains Jiabao and Donohue will have the authority to take any necessary action. We will prepare the soldiers and troopers for dispatch as soon as we can determine safe landing spots." He then spoke into his communicator. "Pilots and flyers proceed directly to the planet with your squads. Details on your missions will be provided later." He hesitated to make sure he put enough emphasis in his final words. "Prepare the craft for aerial combat and ground support."

Chris gave Elinor a passionate kiss and turned on his heel to join his squadron. "I love you," she called to him. She had never said that to anyone but her parents. She shuddered at the thought of him never returning. He turned and blew her a kiss. She forced herself not to call him back. His squadron was needed on this crucial mission. Still she hadn't gotten the chance to tell him the big news. What if he never knew that he was the father of what she was sure was the first human child conceived off the Earth? Well, other than Corens perhaps.

She patted her stomach. "Well little one, your Daddy is going to be very surprised with our news. You certainly surprised me," she whispered. For years, she didn't want to have children. Now she was on the verge of becoming as obsessed as her mother about babies. The constant nagging for grandchildren used to infuriate her. Now she wanted to talk with her mother more than anyone.

She headed for the room where she and Morrow monitored the visuals from the jets and fighters.

Chris sat in the cockpit waiting for his new mechanics to complete their preparations. He looked at the small bulge on the nose of the jet that housed the recorder and thought of Elinor reviewing what he would see. He hoped that didn't include his jet disintegrating. Suddenly his craft moved forward jarring him out of his reverie. After more than a 100 flights together, Armstrong acted in anticipation of his commands. He had a hunter mentality. *How much of that is programming and how much is a reflection of me?*

Following him were 39 craft, mostly fighters piloted by flyers including Don and Hue. They slipped into the atmosphere and streaked toward the planet. Turing supplied the coordinates for their first mission. "You're to provide air cover for a large group of citizens gathered on the west side of Onnapozzen. They're under constant attack."

Wxdot Gruumon looked at his laser rifle in disgust. Although he'd treasured it as a symbol of defiance against the Rulers, it had no effect on the aircraft that bombed and strafed the citizens under his protection. In the distance, he could hear the rumble of Marauders. His weapon wouldn't stop them either.

Thousands of citizens gathered in his neighborhood, hoping

to flee into the hilly countryside west of Onnapozzen. Ruler aircraft had struck every group that tried. Mangled bodies of dead citizens lay scattered everywhere. The buildings were in ruins and thick clouds of heavy, black smoke blocked the sunlight. In the midst of the devastation, survivors huddled waiting for the darkness of nightfall when they might slip away a few at a time.

Howls from the wounded and the frightened pierced Wxdot's body like a knife. He knew if the rest of these people stayed here too much longer, the Marauders would find them.

The scream of aircraft flying overhead shook him out of his funk. Through the clouds he caught glimpses of what looked like Ruler machines. Among them flew two disc shaped craft that emitted a piercing whistle. He'd never seen anything like them before. They had to be new Ruler weapons. The formation wheeled over the city followed by a similar one and their sounds faded.

He remembered his mother telling him not to raise his fist against the Rulers because of their endless power. Another squad of aircraft approached. He counted 11 Ruler craft lining up for a strafing run at his district. As he yelled for everyone to take cover, the strange craft re-appeared shooting streaks of light at the Ruler machines, which crumbled into clouds of fine particles.

This time Wxdot noticed small wings near the nose of what he thought were Ruler machines as the formation roared off over the city. A few minutes later, another flight of Ruler craft bore down on his location. Once again the strange formation returned and destroyed them. He cheered loudly even though he'd no idea who his protectors were.

Emboldened by Wxdot's whoops, citizens cautiously emerged for their own look. As he recounted the battle in the air, they broke into cheers and excited chatter. After the disasters of the last few days, this small triumph brought them hope.

He couldn't report the new craft or learn about the fighting elsewhere because his communicator had died. "Stay here and don't wander in case the Marauders come. I'll find out what's going on," he shouted to the Pozzens he'd been guarding.

Jogging through block after block of ruined streets, he dodged piles of rubble and destroyed vehicles, relieved to see few bodies. He spotted the occasional frightened citizen peeking out a window or doorway. Once again, the strange formation returned and dove on a nearby district firing at targets on the ground. Wxdot hoped the booms were exploding Marauders.

He ducked into an alleyway when he heard the whir of an electric vehicle. An old open cab truck rounded the corner. He jumped out and waved. The driver and two passengers belonged to his troop. The vehicle screeched to a halt and its occupants all talked at once. Wxdot raised his hands. "My communicator is broken. Who's attacking the Rulers?"

Sommon Prozen, an old school mate, said, "Your uncle Nardum has come with help called Terrans. They destroyed the Ruler aircraft and Marauders. They are sending warriors to protect us. He's landing at the park with them. Let's go."

"What about all the citizens around here? We have to tell them something." Wxdot's duty was to protect his neighborhood although he wanted to hear more about his uncle.

"We'll drive through the streets telling everyone the news and they can spread it," Sommon said. "Come on."

Wxdot climbed onto the back of the truck and the vehicle rumbled off. It stopped every block or so as they took turns yelling out the news. Their throats had become hoarse from shouting when Aannder Hilokvon spotted the shuttles.

Sommon revved up the vehicle and they lurched off bouncing violently because of the rigid wheels. The scream of the approaching shuttles frightened most people into hiding and their vehicle arrived at the park without having to slow down.

"They're supposed to land their craft there," said a defender who pointed to the center of the circular field as he tried to get a few curious citizens to move back. "Machines and warriors will come out of them. After they leave, others will take their place."

The first shuttle touched down blowing a cloud of dirt and debris into the air. Several others landed beside it. The back of the craft opened like a giant jaw and uniformed figures dashed out to press small sticks into the ground. When they got closer, the figures looked like short citizens in grey shirts and pants.

"They're marking landing spots for more shuttles," shouted the defender who'd cleared the park.

Four figures stood near the back of the shuttle. Spotting the defenders, they strode toward them. As they drew closer, Wxdot recognized his uncle and ran to greet him. He could hear his pals following. The joy on Nardum's face quickly drove any thoughts of a trap. The other creatures wore helmets and brown and gray uniforms. In their arms, they cradled laser rifles that looked a lot more imposing than Wxdot's.

While he hadn't hugged his uncle since he was a youngster, in his excitement to see Nardum, he threw his arms around him. The armful of weapons made a full hug almost impossible.

His uncle smiled broadly and then hushed the defenders. "We have to move away so more shuttles can land. I need to explain how to guide the warriors."

When Wxdot saw the faces of the others, his hopes shattered. "They're things. Where are the warriors?"

"There is much to explain so listen as we walk," Nardum said, beckoning the four closer. "The ones that look like things are Terrans. They come from a faraway planet. The ones that look like us are called troopers. You can speak to the troopers. Both are very brave warriors. They can help rid us of the Rulers. The next craft will bring big machines and more warriors. You will guide their squads."

Shuttles landing in the park drowned out his next comments so he pinned buttons on the front of their jackets. When the commotion subsided, he said, "Now you can hear all the communications among the warriors." He pointed to an approaching Terran. "Lieutenant Feldez is in charge. Permit me to make some introductions. This is my nephew Wxdot."

Juan raised his right arm for a handshake. "Oh, they will not understand that." Nardum completed the handshake. "This is a Terran greeting."

Wxdot extended his arm. There was firmness in the Terran's grip.

Pointing at the communicators, Juan said in Beingish, "They'll enable us to track your location. We'll issue communicators and weapons to other defenders."

Turbulence rumbled through the park again as shuttles departed and more landed. Troops poured out of them and took up positions in units of six in lines spaced from the shuttles to where Nardum and the others stood. Then tanks floated out.

"Finally, something that can attack the Marauders." Wxdot raised an arm in triumph. A Terran and five troopers climbed onto each tank. With a whistling sound, the machines headed toward Juan.

"I need a guide for this squad," Juan said. "Although the tanks are programmed with maps of the city, there may be better ways of getting around the damaged areas."

Only four warriors rode on the first tank. Juan and Hukaru climbed on and beckoned for Wxdot to join him. "Nardum will help organize the reinforcements."

Wxdot clambered up and the machine surged forward. He managed a weak smile at the other warriors. One held a small black box. In response to a command from Juan, the warrior dragged his finger across it and the tank gained speed. Soon the convoy headed down a main road faster than Wxdot had ever traveled. Startled knots of citizens peeked out of doors and windows at the tanks. He stood up to greet them and almost fell off. Hukaru grabbed him and pulled his hand to a ring. Hanging on tightly to it, he waved again hoping the citizens would realize his presence on this alien machine meant the liberation they'd all prayed for had become a possibility.

After several kilometers, a small group of citizens appeared holding up their crossed arms. "That means danger," Wxdot said.

"All tanks halt," Juan barked. The troopers jumped off as they slowed. Wxdot leapt after his new mates. One caught him as he stumbled and directed him toward Juan. "Find out if any Marauders or Rulers are nearby."

Although Wxdot waved at the citizens to keep fleeing, a few stopped to peer at the tanks and point at Juan and the troopers. "They have come to help us," he shouted. "They gave me this." He held up his laser rifle. It made him feel a lot braver. The citizens pointed anxiously behind them at the sound of distant screams and yells and the hiss of laser weapons.

He relayed the information to Juan who ordered the soldiers and troopers to spread out. "Wxdot, if there are any more defenders, we'll give them communicators. No point in shooting them by accident."

Wxdot ran ahead, screaming at citizens to hurry past the troops and the tanks. After a few minutes, he spotted another defender. Makust's right arm dangled awkwardly and he limped behind a group of citizens. "The Rulers are in for a surprise," Wxdot said when he reached him.

"What are they?" Makust demanded nodding at the tanks and troopers, wincing with every movement.

"Terrans. They will rid us of the Rulers."

Makust didn't look convinced.

"We'll have someone here soon to treat your wounds," Juan said. "Are there more citizens and where is the Ruler army?"

He swayed on his feet. "Citizens everywhere," he muttered. "Rulers that way." He tilted his head to indicate the direction. "While we tried to slow them down, the Rulers have too much firepower."

Makust teetered on the edge of collapse. "Why don't you sit down for a few minutes?" Wxdot said. He took an arm to help Makust ease himself to the ground. "Do any other defenders have communicators?"

"Haven't heard from any in a while."

"We have to warn them about the Terrans so there are no misunderstandings," Wxdot said.

Makust held out a battered brown box to Wxdot who immediately pushed the alert button. "If any one received that, we will receive return signals," he told Juan. The box beeped several times. Wxdot put the unit in front of Makust and pushed the speaking tab.

"Wxdot Gruumon brings help," the wounded defender said.

"They're wearing brown and grey uniforms and some of them look like us and some like things," Wxdot said. "Do a quick fallback to their positions. They'll give you better weapons and communicators."

Makust had closed his eyes. He opened them when a Medbiot sprayed a liquid on the laser burn on his right arm.

"You'll feel a lot better when you wake," the Medbiot said. "This will help heal your wounds. A vehicle will take you to a place for treatment."

Before he lost consciousness, Makust pointed shakily to Wxdot's weapon. "Shoot one of the bastards for me."

Spotting a couple of citizens racing down an empty street toward them with a Marauder in pursuit, Juan and Hukaru slid the power setting on their rifles to medium and fired. The blasts rocked the machine and their second ones brought it to an abrupt halt.

No other Marauders followed so Juan sprinted to it and vaulted up onto the small flat spot in the middle of its top. He flipped open a port and waited. When no one fired at him, he peered inside. "*Enterprise*," he barked over his communicator. "The Marauder is crewless. We saw it tracking and firing at some citizens so it must be analyzer controlled. You can probably see it all on Hukaru's visual. Perhaps a full charge stun gun would disrupt its analyzer."

He waved at two citizens cautiously approaching the machine. Suddenly, one shrieked in horror. Another Marauder rumbled toward them.

"How convenient, here comes our test subject." Juan swung his back pack in front of him and drew a stun gun from a side pocket, selected maximum power and fired at the approaching Marauder. It coasted to a halt as a blue haze flared around it. He cautiously advanced with his rifle pointed at the machine. "*Enterprise*, the stun gun worked."

"It's running," Hukaru shouted. "It could be dangerous."

"It sounds off line," Juan said. With a grunt, he added, "I'm boarding it to find out."

Gnoorvants said, "The jets still have the electronic signal generator. We'll see if it incapacitates the machines."

Wxdot examined the first Marauder before cautiously approaching the second one. He shook his head when Juan explained how the stun gun had stopped it. "After all the killing and suffering those machines have caused and they could be defeated that simply."

"*Enterprise*, I'm on top of my Marauder. Hukaru is inside. Check his signal. We need help figuring out its analyzer system. Can we reprogram it to attack the Rulers?"

"We'll examine his transmission."

Defenders clambered on board and peered at the ton puzzling over the control panel. "Know how these work?" Juan said. They looked at one another blankly which he took for no.

"While we're getting good images of the controls, we cannot understand them yet," Atdomorsin said.

The next transmission started with a hearty snort from the reclusive Cubunowres. "You're too young, Atdomorsin. Machines like that were common on our world before Transformation. This one appears to have the same kind of analyzer unit. Ton Hukaru, push the triangular button to the left of the main display."

Rows of images appeared on the display. "Put your finger on the first image." It depicted a citizen. "At the bottom of the display are light and dark dots. Push the dark one. That'll tell the analyzer not to attack citizens." The citizen image flashed. "The analyzer is confirming the change in command."

"So I push the light dot for targets the machine is to attack and the dark for no's."

"Precisely."

"How would the Rulers protect themselves?" Juan inquired; impressed he could follow the conversation between Cubunowres and Hukaru.

"They must wear a badge that the analyzer would read as

friendly."

After the citizens came images of buildings and other structures. Finally, various war machines appeared and Hukaru touched the light button. The double-check symbol flashed and the trooper pressed the dark button again. The Marauder would attack its buddies and none would know to shoot back.

"That symbol means the program now is complete," Cubunowres said when the main display flashed repeatedly. "When you push the triangular button, the machine will start up again after a delay of about twenty seconds. You should get off before it goes into action."

"We want it to retrace its course so it'll find other Marauders," Juan said.

Cubunowres exhaled heartily. "Good plan. Push the triangular button a second time and then the symbol pointing downwards."

Juan reached down to help Hukaru out of the machine as he spoke to Cubunowres. "Thank you, sir. I'd like to shake your hand when I return to the ship."

"And I yours, young Terran. Humbaw was right."

Juan waited for Cubunowres to finish the statement, but he didn't. "I'd better put a communicator badge on this machine so we know it's on our side."

Several tanks arrived. Juan signaled to their operators to follow his Marauder, which had trundled off in the direction it had come from.

They traveled several blocks in single file before they found another Marauder. Spotting the newcomer, Juan's Marauder aimed at it, but its salvo blew a gaping hole in a building behind it.

Juan pulled out his stun gun and fired at the new Marauder. A blue flash of light swept over it. "One nothing, dummy," he called to his machine. It read the other was disabled and didn't fire at it again.

"I take it back," Juan said. "You're not so dumb after all. If anyone wants their own Marauder, all they have to do is zap it, open the cover on the turret and follow Cubunowres' instructions for reprogramming it. The troopers will know how to do it." Genghis jogged toward the disabled machine.

As soon as he had the second machine running, it joined the other Marauder at the front of the column. It turned left at a T intersection and down a broad thoroughfare into a column of advancing Marauders.

"Show time," Juan called over his communicator. "Stun guns on max."

Chapter 25
The Felauders Attack

When the two reprogrammed Marauders opened fire, the turrets on the Ruler machines scanned back and forth as if searching for their attackers.

"They don't realize we're right in front of them," Juan said. A squad of soldiers and troopers slipped behind buildings and ran down alleys to get into position to start knocking out the newly-arrived Marauders with their stun guns. His machines hadn't caused much damage before the enemy was disabled. Troopers climbed on to reprogram them.

With the takeover completed, Juan sent the nine Marauders in advance of his 14 tanks. "We should call them Fernandez's Marauders or just Felauders." Hukaru slapped him on the back. "For a Prim, you're a smart dude."

Felauders had their limitations. "They halt all the time to look for targets when we want them to lead us to the Rulers," Juan grumbled.

Wxdot and other defenders took advantage of the frequent stops to call to any citizens who might be nearby. The troopers soon learned his message and boomed it out as well.

"Do you think there's anyone in this city, probably on the whole planet, who can't hear them," Juan said. "Any louder and they would deafen me and cause buildings to collapse."

Juan's units were near the center of Onnapozzen. The washed-out grey buildings appeared almost identical. "Must be a shortage of architects," he muttered.

Atdomorsin's voice crackled over the communicator. "Marauders are advancing westwards up the road you are about to intersect. There are attack craft coming at you as well. Fighters are moving to intercept."

"We'll wait here for the rest of the tanks," Juan said. "Also the soldiers, troopers and defenders are checking the neighborhood for citizens."

At that moment, a defender shouted from a doorway down a side street. Wxdot ran to him, and after a short conversation, called over his communicator. "Where are the healers? There're a lot of wounded citizens in this building."

"They'll be here soon," Hukaru said. "Can the defender stay

with them?"

"He doesn't want to leave the wounded unattended upstairs, but if he doesn't stay in the street, how will healers find this place."

Juan pulled a silver cylinder from his pack and tossed it to a trooper. "Stick this in the rubble near the alleyway. The next column will receive its signal and know Medbiots are needed here." Juan keyed his communicator. "A lot of bad guys are headed our way. Troopers and soldiers fan out. We'll send our machines to engage them."

At first, the Felauders and tanks encountered more Marauders. The laser battles lasted until the stun guns took care of the opposition. Then Supermarauders arrived. Not only were they bigger and more heavily armed, the stun guns didn't stop them and they destroyed the Felauders after a short fire fight. "These new machines must be operated by Rulers, not analyzers," Juan said. When the tanks entered the battle, it became a slugfest between heavyweights that rocked the city.

"The tanks have to score a couple of direct hits to knock out the big guys," Juan told *Enterprise*. "As soon as the Super Marauders come under attack, heavily-armed Rulers run from them. It sounds like more of those machines are approaching."

As well, small aircraft buzzed overhead. Figuring they were surveillance drones, Juan ordered the troopers to shoot them down. Hukaru hit one with his second try and it exploded in a shower of debris.

Laser blasts flashed up and down the street, frequently striking buildings. Chunks of blasted machinery and building debris piled up. One tank was disabled by a direct hit, but kept firing. A second exploded after a direct hit while several Supermarauders emitted clouds of acrid fumes. The buildings along the road amplified the noise of the battle and kept the smoke and dust from blowing away.

Overhead, jets and fighters swooped down on Ruler aircraft. As much as he wanted to stay at the front, Juan hung back to wait for reinforcements and direct his units. In addition to the 27 tanks in action, he had numerous wounded soldiers and troopers to gather up. Guided by defenders, soldiers and troopers ranged through the surrounding neighborhoods eradicating pockets of Rulers.

"When you find a secure spot, we'll send shuttles there with reinforcements and remove the wounded," Atdomorsin told him.

"There're two more columns of tanks and troops coming from the park. There's also a small group of Marauders moving in behind your position. We've highlighted them on the tactical analyzers."

Juan and Hukaru headed back to the intersection to dispatch tanks to meet the latest threat and arrange for the collection of wounded soldiers and damaged troopers. The reinforcement column reached it just after he did. Lieutenant Boris Malinkoff from the Russian Army jumped off the first machine.

"We need tanks and troops to intercept Rulers sneaking up behind us." Juan pointed northwards. "The rest of your unit will go to the main battle, about five kilometers that way." He indicated in an easterly direction. "Watch for debris and aircraft. You decide who goes where, but we need you at the front to direct our forces while we gather the wounded."

Boris ordered the column forward. He called a halt and ordered the last six tanks to take the other road and intercept the approaching Marauders.

Trotting behind Boris's tanks, Juan spotted a large crowd watching Medbiots tending to wounded citizens. "Send visuals of this scene to the ships," he told Hukaru. Two citizens holding youngsters anxiously waved and he returned their greeting.

Despite the smoke and devastation, more citizens appeared calling greetings to each other and blessings for their deliverance. The celebration didn't last long. The scream of approaching aircraft sent the citizens rushing for cover. Juan had the first craft in his sights when it abruptly plummeted to the ground and exploded. "Damn pilots," he grumbled, "taking all the fun out of our adventure." He found it strange that he hadn't heard the whistle of a jet or the crunch of a laser beam hitting the aircraft. In fact, the city had become eerily quiet except for the occasional tank blast at gangs of Rulers.

"All units report," Atdomorsin called over his communicator.

"The Ruler machines stopped operating and their aircraft crashed," Juan replied. "It's like they were turned off. What's going on?" Similar puzzled observations poured in from elsewhere in the city.

"We have destroyed their communications link for Onnapozzen and they cannot function without the signals," Atdomorsin explained. "Proceed with eliminating any Rulers."

"We've got defenders, soldiers, troopers and tanks mopping up the last squads of them," Juan radioed Boris. "We'll look after gathering up the wounded and organizing patrols out of those who can still fight."

"We'll need lots of transports," Boris said.

"I'll assign my ton and Genghis to that." They dashed off while Juan created seven patrols out of a mixture of defenders, troopers and soldiers, who were all as hot, dirty, and thirsty and exhausted as him. The troopers needed a way to cool off. All they could do was wave their hands back and forth to dissipate their internal heat. "It will be a fight to the death with any Rulers you find so be careful."

The tons rounded up nearly 20 tanks still in operating condition along with a few Marauders and even some Supermarauders. Also there were units that could be towed like wagons.

"Good work. Get whoever you need to drive them back here collecting the wounded as you go," Juan said. "If you find any citizens who need help, mark their positions. *Enterprise* is organizing a full sweep of the city by defenders and our troops to look for them and any remaining Rulers."

The convoy arrived with Hukaru and Genghis sitting on the lead unit, which carried a defender pennant on a hastily rigged pole. Wounded soldiers and damaged troopers covered several machines already.

"What happened to the Rulers?" a wounded soldier asked when he spotted Juan. "We ended up behind a building that had exploded and the patrols couldn't hear us because of the noise."

As Juan recounted the battle, citizens appeared. When Wxdot returned to announced his patrol had killed every Ruler they could locate, the crowd burst into cheers and began dancing and singing.

Chapter 26
The Link to Earth

Ruth Huxley's first two months at Mandela had passed in a blur of activity. It was mid-summer and yellow and orange flowers dotted the shrubs. Crops planted in the early days of the settlement swayed in the breeze. The harvesting of vegetables was underway. It would be a while before the sweet corn was ready, she noted wistfully during her morning walk. She looked forward to that treat.

She always walked around Mandela on her way to and from her laboratory both at the hospital both for the exercise and to see the steady progress in the community. The home building continued with the Corens doing much of the work under supervision by Constructbiots. Children trekked to school. The youngest chattered in excited voices. They hadn't taken chemicals as long and the effects on them were far less. The older ones said little and still showed hints of the disconnected Nameless appearance.

Ruth planned to spend time in the classroom to observe how the young Corens adjusted to learning. Their parents had been trained for specific roles and little else. She'd hoped that they would understand the importance of the schools to their future. The majority of Corens still underwent rehabilitation from the chemicals as well as learning to look after their homes and how their new society worked.

As usual, her three tons, Huxton, Altaton and Florton, and Umet, her new assistant, accompanied her on the walks, peppering her with questions. Few Terrans lived on Mandela. As a result, the tons had become Ruth's companions. They paid close attention to her and if she ever felt despondent or lonely, they immediately set to cheering her up. She finally realized they wanted to become more than her assistants. They wished to be her friends.

At first, she'd found their queries simple to answer. Lately, they'd delved into Ruth's research into memories and the working of the human mind that might lead to ways to improve the recovery of the Nameless. She stayed up late at night finding answers to their questions. Whatever she read, the tons would study as well triggering even more questions.

She had the perfect academic life. Mandela was her Institute and the Corens her research project. Her research had started with Micheline Azwatta's observation that "rehabilitating the Nameless is a lot like treating people emerging from a long coma. Except that we aren't explaining to them what they missed during a few months or years. We're preparing them to live in a society where they're in charge."

Ruth decided to stop to observe a construction team organizing its work for the day. When Umet and the tons moved beside her, she said, "My goal is to see if the Nameless have any memories of their past. I began interviewing them following the removal of the controller to establish a baseline of what we can expect them to know.

"Right now, they learn by watching us and the Biots. Most recall little beyond family members and the role the Rulers assigned them. I've kept at it hoping to spark thoughts beyond the numbing routine of the bases."

Shaking her head for emphasis, she said, "As despicable as the Ruler treatment was, the chemicals certainly were effective. The Nameless did what they were told, when they were told and nothing more. They certainly couldn't have caused any trouble. I'm gathering all these snippets of memories. So far, there's not enough to guess at their meaning. Someday, it might all become clear."

Umet frowned. "I have much to learn, but at least I didn't go through what they did." She'd gained access to the files in Hippocratica, the medical Controlling Unit. "The Medbiots love to teach me things."

Umet was adjusting to Mandela faster than the other Corens. Ruth knew Juan's messages of encouragement helped her a lot.

"Piecing together the Nameless memories is like finding a few pieces of jigsaw puzzle and trying to imagine what the picture is," Ruth said. "What's really frustrating is some of them appear to possess memories that are blocked, probably by the influence of the chemicals."

When Umet and the rest of Sinomla's Corens had arrived on Mandela, they'd been kept separate at first to allow Ruth to study them. After their integration with the others, Umet had volunteered to help the Nameless after the removal of their controllers.

Sinomla often accompanied Ruth during the interviews. "I may be able to pick out something you would overlook or not fully appreciate," he'd said.

She rather enjoyed his company. "It would help the medical team a lot if, like Umet, you could talk with the Nameless every day," Ruth said. "As they recover, they become curious why Corens and Terrans are so much like them. We need to convince them they can become like us."

Sinomla nodded and Ruth beamed at him. "Micheline and Henri will continue their projects to improve the medical health of the recovering Nameless and ease them onto a solid diet. Few of them can yet handle Terran food and the Supershake is still the most popular meal."

The tons and Umet all laughed. "You would think they would tire of it," Florton said. "Their food must have been really terrible."

"Dr Azwatta is concerned that even after the controllers are removed, the Nameless continue to suffer mysterious diseases and conditions," Umet said.

As they reached the hospital, Henri joined them. "So how are your interviews coming? Your subjects tell me the questions are very confusing."

"We think some have memories that have been blocked by the chemicals. Although I'm stumped by how to help them, I want to continue the interviews." The doctors considered her memory recovery project mostly wishful thinking.

Later in the day, Ruth strode from her lab with a big smile on her face. She found the doctors in a Conference Room examining X-rays of Nameless patients. "Finally, I may be getting somewhere. There's a teenager Brona who can recount some events."

"Wow, now that's unusual," Micheline said pointing Ruth to a chair.

"After describing games she played as a kid and who her friends were, she looked at Sinomla and asked, 'Are you from our home?' He was surprised and asked her where she was talking about." Ruth pulled out her portable analyzer and said, "Here's the pertinent part of the interview."

On the display, Sinomla said, "We always lived on the other planet until we moved here."

"We come from far away." Brona looked dejected. "This is not our home."

Ruth froze the image and said, "Brona was from one of the first bases." She let the interview resume. Brona's face was screwed up in concentration. "It has been a long time since we were taken from our home. Many, many ages. My grandmother said where we come from was a lot nicer than where we lived. She told me a lot more that I can't recall."

Ruth stopped the recording. "We have to retrieve the rest of the girl's memories."

"Before, you said that seventeen Nameless had vague memories of being different because they come from somewhere else." Micheline looked at her ton for confirmation. She nodded.

"Hippocratica says that even with Brona's recollections, the information is insufficient to postulate any theories about the origin of the Nameless," Ruth said. "However, I told Arthur Lorne, a colleague back home, about the scattered memories of a faraway world. As they clearly originate from Earth, he is looking for possibilities."

The next morning, Brona sat in Ruth's lab with her head in her hands. "I can't remember anything more."

Henri entered the lab just as Brona spoke her last sentence. "You could try hypnosis on her." Brona looked at him blankly while Altaton and Huxton consulted data files. Umet put her arms around Brona to console her.

"Henri, do you know how to do it?" Ruth asked.

"I participated in some sessions on it during my hospital training. While I'll need to update myself, I'm sure we can make it work. Especially with all our helpers," Henri said.

Although it didn't take long for Henri to hypnotize Brona, after several hours her memories hadn't become clearer.

Ruth was asleep when Altaton pounded on her door. "Brona remembers more. Come quickly."

The girl lay in her bed, tears streaming down her face. Wiping her face with a sheet, she recounted her restored memory of her grandmother's tales of coming from another world as Altaton recorded it.

Before breakfast, Ruth played the recording for the other doctors and Medbiots in the medical conference room. Brona stifled more sobs as she stared at the visual of her spilling the long buried memory. "How would I have remembered without the help of the doctors? How was I supposed to fulfill Grandma's wishes?"

Umet quieted her before saying. "We transcribed her comments to remove all the interruptions."

On the screen Brona appeared recounting her story.

"Grandma did not know anything about the Old Masters other than they could change their appearance to resemble us. She doesn't know what they really looked like. The knew their vessel had broken down and they could not tell if their call for help was picked up by others of their kind so they set up a colony and gathered some people to work for them. The Old Masters had wonderful machines, everything was bright and there was lots of food. After many, many years, a rescue ship came. Rather than leave any trace of their presence, the Old Masters destroyed where they lived and took away the people who worked for them. Grandma didn't know how we came to be under the control of the Rulers instead of the Old Masters. They were quite different."

The room was silent as everyone digested the story. Umet pointed at Ruth. "You and I come from the same planet as her. Someday, we will go there." She held Brona as tears again streamed down her face. Umet's face was wet as well.

"I'll send this information to Arthur to see if this helps him," Ruth said. "We should try hypnosis on the others who have memories of the other world." Ruth put her arms around the two women.

The doctors agreed. "We'll inform Humbaw and Hector about what've learned," Micheline said. "Humbaw thought the genetic and DNA difference between the Nameless and us was probably nothing more than living on different planets."

"I will tell Elinor," Ruth said. She sat on the other side of Brona and stroked her hair. "You may remember more in the coming days. You must tell us about anything that comes back. When you're ready, you will have to recount your story for all the Corens because it's their story too."

"The Renegades or their predecessors must have had a rigorous breeding program because there's no evidence of inbreeding," Henri added. "Of course, they would've killed any children that weren't right."

The fulsome congratulations and praise from Humbaw and Hector for the discovery embarrassed Ruth. "Micheline, the other doctors and my assistants helped a great deal. We'll inform the Secretary General. Our conclusion will generate plenty of controversy."

"The credit must go to Ruth," Micheline interjected. "Her curiosity got us started. She worked tirelessly on it. The Medbiots helped a great deal. Nothing fascinates them more than a deep mystery."

Humanity's Saving Grace

Chapter 27
Ye Olde Castle

The *Enterprise's* Command Chamber was still celebrating the shutdown of the Ruler war machines when Chris Donohue made his big discovery far to the west of Onnapozzen. "I'm flying toward what looks like an old castle with high walls and a massive keep. On its roof is a tall mast dotted with round and rectangular contraptions that must be communications dishes."

"We have your visual now," Fassad Hurandi said.

"*Enterprise*, there are no signs of any Rulers or Marauders," Chris reported. "We'll make another overpass so you can get a better view. Here we go." The excitement in his voice bubbled from the displays' speakers. "We'll spread out our approaches to give you a full view of this place."

"The hills behind the castle are an area that's closed to us," Nardum said. "There were always rumors it contained a Ruler headquarters. A place of evil, but it does have an air of majesty to it."

As they waited, Fassad explained the historic roles of castles on Earth to the puzzled Beings and Pozzens. The displays showed different views of Pozzen terrain from the sharply banking jets and fighters in the patrol. The view of the castle became clearer as the jets closed on it.

"*Enterprise* to Donohue, take out the mast," Gnoorvants ordered.

"Follow me in and fire at it until we are past," Chris said. The sound of his lasers firing rang through the Chamber. The mast reeled and swayed from the laser blasts, but remained standing. Chris banked sharply to line up for a second attack.

Mig was next. The displays showed his visual until he was past, and then switched to Don's craft. As he fired, the tower slowly toppled, bounced on the edge of the keep and tumbled end over end as it hurtled downwards. It landed on several small buildings, scattering debris and electrical charges through the courtyard.

"Nice shooting," Atdomorsin said. "We'll send soldiers and troopers to reconnoiter the area."

Silence greeted the shuttles that landed outside the castle. "The first squad will reconnoiter and open the gates into the courtyard," Vasile Stocia ordered. "Then we will check all the buildings. *Enterprise* says there are no Rulers here, but remain vigilant."

Cubunowres stepped cautiously from a shuttle. "Finally, I might be useful."

A trooper scaled the wall, dropped down and opened the gates from the inside. The soldiers and troopers fanned out through the courtyard, stepping warily around the toppled communications mast. They reported that the smaller structures were for repair and maintenance of the attack machines.

Vasile headed for the entrance to the keep until a trooper called out, "You might want to look at this, Captain." He and a couple of others had opened a double door on the side of the keep and found a descending staircase and elevator.

When Vasile reported the finding to *Enterprise*, Atdomorsin said, "Check out what's down there first. Our surveys didn't show anything underneath the keep it so it must be well shielded."

Vasile sent Shaka and a few troopers to explore the keep and stationed a couple at the double door while the rest of the inspection team cautiously descended the stairs with several troopers in the lead.

About 150 meters underground, they entered a large room packed with analyzers. "By all the flashing function lights, these machines must still work," Whiz said peering about. "What were they for?"

"They relayed orders to the machines and aircraft across the planet although without the communications mast, their commands won't be going anywhere," Cubunowres said.

"Maybe not everywhere else," Lxoc grumbled. "The Rulers had cables all over the planet. We tried to map their locations."

Cubunowres stared at the Pozzen, and with a nod of his head, strode to a bank of tall machines dotted with flashing lights. "These are the main control units for this facility. Everything else will be linked to them."

Once everyone gathered around them, Vasile said, "We have to get them out of battle and communications mode." Despite the troopers pushing buttons and uttering commands, the lights on the machines still flashed.

Nardum walked about the room in wide-eyed amazement. "The Rulers have a place called Sanctuary. But we don't know where it is."

Cubunowres coughed. "No wonder. It's not on this planet." He'd shuffled to a large black machine that had a keyboard. He ran his fingers over buttons and keys, which caused strange symbols to appear on its display.

The inspection team gathered around Cubunowres. "Similar devices from the era before Transformation existed when I was young. The High Council later had them destroyed. To show you I'm not a raving old coot, I'll shut down the rest of the war machines on this planet."

For several minutes the team watched in awe as the old Being's fingers flew across the keyboard. "Ask *Enterprise* what's happened."

Atdomorsin confirmed all the Ruler machines on Pozzen had stopped.

"When that gentleman," Cubunowres nodded at Nardum, "said there were cables all over the planet, I knew the Rulers had a backup system in case the mast malfunctioned."

Cubunowres' fingers continued to roam over the large keys of the machine and more symbols danced across its display, their meaning clear only to him. Finally he let out a triumphant roar. "I have found the location of their Sanctuary. It's on a large asteroid about a half light year from here.

"Most Rulers left Pozzen more than a week ago after putting their war machines on attack mode to work with the troops they left behind." His voice became steadily shriller. "The Rulers can signal this planet from their Sanctuary. Or they could. Perhaps it's a refuge in the event of a rebellion. The Marauders and troops would deal with the rebels and they could return when it was safe.

"Arrogant bastards never hid the location of their Sanctuary in their analyzer records. They must have thought no one else would ever gain access to them. It was easy to break into and figure out. They'll all die because they believed they're better than the rest of us!" He said no more although the many lines and creases on his face all ran together in an immense smile.

In little more than a day, the last scattered groups of armed Rulers had been hunted down. Gnoorvants decided to wait for the arrival of *Alliance* and the rest of the fleet before attacking the

Sanctuary. He shared Cubunowres' view that the Rulers wouldn't flee their refuge.

"It'll take all the troopers we have to help collect the Ruler weapons and machines and disable their military capacity so the Pozzens can use them as transports," Juan had said in a report from the planet. "While they're here, the troopers can also restore power and water distribution systems and set up supply centers. We've found lots of food on the planet tucked away in storehouses and some rather posh residences and retreats. The new government can deal with them."

Gnoorvants had replayed the next part of Juan's report several times. It made him feel confident about the future.

"We found many Rulers alive mostly because they were too badly wounded to kill themselves," Juan had said. "To my good fortune, I don't know what they said to the Pozzens. It was so disgusting my ton wouldn't translate it. At first, I instructed the soldiers to help them. Now we just inform the Pozzens of their location and leave it at that. The only condition is not to torture them although I suspect their deaths are rather unpleasant. I don't ask."

The cleanup on Pozzen continued until the other galaxyships arrived, and their victory celebrations resumed.

In her report, Elinor showed citizens gathered in a park walking about, hugging and singing. "The Pozzens from the three bases along with the twenty-three we captured in the first raids are preparing for a homecoming few dared to hope for--a world without Rulers."

She included an interview with Nardum. "The celebrations will carry on well into the night," he said. "That will be special for us because unless we were required by the Rulers, they would kill us if we were out of our places after dark."

Hector and Humbaw had spent many hours with the Pozzens on the trip to their home world discussing what the High Council expected of the new government as well as the assistance the Beings could provide. Earth would focus on helping Mandela.

"We set out to end attacks on our worlds and discovered much more than we could have imagined," Humbaw said in his interview for Elinor's report on the discussions. "With the Rulers eliminated, a new era of peace and progress will begin in our own region of space."

When Nardum joined the interview, Humbaw asked him, "Can you suggest Pozzens who might be willing to serve in a provisional government?"

"There're many, but it will depend on who is still alive," Nardum said. "I'll prepare a list that will include me."

With Pozzen in the hands of the citizens, that left the Sanctuary as the last task. Humbaw put on a solemn air for the recording by Morrow of his discussion with Hector in the Conference Room. He had wanted to put his remarks on the record in case the General's actions were ever questioned.

"To avoid placing you in a conflict with your orders from the Secretary General, I recommend all members of FEEF remain here. We plan to send the cruisers and armed transports to the Sanctuary. My orders from the High Council are to destroy it to obliterate the Rulers."

"Do you feel ready to take command of such an operation?" Hector asked.

"Gnoorvants and Atdomorsin have shown they possess the fortitude for it. When we're done, we'll take you home."

Hector reflected on all that the Feefers had accomplished in almost 14 months in space. His posting at the UN had left him in despair of mankind's future. Now a small slice of humanity had shown it could be a lot better. Hopefully, the rest of Earth would draw inspiration from FEEF's accomplishments. They had won the admiration of the Beings and the friendship of the Biots. The grim future he expected for his grandchildren looked more tolerable. He envied the Beings' long lives.

If he asked for volunteers, many Feefers would agree to help the Pozzens even though it meant an uncomfortable environment and few facilities and rations. He had no doubt that like him they would prefer to accompany the Beings to the Sanctuary to see the completion of their mission.

He also wrestled with the fate of the Rulers. As much as he abhorred the destruction of thousands of lives, he could think of no reason to spare them. It was hardly genocide. The evil they'd inflicted on the Corens was more than sufficient grounds for their execution. What they'd done to their own kind sealed their fate. The Rulers could be the Devil's henchmen.

Humbaw waited patiently for Hector's response.

"I wish to discuss it with my senior officers," he finally said. "Many will want to stay on your ships as that wouldn't violate our orders. No one could argue that we should've stopped the destruction of the Sanctuary. I can't even think of a reason to try to dissuade you. I've seen what the Rulers did and would feel uncomfortable thinking they would someday be able to resume their war against you."

"We could leave a couple of ships to guard Pozzen and take anyone who wishes on the others," Humbaw replied. "We would like Ms Brady to come."

"I think it would be best to offer everyone the choice."

Humbaw stood to leave.

"There are a couple of other issues to discuss," Hector said. "I'm not sure that all my people are ready to go home. They've seen a lot and many think it's unlikely they'll ever get a chance to travel in space again. Younger Terrans with no families of their own may wish to stay behind to help the Corens."

Humbaw smiled. "Sinomla has requested additional help from FEEF. There is a young woman who hopes Sergeant Feldez will stay."

Hector chuckled. "I've lost track of how many people told me about her and him."

"Madame Huxley and Dr Azwatta are very impressed with Umet," Humbaw said. "We will visit the planet regularly and can arrange to return any of your people to Earth if they wish."

A few days later, *New Jersey* detected a large asteroid dotted with structures and docking stations. It was hollow and teeming with activity.

After encircling the asteroid, the cruisers pummeled its protective screen with laser cannon salvos, steadily draining its energy reservoir until it became defenseless. The Beings made no attempt to contact the Rulers in the Sanctuary and heard nothing from them. The transports joined in the relentless bombardment that weakened the asteroid. It cracked open venting bodies and debris that were vaporized by the ongoing laser barrage. Soon only a cloud of sand marked the location of the Sanctuary.

Chapter 28
A Wish Comes True

Hector strode toward the main bay of *Enterprise* mulling over requests from more than 300 humans to remain on Mandela. He had no reason to deny any of the requests, especially Micheline Azwatta's offer to take on Juan as a medical student.

As Hector stepped into the bay, he paused to survey the surroundings. He'd never seen so many Beings, Biots and humans in one place before. The scene would be replicated in all the cruisers and transports of the Being. Pilots and soldiers stood alongside the troopers and flyers.

As if Hector's arrival had been a cue, the Biots broke into a raucous rendition of *For They Are Jolly Good Fellows* followed by three loud Hip Hip Hoorays. The sound filled every ship in the fleet. Then to complete their own tribute, the Biots sang *When You Wish Upon a Star* in the lilting brogue of John McCormack followed by *What a Wonderful World* sounding like thousands of Louis Armstrongs. They finished off with New Queen's *We Are the Primitives*. While few humans knew the first two songs, they joined in the last one.

The Beings stood in quiet amazement. Hector imagined them wondering how they would cope with their helpers' love of music and if their worlds would ever be tranquil again.

Finally, senior Beings and human officers appeared on platforms in front of the assemblies. "For all of you we have a medal to mark your participation in the defeat of our enemy and the discovery of our new partners in the Galaxy," Humbaw said. "It was made from metal salvaged from destroyed Ruler machines."

With that, the officers worked their way through the rows passing out the medals.

Next was a bravery medal that was given to humans and Biots selected by Humbaw, Gnoorvants and Hector. Vasile Stocia, Juan Feldez, Ben Kennedy, Chris Donohue, Lin Jiabao, Sergi Konstantinov, Genghis, Bolivar and hundreds of other flyers and troopers received them.

When the celebration and congratulations subsided, Humbaw asked for order before his next announcement. "Earlier today," he said, "I received a communication from Chief Councilor Dormmundar. He writes that in recognition of their bravery and dedication in stopping the Nameless attacks, liberating the Corens and Pozzens and restoring Hnassumblaw, the High Council has unanimously agreed that from this day, the Biobots are full citizens of the Being worlds."

For a moment, silence reigned throughout the fleet as his words sank in. The Biots looked at each other in disbelief. Then a roar of jubilation rolled through the ships. The humans applauded as Biots yelled, cheered and hugged each other. Genghis jumped up on the podium and approached Hton with his hand extended. "This is your triumph." Moving to Dton, he said, "Thank you for sticking with him. You two never lost faith that the Beings would understand and the Terrans would make the difference."

Genghis walked up to Humbaw. "Please express our appreciation to the Council. We'll be good if somewhat noisy citizens." He stepped forward so all the Biots could see him in person or on a display. "This time for Hton and Dton, our heroes."

The Hip Hip Hooray was deafening. Then the Biots sang their anthem, an ode in Beingish to life and the universe set to the music of *A Song for the Moon*.

When it ended, the bays buzzed with conversations. Once again, Hector had witnessed history happen. This was the best one yet. He pushed forward to congratulate Hton as in the distance other Biots gave him thumbs up.

When the hubbub subsided, Demmloda spoke up. "The Chief Councilor's message also says the Biobots will have the same rights and responsibilities as all citizens. To make that meaningful, the tons of the Councilors are appointed members of the High Council." Smiling slyly, he continued, "Of course, as they have been running their own High Council, this should not be a difficult transition. In time, the Biobots will elect their own representatives."

Hector snapped of his reverie as Hecton approached with his hand extended. Other tons surged in his direction. A Biot's smile said as much as anyone's.

After the ceremony, the galaxyships returned to their home worlds for well-deserved rest before resuming their regular duties. *Alliance* and *Enterprise* headed for Mandela to drop off the volunteers. *Enterprise* would return the rest of FEEF to Earth.

The trip to Mandela left the Beings and humans with a mystery. While the attack on Pozzen was under way, a transport carrying Nameless to Mandela had developed propulsion problems. It came out of galaxy speed into an unexplored solar system. Mostly for something to do while repairs could be completed, the Biots studied the planets in the system. They found the second one had a breathable atmosphere and catalogued it for future exploration until the imagers discovered an artificial dome surrounded by thick jungle.

"The dome is an energy field unlike anything we know," Nonforense told the morning briefing. "The ship could not see inside even with a shuttle that flew close to it."

With *Enterprise* and *Alliance* overhead, a shuttle landed Vasile and Whiz for an inspection of the dome. "There's no sound coming from it," the ton reported. "It's transparent."

Vasile pushed a stick against the dome. The surface gave a bit but the stick didn't penetrate. He couldn't shove his hand through it. Neither could the ton. "While it feels cold as ice, it's actually the same temperature as the air," Vasile said.

They walked alongside the dome for several hundred meters. "On the inside, we can see identical looking buildings with paths leading toward the center. However, there's no one moving about." After a few minutes of contemplation, he resumed his commentary. "If it won't admit us, maybe we don't belong or we're doing something wrong. Could we make ourselves more presentable?"

He shrugged off his rifle and placed his pistol and knife on top of it. He smiled at Whiz and knocked on the dome. On the third rap, his fist passed through the energy field. Feeling only a slight tingling, Vasile stepped through the barrier into a brightly lit world that was warm and dry. It would be the perfect holiday destination. The ton shed his weapons and followed.

They gazed about. The buildings were in a vast array of colors repeated in patterns. They had many circular openings, but no doors or windows. Trees and flower coated shrubs grew everywhere.

"Hello," Vasile called out, "Anyone home?" The only response was the gentle caress of a light breeze.

"Maybe they're all somewhere," Whiz suggested. "Let's go inspect. It certainly feels like there's someone around. We just can't see them." Pointing at the ground, he said. "There're no footprints but ours."

After walking for about 10 minutes, their surroundings appeared the same. Inside the buildings, they could see furniture that looked like chairs and couches. "Why can't we find whoever lives here?" the ton said. "This is such a lovely place. Wouldn't humans consider this paradise?"

Tears poured down Vasile's cheeks. He said something that caused Whiz to stare at him. Then a gentle breeze dried his face. He patted his ton's shoulder. "It's time to leave. We've seen what we're meant to see." They retraced their steps, stepped through the barrier, retrieved their weapons and walked to the shuttle without another word.

As they boarded the shuttle, Whiz transmitted his visual of the exploration of the dome to the Conference Rooms on the galaxyships. Nonforense told them the words the ton hadn't understood were in Romanian. "Granny, you were right, there are mansions for angels in the stars."

The shuttle flew to *Alliance* for a meeting with Humbaw and Hector. "You saw everything we did," Vasile said. "The dome told me it admitted us to acknowledge we'd righted an ancient wrong by liberating the Corens. However, the dome is not a place for us, at least not for now."

When asked by Humbaw about the reference to his grandmother, Vasile said, "When I was young, Bunica looked after me a lot. She told all sorts of tales and stories of the old days. But every now and then, she would talk about angels and how they lived in special places in the stars. When I said angels were just an invention of storytellers, she scolded me and said there are some things that can't be explained by even the smartest people. Later, I found the Bible talked about mansions in heaven and I thought that was what she meant."

"We'll mark this planet as closed to exploration and habitation," Humbaw said. "Now if you will go to the holograph chamber, we have something to show you."

When they reached it, Humbaw's voice flowed through their communicators. "As you know, after we found the ruins on the other side, we put all the data we had collected about them into Turing and Nonforense to see if they could make holographic copies. They made some interesting, but inconclusive, conjectures about the ruins."

Humbaw kept talking as they entered the chamber. "With the help of the main Controlling Unit on Hnassumblaw, they developed models of what those settlements might have looked like when they were intact based on what we learned on Kendo."

Vasile and Whiz stopped a couple of paces into the room. The door rolled shut behind them. The overhead lights faded and the first settlement came to life. The buildings were whole with their roofs in place. Neat pathways linked them and ran down to the two flat areas in front of the settlement. After a few minutes, the image morphed into a depiction of what the second settlement might have looked like the day after it was abandoned. It too was neat and ordered. The much larger settlement from Kendo appeared next. "All that's missing is who lived there," Stocton said.

While the display had finished, the room remained dark. "We have another treat for you, but it will be erased after you view it to respect the dome's wish for privacy," Nonforense said. With that, Vasile's mansions of the angels appeared.

"You were right, Whiz. It's paradise."

After a few minutes, the ton tugged on his sleeve. "It's time to go."

Vasile resisted and then followed. "You're right, partner." He didn't try to hide his reluctance to leave. He could stay here forever and dream. They strolled out of the chamber taking one final look back until the image vanished. Whiz crossed his fingers when he said his recording of it had been erased.

Humbaw and Hector waited outside the chamber. "A consortium of universities on Earth and the Being worlds wants you two to lead a study of the ruins and their inscriptions," the General said. "You will have access to the top archeologists and all the data from the derelict spaceships found by the Beings."

"Whiz can also assist Terran scientists who are studying the Biots for ways to improve robots," Humbaw said. "While the Biots on Earth have already contributed, his partnership with you might provide more insight."

"Sounds like a great gig, partner," Vasile said as he and the ton shook hands.

Another report came from Mandela before the ships reached it. "As you know there're far more females than men so the women here decided that each man should have two or three wives," Michelle Azwatta said. "They think it's important to increase their population and Mandela is the place to do it even if it isn't their world. General, I will leave it to you to explain this to the Secretary General."

Hector could well imagine the political problems Benjamin would have with the ultra-conservative factions on Earth. The

Secretary General already had his hands full with speculation the Corens had to be descendants of humans who were slaves of the race that had created Atlantis.

Elinor had several more stories to report before she reached Earth about three months later.

Dormmundar had stepped down as Chief Councilor and recommended Hton succeed her. He agreed as long as she remained as Deputy Chief Councilor.

Next was the birth of Ruth Joan Humbaw Donohue.

The last was passing the satellite that witnessed the departure of *Alliance*.

The hero's welcome for *Enterprise* and its valiant captain she left for her journalist colleagues.

CPSIA information can be obtained at www.ICGtesting.com
Printed in the USA
LVOW05s0100191113

361801LV00001B/16/P